The Copy Candidate

by

Alexander Francis

The Copy Candidate

by

Alexander Francis

Copyright ©2016 by Alexander Francis

Arcus Verba Publishing
P.O Box 210
De Forest, Wisconsin
53532
www.arcusverba.com

Cover design by Alexander Francis

ISBN: **978-1-942420-20-0** print edition
ISBN: **978-1-942420-21-7** e-book

Table of Contents

Foreword

When Ronald Reagan was elected president, I observed and studied him, both as a candidate and as President. In truth, I didn't support or vote for him in his first attempt at the White House, but I did thereafter and was never sorry for it.

What I remember best was his gifted ability to make a speech. At first I passed it off as part of a long acting career and experience being in front of the camera, but I began to realize that we were seeing the actual person, not an actor and not just a polished politician. His sincerity came through, and most Americans loved him for it. Wouldn't we wish that he could reappear by some magic so we could have a leader that we trusted and believed in again?

In this tale I have created, Ronald Reagan does come back. Needless to say, this is pure fiction, and that means that literary license was taken with any and all conspiracies implied in the book. I am not stating or suggesting that any of our representative parties are corrupt or would act against the interests of the United States of America.

Or would they?

Alexander Francis

The Copy Candidate

Alexander Francis

Chapter One

A Collective Gasp

Jill nearly caught the moving heavy glass door but missed, and it shut silently, sealing in the noise from the lobby for a moment. The burly male, who had let it close on her, moved away indifferently, his back to her. Male deference toward women was a thing of the past, she knew, but basic human decency and consideration were fleeing as well. As footsteps and conversation from behind came closer, she pulled the chrome handle toward her with a fierce lunge, slipping in and letting it go while not looking back. She could play that game also.

Inside the wide lobby, she threaded her way between small groups engaged in ardent conversation but distributed in random clumps making passage toward the large entrance to the hall an ordeal. She wanted a good seat in case there was a need for photographs, and besides, she didn't recognize a single person. The gear on her left shoulder hung like a substantial anchor on a boat underway. Useless...for the moment, and heavy. As she passed through the large opening at the rear of the amphitheater, she encountered more obstacles. This time it was gear...cameras mounted on heavy platforms supported by dirty, well-worn casters. Thick electrical cords crisscrossed the floor, and several crews bent to their work getting ready. This announcement was going to be a big deal, she could see. Her editor, Mr. Burns, didn't tell her what to expect or, more likely, didn't know himself.

Jill stood on her tiptoes scanning the room for the ideal spot to occupy, one that allowed extra room for swinging the long lens around. Then she saw the sign, actually there were several, printed in bold red type using six inch letters. "Absolutely NO Cameras," it read. Rats.

"Excuse me, Miss," he said, tapping her on her shoulder. Jill turned toward the interloper, wide-eyed with expectation. "Camera in that bag?" he asked pointing to her camera bag, the one marked "Photo Gear."

"I know...I saw the signs," she replied. She noticed that he was neatly dressed in suit and tie and had groomed blond hair over a close shave. A very attractive fellow, she realized, and roughly her age. A metal tag announced that his name was Ted and another one, more badge-like, identified him as a member of the RNC, the Republican National Committee.

"If you attempt any photography, you will be escorted from the room. You don't want that, do you?"

"Wish I would have known," Jill said, looking a bit beat. She continued to scan for a good seat, ignoring Ted for the moment.

"I would be glad to take your bag and keep it for you," he suggested, beaming her a big toothy smile while extending his arm as if to encourage her to hand it over. Jill hesitated. The gear was expensive and belonged to her newspaper. She couldn't afford to be charged if it turned up missing.

"I promise it will be safe...in fact, I guarantee it." He looked sincere enough, but she didn't know what to do. She studied his tags again trying to make up her mind.

"Can't I just keep it with me?" She responded, unsure of what to do.

"Tell you what. Just let me carry it for you, and I'll let you sit right beside me on the front row. You can put your bag under your seat. Will that be all right?" He smiled and eased the heavy bag from her shoulder without waiting for her to decide. After he slung it on, he gently offered his other arm to her. Wow. She regretted thinking that all males had regressed into early hominids. She smiled up at him and patted his hand.

"My name is Jill. I can see that you are Ted, and you work with the RNC. Anything else I should know?" They slowed to step over a group of cables.

"Any chance that you are a reporter, Jill?" he laughed and pointed to an opening between two groups of men in animated conversation.

"Any chance that I'm not?" Jill responded. "I mean, this room is full of them. I've never seen so many in one place."

"So, that means that you are not from Washington. Small town paper I'm guessing?"

"Very small. Just the way I feel right now. Small and unimportant."

"Nonsense!" Ted laughed. "You found me, and I can't believe your luck!"

"Now I have to ask, Ted. How would that make me lucky?" Jill had a serious face, her brow wrinkling in concentration.

"Luck in that I'm captivated by your little-girl-lost look, especially since the little girl is so attractive. You don't know this yet, but I'm the go-to guy for information. You'll see." He laughed again and swept his blond hair back with his free hand. It was a typical masculine gesture but seeing him do it was memorable for some reason. She looked again at Ted. This time taking him in, measure by measure. Yes, this was a handsome fellow for sure, and a confident one.

"I'll have to let you know later, Ted, I mean, if you are right. Now tell me what this show is all about. A quick summary, if you will."

"No one, even me, knows for sure. And I mean no one. The rumor is that it is big. Very big. You can see all the networks are here, and that should tell you something."

"What, exactly, is the rumor? Come on, you can tell a lost little girl *something* at least. You are the go-to guy, remember?" She playfully tugged on his coat sleeve.

Ted guided her to her seat and motioned for her to sit down. It was on the first row, all right, just as he promised. Jill was feeling lucky after all. She shoved her camera under her seat, sat up and looked his way, waiting.

Ted leaned toward her and spoke softly into her ear. "Kid, I tell you this, and you have to promise that you'll never credit me. Promise like you mean it."

"I promise. I never heard anything from you," she whispered. She waited.

"Now promise me that you'll have dinner with me tonight," he added, just as secretively.

"I promise to consider it. Now spill. You have my reporter blood up."

Ted looked around again just to be sure that he wasn't overheard and leaned closer, nearly touching her ear. "You smell wonderful," he murmured.

"Am I just a pick-up?" Jill reacted and started to stand, but his arm restrained her.

"No! Don't leave. I'm serious about being the go-to guy, and I'm also serious about your perfume. Sorry if you found me rude, and you have my apology. Let me try again. Please."

Jill resumed her seat, but she folded her arms across her chest and looked straight ahead.

"This event is to be an introduction of a heretofore unknown politician. A candidate for President of the United States. We have been assured that we will recognize him but have not been told his name. We are all in the dark except for a couple of insiders who organized this event. It's a surprise, but given all the publicity, it better be good." He looked around again just to be sure.

"That's it? That's all you know?" Jill sniffed. "Hey, I knew almost that much. Some secret."

"You don't get it, Jill. This man, whom we will all know, is an unknown. Does that even make sense? It doesn't to me."

"Let me ask you this," Jill whispered, leaning closer. "Can a person, who has already been president, run again?"

Ted shrugged and pushed his lower lip out in contemplation. "We discussed this yesterday, wondering the same thing. You know that Teddy Roosevelt tried that but was unsuccessful. We didn't remember any other person who even tried, and certainly none were elected. I don't think the voters would want that. Besides, presidents are usually old when they retire. Why would they want to run again. It's crazy."

"Then a general...like Ike, you know," she asked.

"Eisenhower was already famous, respected on a scale that no one today measures up to. No, it can't be a general. I guess we'll soon find out. Now, about that date tonight?

Ignoring his question, Jill put her finger in the air and smiled, "I know! An actor or TV personality. That's got to be it."

"Sure. We thought of that, too. But then why the surprise? Don't you think we would have gotten hints by now? Did you hear my question about dinner. Around six?"

Before Jill could answer, a sound made her focus on the stage in front of her. A technician was tapping on the microphones, one at a time, and adjusting some unseen controls under the podium. Satisfied, he waved to someone offstage and walked off the other way. There was a quiet that came over the attendees, and Jill strained her neck to look around. She judged that the audience numbered well over two hundred, seated that is, with more around the large camera units in the back of the hall. Most were obviously press and either were attentively working with their cell phone or adjusting and marking papers in their laps. Possibly a third were women, and none of them, other than her, were seated on the first row. Yes, this was a lucky break indeed, Jill agreed. She tapped Ted lightly on his shoulder, and when he turned, she nodded affirmatively and mouthed, "Yes." Ted smiled back and nodded approval.

Approaching footsteps heralded the announcer who sedately made his way toward center stage while acknowledging several audience members with little waves and a quick smile. He was older, grey, but groomed like an advertisement, dressed in a black tuxedo. Confidence and command radiated from him like that of a president, or at least a confidant of one. He was lean, fit, displaying a sharp tanned face complimented by a prominent patrician nose.

"Who is he?" Jill asked quietly. Ted flipped the back of his hand toward her in dismissal, while focusing intently on the man, who now had assumed his position at the podium and was looking at the crowd. For a brief moment, he glanced down at Ted, his eyes darting to Jill, then back again. She could swear that there was a fleeting display of amusement on his face, a knowing kind of look, then it was as quickly gone.

"Greetings and welcome," he began. "For the few of you who don't already know, my name is Lance Waterson, and I am the Chairman of the Republican Party." He smiled again, noting, by pointing in turn to, various people below him. He put his hands out and forward, palms facing the floor, to bring the noise level down, and like a cue from Merlin, it worked.

"There isn't any way to describe what is about to happen in this room, but I can assure you that it is earthshaking. Nothing like this has ever happened before, certainly not in the United States of America. We on the committee are as stunned as you are about to be, to put it mildly. We are assembled today to enable an introduction, and only an introduction, to someone who wishes to be considered a candidate for president. We, nor the Candidate, are prepared for questions and answers...not yet...and this view of him will be short, too short for most of you."

"I already know the questions which will arise, and I want to answer truthfully right now. I don't know." He paused and looked around expecting some eruptions, but the audience was still trying to determine why they were there, not yet knowing what to ask. After a pause, he continued, "At this moment, we don't have the most fundamental answers to the most obvious questions. It's going to take some time and effort on all our parts to ferret out the truth. Let me be clear on one thing: the Republican National Committee is not endorsing this candidate whom you are about to meet. We are providing an introduction and a limited one at that. There are too many facts yet unknown for an endorsement or even official encouragement. That being said, I also want it to be known that I, personally, am wildly enthusiastic about the possibilities."

Chairman Waterson paused again looking sternly back and forth before pushing away from the podium and walking around to stand in front of it. "I am a convert, a believer, and I predict that all of you will be also." He looked toward stage left and extended his arm as if signaling for someone to come forward. All the heads and cameras present followed his arm and focused breathlessly on the curtain.

Jill leaned nervously forward, quickly glimpsing back and forth, becoming aware that most of the audience were focused as intently as she. The room settled into dead quiet, then footsteps were heard approaching from behind the curtain. With all the anticipation in the atmosphere, she wouldn't have been a bit surprised to see King Kong emerge, complete with a blonde in his grasp.

Before she could look back at the stage, she heard a collective gasp, a whoosh of air inward, lungs being inflated involuntarily. At first, all she saw was a notably handsome man, dressed in a dark blue suit with crimson tie, striding confidently toward the outstretched arm of Chairman Waterson. The man was smiling, in a somewhat familiar, asymmetrical but endearing way. He had full, dark hair swept backward across his head, hair that was groomed and combed meticulously, giving the impression of something.... "Damn!" she exclaimed out loud as her memory jolted her into comprehension. She couldn't bring the words rapidly streaming into her conscious thoughts together in time to be the first to remark: "He looks like Ronald Reagan...exactly like Ronald Reagan!" The words came out from various areas of the audience at once, nearly forming the start of a chant. Some stood to get a better look, and the din of noise rose quickly.

The Candidate was met by Chairman Waterson just prior to attaining center stage. They embraced warmly, and Jill noticed that Chairman Waterson spoke briefly into the man's ear. He nodded, smiled, then continued toward the podium. Once there, he looked directly at the audience and they him, eyes meeting on a grand scale. He smiled warmly and made a motion for everyone to be reseated.

Jill grabbed the arm of her new companion and pulled him down toward her. "Are you seeing what I am?" she asked rather loudly. Ted nodded affirmative but didn't take his eyes off of the stage, even for the briefest of seconds. The audience murmured softly, but everyone seated themselves, while gaping in awe toward the man on the stage. Chairman Waterson discreetly withdrew, no one even noticing his departure, so fixated were they on something they didn't begin to understand.

The Candidate tapped on the mike in front of him, both to assure that it was working and to signal that he was about to speak. Again, the room fell absolutely silent, waiting on the voice to emerge and preparing mentally to judge whether it was as similar to what they remembered. Jill figured that about half the room was old enough to have a clear, first hand, memory of President Ronald Reagan, and most of the others had, by now, heard and seen videos of the former president. Jill wondered if anyone other than she had seen most of Reagan's movies. If there was a movie he had been in that she had not seen, it would be remarkable. She had seen them all and, long before this day, had a crush on the handsome actor. Yes, she remarked to herself, this man was a visual copy, a perfect one. She quickly judged his age and realized that he appeared much younger than the president had, even in his first term. This was a man in his prime, much like the younger actor who had mesmerized so many women of his generation.

"Greetings and thank you for attending," he started, continuing to bathe the audience with his infectious smile and his twinkling eye. Jill was absolutely convinced. Even the voice was the same. Same timber, same timing and inflection. She couldn't believe her own senses. It was impossible, but there he stood.

"My name is…" he hesitated briefly, masterfully, waiting that brief time for the impact to be enhanced even more. A punch that you know is coming, made that more intense by expectation. None among the audience would have presumed any other name to emerge...but... "Ronald Reagan." He quickly put up his hands in a mock defensive gesture, by this, warding off any negative comment with a touch of humor. "Yes, you can believe your eyes, your ears and your memories. I am Ronald Reagan." The audience was immediately back on their feet, questions loudly shouted at the stage from dozens at once, generating a garbled white heat noise. The feelings aroused could not be silenced, and Chairman Waterson emerged, frantically waving his arms in a vain effort to quiet the room and regain control. As soon as some sat down, others rose as if their questions had compelled action. The seated ones stood again, and for a time it seemed as though everyone was trying to be heard all at once. Except Jill. She covered her ears and shrunk back in her seat, her wild eyes trying to follow events but shielding her ears from the intensity of the moment. The place was in chaos, and there was no controlling the crowd, enraged with questions as they were, partially from surprise and partly because of the lack of plausible answers.

Chairman Waterson glared at the audience, a disgusted frown contorted with a sprinkling of fear on his tanned face. Without explanation, which would have been impossible anyway, he took the Candidate's arm and led him quickly off the stage to the disapproving roar of the audience. Jill fully expected that if there had been beer bottles present, they would have been in the air just then, headed for the stage and the back of the Chairman.

Minutes passed without any living, or even dead, person on the stage, metamorphosing the roar into hundreds of heated conversations, finger-pointing and general furor.

Ted leaned toward her and gently pulled one of her hands from her ear. "I think it's over out here. Want to come backstage with me?" She couldn't believe it could even be possible and the idea of going backstage in front of this mob...no, she wasn't sure it was a manageable feat or even safe. She shook her head "no" and put her hand back over her ear.

Ted patiently pulled her hand away again and loudly whispered, "I know what your brain is thinking. Don't worry, I know another way in there. I can get us in...safely. Willing to try?"

This time she signaled her willingness by retrieving her camera bag from under her seat and, when she was ready, by looking expectantly up at Ted, who had remained standing. He smiled conspiratorially at her and nodded, pointing with his eyes toward the back of the room. They were going to look like they were leaving, while the bulk of the audience remained in hope that the creature, who was, no doubt, an alien copy of Ronald Reagan, would again emerge. Until they were absolutely sure he wouldn't return, they weren't about to leave or be quiet. Besides, leaving prematurely would enable their competitors to scoop the facts ahead of them, a clearly intolerable calamity.

Ted led, his right hand holding the heavy camera bag, using it as a wedge to push people aside and encountering hostile looks as he did so. His left hand held Jill's, who was following along behind, trying not to return questioning stares from those they passed. She could imagine their thoughts: "Why is she leaving? Does she know something? Where is she going?" Once in the hall, she pulled Ted to a stop and looked around. The hall was entirely empty. Every single attendee was in the big room, clamoring for information, for pictures, for a history of some type. She smiled up at Ted, showing her appreciation but also trying to restrain herself just a bit to avoid later expectations. They walked arm in arm toward the rear exit, and as they pulled away, the noise diminished enough so that they could converse normally.

"Wow!" she exclaimed. "I would never have imagined that, even in a dream. It's not possible...is it?"

"Caught me by surprise as well, Jill. Truth is, I'm somewhat angry at being kept out of the loop. They expect me to be a source for the press and then keep me ignorant of any facts. But don't worry, they will have to talk now. Listen up, Jill. Don't say a word in there about being a member of the press. You understand?" He seemed firm, even a bit aggressive about it.

"Here I am with a thirty pound camera bag marked photo equipment. Think they won't see it or something?" she asked, just as he pushed the heavy glass door outward, allowing the warm, moist air to bring them back to earth as they emerged into sunlight.

"I plan to put it in the trunk of my car which is just over there...unless your car is parked close instead?" He smiled again, the little boy smile that she found so attractive. She understood why he was chosen to speak to the press. It was his ability to disarm by his looks and natural charm, much like Ronald Reagan had done to much of the free world...and apparently will do again. Jill didn't answer, other than a little female shrug, and they headed for Ted's car, glinting in the sunlight. After a few long strides, Ted popped the trunk open and tossed the bag in rather carelessly.

In anguish, Jill put her hands to her mouth, seeing her expensive equipment treated roughly. "I hope you didn't break any of that. They'll take it out of my salary."

"Let me know if it's broken, and I'll pay for it personally," Ted said and again began to pull her back toward the building. Jill broke free and stood with her hands on her hips, her legs slightly apart in defiance.

"Hold on there, Bub. First answer some questions," she said.

"Jill, we have to hurry before the Candidate leaves. You'll want another look, I presume."

"Why, Ted? Why me? They don't want reporters in the back rooms, I'm quite sure. Just what is all this attention about?"

Ted stopped and turned toward her, his hands at his sides. For a moment he hesitated, then decided to level with her. It was the right thing to do. "Want the truth, eh?" Starting only led to another awkward pause. "Truthfully, I'm attracted to you. I'm not sure why...yet. It's just you looked so needy when we met. And it's an accurate assessment, don't you agree, that you needed some help just then?"

"I surely did. Still do, in fact. But a question for you, and I expect you to be honest. I can always tell a lie from a man, you should know. Just what are you expecting to get out of helping me?" She had to restrain herself from protruding her lower lip, but mentally, she did anyway.

"I don't expect anything, Jill. I'm giving, not getting. Now can we go inside?"

"Nothing?" Jill asked, standing her ground.

"Other than the privilege of having your company tonight at dinner...no, nothing at all. Please, no more delays. We need to hurry."

Jill had heard enough, and she rushed forward, tugging Ted along behind her. Her thoughts had returned to the subject at hand. Is the man inside for real, and what is his story? Ted caught up, laughing at her, and when they arrived at the side door, he gently pushed her behind him. "For the record and for the ears inside, you are my new assistant. Got it?" Jill nodded that she understood and gave him a big smile in appreciation. Ted knocked loudly on the door using a key to intensify the sound.

After an awkward moment outside, and just when Jill was deciding that Ted was in error about gaining admission, the door opened about half-way. Blocking the entrance was a rather burly fellow, his round, unshaven face appearing rather like the moon high above her. His eyes took in Ted and Jill and spent more time on her than was comfortable.

"I'm not supposed to allow entry through this door," he growled. "This is an exit only," he added, remaining in position.

"Come on, Bob, open the damned door. We are in a hurry. Is he still in there?" Ted pulled the door open forcefully revealing the full size of Bob who was as massive as a side of beef and also armed with a large black handgun hanging menacingly at his side. Bob backed up and regarded Jill with undue interest as they both came across the threshold.

"Still here," Bob answered curtly before returning to his chair beside the door and sitting down heavily. Jill could feel his eyes pour over her as Ted led the way down a corridor. She could tell that her hands were wet with perspiration and hoped Ted wouldn't notice. There was a small recording device in her purse, and she wondered if it would be spotted if she managed to retrieve and activate it. Better wait, she decided. Ted stopped in front of a large door and leaned forward to listen. He evidently didn't hear what he was seeking, and they continued walking in silence.

Ted stopped in mid-stride, and this time Jill could also hear voices, murmuring voices, from several sources, the sounds seeping from behind a particular door. Ted knocked this time, respectfully and with restraint. The door opened a crack and an eye appeared, looking them over, then the door opened fully. At the far side of a rather extensive room was a set of furniture, including a large leather couch, on which sat the man calling himself Ronald Reagan. His legs were comfortably apart. He had taken off his shoes and was smiling, engaged in conversation with a fellow in a dark tailored suit standing just in front of the couch. Chairman Waterson was seated in an upholstered chair just to his left. As Jill watched, wide-eyed, the Chairman glanced in their direction, a knowing look and small smile came to his face. He crooked his finger toward Ted, signaling him to come forward. The Candidate also noticed and was looking directly at Jill, or so she felt. A lump came into her throat. What in the world is she doing here, she asked herself.

On the way in, Ted exchanged a quick back slap with the door man who evidently knew him well. Jill made a momentary and involuntary hesitation before being nearly yanked forward by Ted. He gave her a quick, disapproving look accompanied by a nod to remind her of her imaginary position. They walked together, Jill lagging slightly behind, and on the way, Ted let her hand go. She stopped, but Ted continued his progress toward the Chairman, his hand extended for a shake. Jill was left alone, an uncomfortable distance from the action, but near enough to be noticed. Then she realized there were other eyes on her from several small groups of well-dressed people, all looking her over at the same time. She felt the urge to straighten her dress, or her hair, or even smile back. But she didn't. She just stood in place watching Ted, who at the moment was shaking the hand of Ronald Reagan.

Jill's peripheral vision noticed that Chairman Waterson was motioning at her, and when she looked directly at him, she realized that he wanted her to come to him. She wanted badly to look around, perhaps for help, perhaps for escape, but there was no choice. The Chairman was smiling at her and looking her over from head to toe. As she closed the distance, he rose from his chair to meet her, and like the experienced politician he was, he warmly greeted her with hand outstretched. Jill had never been this close to power before, nor this level of potent, practiced charm. She smiled at him as convincingly as she was able.

"Hi, I'm Charles Waterson, but you may call me Charlie like my friends and supposed allies do." He smiled, displaying his perfect white and even teeth. Jill noticed a manly, continental perfume as she got closer. She allowed the handshake but realized that Charlie had moved close enough to nearly touch her. "And your name, my dear?" he asked in a melodious, disarming voice.

"Jill, Jill Longley, sir. Glad to meet you." Her voice sounded normal enough, surprisingly so, given the circumstances.

"And, lovely Jill, for you are a lovely little thing indeed," his eyes searched her hair and neck as he spoke, "what, may I ask, is your claim to fame?"

"Sir?"

"What do you do for a living, Jill?" he asked patiently. Jill could sense rather than see, a figure move closer, just beside Charlie. She dared not look away from Charlie's face at the moment.

"Well, I'm with Ted. Didn't he tell you?"

"I saw that, Jill, and yes, he mentioned you. But I wonder, what are your skills, besides being an attractive young blonde, I mean. What *do* you do?" This time some of the smile had faded, and Jill realized that this was becoming an interrogation. The Chairman meant to discover her true nature, and in as short a time as he could manage.

Jill was trapped unless she could have, or invent, a believable cover story. "I'm a writer, Charlie," looking him in the eyes with as soft a feminine look as she could muster. Female sexuality disarms most men, but not this one, or this type, she realized, too late to change tactics.

"Oh, a writer. What do you write, if I may ask. You see the need for me to understand, don't you?"

"Most certainly, sir." She reverted to the non-personal to gain room and time to think. "I write books. Had one published, and it's doing rather well."

"You don't say," Charlie said with too much sincerity. "What is the title?" he grinned at her, assuming that he had her trapped.

"*Geminknot.* It's a true story made into novel format." She smiled, the truth is always an ally when you need it. This time she looked toward the second person and realized she was an older woman, busy with a handheld electronic device of some sort.

The Chairman waited for something, and so did Jill. Frozen in place. Out of her peripheral vision, she noticed Ted, who was still engaged with Ronald

Reagan. She thought she saw him glance quickly in her direction.

At last, something happened. "Got it," the woman said holding the screen so that he could see it. "Good ranking, too. Guess she's telling the truth, there's even her photograph here." She tapped the screen in the correct place. Charlie smiled vaguely and murmured thanks as the assistant withdrew.

"A real writer, Jill. Not one of those..." he let the word go, being too experienced to ever make a verbal slip. "Stick around, Jill. We just might be able to use a good writer like yourself in the near future. You never know." Charlie looked away, and she realized that she had been dismissed. She could see Ronald Reagan's head, or at least part of it, the rest hidden by a dark suit standing between them. His eye was on her a little too long to be accidental. He had noticed her. Generally, for a young single woman, being noticed is a good, a very good, thing, but given the devious way she had entered this environment, it made her feel like the interloper she actually was.

When the Chairman moved away, Jill was left standing alone, exposed to the interrogative looks of interested parties. She watched Ted work his magic on those around him. He had charm and looks, she had to give that to him. And he was persistent when he wanted something. It was hard not to be impressed. As if he were aware she was watching and thinking about him, Ted turned, looking at her with a smile and wink. He made a discrete motion for her to join him, and somewhat hesitantly, she did.

Ted placed his hand on her shoulder lightly, a slightly possessive touch, and introduced her to the man of the hour, the Candidate, who was watching her with amusement. "Sir, I would like to introduce my assistant, Jill. I'm pretty sure you'll see her again after today."

Ronald Reagan rose to his feet, then looked down and laughed. "You'll have to excuse my feet, Jill. What a way to greet the most lovely woman in the room!" He laughed again, showing the small wrinkles around his eyes. "I noticed you when you came in. It's a delight to finally meet you face-to-face." He gave a very slight bow, really only a nod of his head, but extended his hand toward her and smiled convincingly at her. Jill thought for a moment that she would faint and be struck dumb. This man was the movie star she dreamed about, the very one she couldn't get enough of by watching his old movies. It couldn't be happening, she had to be asleep. But when she found his hand, it was warm and alive, and he used just the right amount of pressure, then lingered a bit while letting go.

"I noticed you survived interrogation, and you have not been ejected or tortured," Ted noted aloud. Reagan shot him a quizzical look before again focusing on Jill.

"Using that remark as a basis, let me speculate...Jill is really not supposed to be here," he correctly guessed. "So, you must be a lady friend of Ted's then." Reagan stood erect and had a more serious look come over him.

"We met today in the auditorium. I don't even know his last name."

"So, Ted," Reagan asked. "I was told that you are a sharp operative, just a while ago, in fact. This sounds like something rather rash. Not that Jill isn't a desirable young woman, but that you don't know anything about her. Shame on you, Ted."

"Sir, there is just something about her...you are correct, of course, but my bet is that I will also be correct in the long run."

"May I ask what you were doing in the auditorium, Jill?" Reagan asked, then sat back down and waited on her reply.

"I didn't know it, but I was waiting for you. Seeing you up close is one of the biggest thrills of my life."

"Come, come. You are a reporter, aren't you?" he retorted.

"I am. From a small town newspaper and this is the first time I have ever been sent away for a story." She paused for a moment looking back and forth between their faces. "And I have written a book," she added brightly, hoping that would somehow make a difference.

"What kind of book," Ted asked.

"I call it a novel, but it's based on a true story. Chairman Waterson's assistant looked me up. Ask her."

Ted looked contemplative then brightened. "I have an idea that we may be in luck finding Jill, sir. Want to hear it?"

"Sure, Ted, but we have to also run it past your organization, don't we?"

Ted ignored the question. "We have to have publicity, correct? The right kind, the right amount and in the right sequence. She may be the perfect newsperson to work through. Look how enamored she is with you. Yes, it's perfect. I can see how much the other news outlets will howl but going through Jill would be, well, controllable." Ted looked at Jill for conformation.

Jill could feel her face flushing before she found the words. "Wait! I'm standing here, you realize. You just said I could be controlled. Just what do you mean by that, and your answer better be good, or else."

Ted laughed. "You can't walk away from a story like this Jill. It's a once in a lifetime opportunity. This will make you a household word. No reporter could possibly refuse."

"Well, I can. I can just go back to my home and write about the little issues, as I've always done. Don't take me for granted."

This time Ronald Reagan reacted. "Please, Jill," he said softly, patting the couch beside him. "Sit down and talk to me. No one will ever take you for granted. I promise you. I think what Ted was trying to say is that you are a person to whom I can tell my story rather than have a reporter dig it out while getting it wrong or purposely putting it in the wrong perspective. You look like someone I can trust. Can you trust me is the question?" He reached for her arm and gently pulled her down beside him. The smile he gave her would have melted nearly any woman and certainly softened Jill.

"You are someone or something I've dreamed about, you should know. I've seen all your movies...all of them." Jill stared at him with a dreamy, adolescent look.

"I've never made a movie, Jill. And I've never been president. I am named Ronald Reagan, and I look like him, but I am a different man entirely."

"You simply can't be."

"There is a lot to my story, Jill, and I'm willing to share it with you, but you have to prove to us that you can be trusted."

"And how do I do that?" she asked, not taking her eyes from his.

Ted squatted down on her other side and tapped her arm to get her attention. "You have to write this encounter today using all your literary skills while keeping in mind that it was a unique privilege to be here, and that we are fully trusting you to do the right thing. After your newspaper prints your article, and we get a look at it...then we will see what comes next."

"Well, Mr. Reagan," a deep voice interrupted. It was the Chairman, who evidently was watching the little drama and decided to intervene. Reagan looked up and waited for the question.

"Most of the crowd has remained. Care to try again or call it a day?" he asked.

"Suggestions?" Reagan responded.

"Yes," Ted interrupted. "I think we accomplished the surprise of the century. Let them stew on it for a few days first. Don't give them too much of the story today. Little bits at a time will keep Mr. Reagan in the news and make the public hungry for more."

"Yes, Ted. I see your point. Is that the way you want to play it, Mr. Reagan?" the Chairman asked.

"When you told me that Ted is a genius at management, I believed you. Now you should believe your own words."

"So be it," he said solemnly, then grinned a thin smile at Ted. "You, Ted, are appointed to go out and face the lions. Tell them whatever you want, but get them out of here before they tear the place apart."

Ted stood, glancing at the three one last time before turning without a word and heading for the hallway. "Wait for me, Jill. I'll be back shortly," he called over his shoulder.

Jill watched him leave and then realized that Ronald Reagan was still looking at her. "Just what *is* your last name, Jill?"

"It's Longley, Mr. Reagan," the Chairman offered. "She's a reporter after all. We looked her up."

"I know. She told me. Did she also write a book?"

"*Geminknot.*"

"Well, even that's true," Reagan remarked, still looking at her with soft eyes. "I think I'm going to enjoy seeing you, Jill. In fact, I'm looking forward to it." He laughed that soft appealing chuckle that he had used on Gorbachev so effectively. It still worked and made Jill determined that she was going to be the one to write his story. She just had to.

Chapter Two

Theodore Philipe Clark

Ted raised his glass of wine, extending his arm toward her and offering his winning smile with the toast. "This is to...," he seemed to hesitate, not wanting to go too far, yet make this first dinner a celebration of some merit, "our new friendship and a productive relationship as well."

Jill accepted and touched her glass against his. They both took a small swallow while keeping their eyes in contact. In the shadowy becoming light, she noticed his small chin dimple as well as the little depressions which formed lateral to the corner of his lips when he smiled. That his eyes were blue was expected, given his rugged blond hair color. Jill hadn't known many blond men or perhaps had paid no attention previously, but this particular one was exceptionally fascinating. She resisted being pulled into his orbit too quickly, because her past experiences had taught painful lessons. Slow is better than fast. It takes more time than you expect to get to know someone, and she had heard from many sources that to really know someone even takes living together for years.

After Ted had returned from the ordeal of dealing with the angry press, he seemed spent, even limp. Ronald Reagan had left earlier, in the escort of several well-dressed men, but before he exited the room, he turned and gave Jill a little wave, which nearly buckled her knees. He was the most magnetic man she could imagine. His natural charm and grace looked to be a perfect fit with his handsome appearance, and the best part was that it all seemed to be so real. By contrast, Chairman Waterson had charm, loads of it, but of a kind more like that of a lethal snake which transfixes his victim before striking.

Ted was harder to read. Was he sincere or just particularly good at becoming what people wanted? Or did any of it matter at this particular moment? Ted was attentive, romantic, undeniably handsome, and possibly the ideal companion for dinner. She decided to just enjoy the experience and not dwell or analyze motives...at least not tonight.

"For the last half hour my charming companion has squeezed nearly every ounce of my history from me, enough that any additional disclosure will be too personal or painful. Now it's your turn, Ted. I want to know everything, every detail, so that I can finally figure you out."

"It's complicated, my dear Jill, and too long for dinner. It would spoil the dessert and ruin the dancing," he answered, his head lowered, looking mysteriously at her while speaking in a barely audible murmur.

"An answer like that would make me think you have something to hide. Where did you grow up, what does your father do, where did you go to college? You can leave out the names of your girl friends or even your enemies. How about starting with how you came by this job?" Jill didn't allow herself to smile at him this time, because she wasn't going to be postponed after disclosing her entire life to him. Then she realized what he had just mentioned. "What dancing?" she asked. As she surveyed the room, she knew that there was no dancing at this restaurant, however fancy and expensive.

"The dance we are going to in, let me see...," Ted paused to look at his wrist with mock sincerity. "In twenty-two minutes. Finish your *digestif*, we still have time."

"No, Ted. I'm sorry, but you remember the news article I still have to write? It's due by midnight, or it won't get into print. Not tonight."

"Oh, I forgot all about that. Yes, I have to be sure you have time to write a really good piece. A lot depends on it. Have you thought about what to write?"

"There isn't anything *to* write. Ronald Reagan looks and acts like himself. He is charming to a fault, captivating, at least to me, and being around him is like traveling back in time. Other than that, I know nothing about him. Nothing at all, and that's the part people will be hungry for. They will want to know if he's related, who his mother is or was, where has he been all this time and why is his name Ronald Reagan? Do *you* know anything about him?"

"It would be better if you got it directly from the source, Jill. He didn't authorize me to disclose any facts, but I'll give you one pearl you can use, if it helps." Ted watched her face for expression before he spoke. Truly, he didn't know how to answer any of her questions himself, because all he and Reagan had talked about was the future, not the past. He wondered if anyone knew, other than the Candidate himself. "He had his name legally changed only six months ago, and no, he didn't tell me from what. That means he can't easily be traced. The facts will only come from his mouth and then we can discover if any of it is true."

"We all are in the dark? Even the Party?" Jill asked, astonished.

"Afraid so. What we know is that he came to us with the same name and appearance as a very revered previous president. The timing couldn't be better, because the Party badly needs a popular candidate at this moment, or we'll lose the upcoming election. It's like too good to be true."

"Well, has anyone thought of DNA? I imagine there are samples from the president someplace. Or fingerprints?"

"Jill, he admits that he isn't the president. I heard him tell you that. What would fingerprints prove? As far as the DNA, Charlie, I mean the Chairman, whispered that Ronald Reagan had supplied that data himself...tests run by a credible lab...and the results prove a match with the former president. He's related...but you can't use that in print until we get permission. Understand?"

"But that's what they will demand. Any hard evidence will be convincing. Please, can't I use it?"

"Negative and the reason is clear. They, the public, the press and our adversaries, will demand to see the printed results and will call the lab for confirmation. I don't have the papers and likely they won't be released until our side corroborates them. No...don't print that either. Now you understand what I meant by being cooperative. This is what it will take to be inside. You will have knowledge that can't be disclosed. Timing is everything in this game."

"In this instance, I agree with you. I won't mention it. But later...I might not be willing to keep quiet. What if it turns out that there is something the voters have to know? I'll be forced to choose between my country or the Party."

"You might...or you might not. Let's cross that bridge when we have to. Not yet. Agreed?"

"Agreed. Back to my hotel now?"

9:00 PM The Arlington Retreat Hotel

Jill started typing while trying to remember the afternoon in detail. She decided to recount the pandemonium in the auditorium first and stopped to think about the right words to properly describe the intensity of it when the phone rang.

"Hi," she answered.

"Hi yourself," Mr. Burns retorted, his familiar voice deep and abrupt, always reflective of his impatient nature. "I'm getting an earful right now listening to the cable news shows. They are showing pictures of a man who looks like...Ronald Reagan. Were you actually there, and where is my copy?"

"Working on it right now, Chief. I'll get it in before midnight. That's the cutoff, correct?"

"Where have you been? What in the blazes were you doing after the event? I mean, hell, that was over before noon. Do you think I'm just sitting around playing chess while the world is on fire with a story this size? This is your first assignment out of town, and you are dallying. Explain!" he shouted the last, and Jill held the phone away from her ear, knowing it was coming.

"Mr. Burns, " she began, only to be cut off by more yelling.

"I'm telling you that this is the last time I'm sending you out. You'll be doing the missing dog reports from now on. You hear me?"

"Wait and be quiet!" she yelled back. "Let me talk...please!" Her unexpected outburst had the desired effect, because there was at last silence on the other end. "Your star reporter was the only one, and I mean the only one, invited backstage to meet Ronald Reagan. I sat right beside him on the couch, and we talked. I went to dinner with the RNC spokesperson, Ted Clark, tonight, and I think I am going to be invited to meet with Mr. Reagan again. Possibility is that I will have exclusive access to him and his story. Now do you feel like shouting at me or dancing a jig?"

"You are serious?"

"You bet I am."

"Damn. Really?"

"Really."

"OK. Then file your story...but it better be good. I'm not going to bed until I read it, so make it fast."

"Yes, Chief. Love you, too. Bye." She hung up feeling a lot better. All bluster, Burns was cursed with a heart of gold. She burned with pride that this story would be the best thing that had ever happened to him and that his unwavering faith in her was justified after all.

She began furiously typing again, then stopped abruptly and looked off into space. Was she missing something, were they all missing something? Why, out of the blue, would appear a man...no, a savior, who is an exact copy of one of the most popular presidents of all time? Then she remembered the book *The Manchurian Candidate* and its chilling story. Were they all dropping their guard because of this individual's looks, charm and voice without any other facts? And right this minute Jill is contributing to the worship without knowing the first thing....no, that wasn't right. She knew that he had changed his name. More obfuscation, more shadows. She couldn't allow herself to be swept up like all the others. She had to keep a clear head. Then she remembered her task at hand. Write this story to make Burns happy, the public interested while not offending the RNC or...Ronald Reagan. That is, if she wanted to be allowed back inside. Only inside was she going to have access, gleaning facts which could be independently checked and verified. It was her duty as an American to keep her access so that the true story could be told. And, she resolved, it would be told, with no detail left out.

6:00 AM

Jill rubbed her hand into her face, still caught in the grip of an interesting dream and not wanting to exit. The bedside phone continued to ring as her brain fog lifted. She saw the time at the same moment she realized that the house phone was ringing. Reaching for it, she laid back against the pillow, holding the phone against her ear. "I didn't ask for a wake up call," she said and rubbed the other eye with the back of her fist.

"We're sorry, but there is a fax which just arrived with instructions to give it to you in person as early as possible," the voice said. "May I send someone up?"

"Yeah, and tell him to have a cup of black coffee with him. Make that two cups and charge it to Mr. Burns." Jill hung up and stared at the ceiling. She had waited until 1:00 AM for any complaint about her work, then gone to bed. The fax arriving momentarily would likely be a copy of the front page. Burns had printed it just as she had written, or she would have heard. First victory of the day was in her corner. Now what? She hurriedly pulled on her robe and just in time, because there was a knock on her door.

The smiling young girl greeted her with a large manila envelope tucked under her arm, while holding a folded Washington newspaper on a tray containing an empty cup and saucer and a small, still steaming, pot of coffee. In addition, there was a large glazed bun. "So you are Jill Longley," the girl affirmed. Her metal name tag displayed "Laura." "I saw the fax. Congratulations. Wish I had been there with you. You know Reagan's photo is in all the papers? Wow, is he good-looking. What did you think?"

"I think I need to fully wake up first. Thanks for the tray and the paper. I'll be sure and leave a tip for you at the desk before I check out," Jill said and moved away so that the tray could be placed on the table.

"Are you staying with us for awhile?" the girl asked. Jill's antenna went up. What was the reason for the question, she wondered.

"Unknown. Why do you ask?"

"I imagine that this place will get very busy if you do, if you know what I mean."

"Thanks for alerting me. That's an extra ten bucks for you. I'll put it in an envelope marked *For Laura*."

"Have a good day," Laura said as she closed the door.

Before sitting down, Jill held open the Washington paper, knowing what she would find. The headline was huge. "Ronald Reagan Returns!" it screamed. There were photos obviously lifted from video but were of excellent clarity. There was one positioned beside a historical photo of the original Ronald Reagan and his facial expression, the angle of exposure, even the lighting were eerily similar. It seemed to be the same man in both photos. She rapidly scanned the article but quickly realized that the paper had no sources other than the reality of the event itself. The article was full of speculation and comment by other politicians, most from the opposition, and most of those belittling the original Reagan. The political heat had just started. One side builds, the other detracts. She turned on the television and flipped until she saw Reagan's handsome face appear. Listening and watching while she started her coffee, she realized the same thing. There *were* no facts, and Jill Longley had the only interview, and it was printed and lying on the table beside her. It would cause thunder and lighting, and she was sure that every television media would want a live interview with her. The gal, Laura, was right. If they found her, she was trapped.

She finished her bun and the last sip of coffee before opening the envelope containing her story. "The best for last," she said aloud.

Someone at the paper had taken the front page and shrunk it to fit letter size for faxing. The headline alone was satisfying: "An Interview With Ronald Reagan by Jill Longley." She scanned the words and could see no changes. Bless Burns's heart, he had let it through intact. She read and thought it over, went through the words one by one. It should do the trick, she smiled.

Jill suddenly sprang to action. Aware she had to leave before the other press discovered where she was staying, she decided on a quick shower before packing. But go where? She had to use a credit card and her real name. Every place would be the same. And whom to ask for help? She didn't know a soul in town other than...Ted. No, asking him was asking for problems. He might expect a return of favors, besides a connection would be discovered, tainting her reports in the eye of the public. But if she left now, how would Ted find her, assuming the RNC was happy with her article? Ted had taken her back last night, so he knew her hotel, but he never got her personal number, nor did he give her his. A dilemma. She shrugged, disrobed and headed for the shower. On the way past the full length mirror, she paused to look at herself. "Exactly what do men see in me?" she asked her image.

Chapter 2

Chapter 3

A Room With A View

Still making up her mind while grooming her hair, Jill's mind raced with all the previous events and possible future ones. Could she influence what was about to happen, or was it simply fate, inevitable fate? Looking in the mirror past her shoulder toward the dark corners of the sleeping area, she imagined the wrinkled faces of the Moirai, the three sisters of fate. What will happen has already been determined by them at her birth, and Jill was along for the ride. She felt her lips purse, about to ask the shimmering image of Clotho what was to happen, when her cell phone rang, jarring her back to reality.

Jill picked it up and looked at the number. Unknown. Hesitantly, she pushed the button and held it to her ear, listening only.

"Jill? Are you there?" Ted's voice said.

"Hi. Didn't know you had my number," she answered.

"I have resources. Had breakfast?"

"A roll and lots of coffee."

"Good. I'll be waiting at the front entrance in twenty minutes. See you." Ted hung up before she could answer affirmative or negative. Likely on purpose. The guy was a piece of work all right. She shrugged. Answers one of the many problems anyway, she thought.

Ted was waiting, leaning against his car, when she walked toward the glass door, pausing to have the automatic opening activated. He smiled and strolled toward her, and she noticed that he was dressed differently, more casual but still expensively. His polished wingtips caught the light when he moved. The car was a heavy German model, glintingly showroom new and still running. He held the passenger door open for her with one hand, the other ready for assistance should she need it.

"Really, Ted, I expected a chauffeur and sitting in the back seat. This is a letdown."

"Next time. We didn't need the company. Now, ready for wonderful conversation over breakfast?" He glanced at her, not expecting an answer, while he concentrated on driving. "Read your piece this morning. Good job, in my opinion. I'll hear more within the hour...and so will you. If you look in the glove box, you'll find another phone you can use. No one can get that number, and I predict you will need it."

"I saw some of the other reports on the air and in print. Your boy really stirred them into a frenzy," she observed.

"It's only going to get more intense from here on. The opposition will try hard to run him down and dig up negative facts. They'll use you if your guard isn't up. Think you can handle it?"

"That mean I'm in?"

"As far as I'm concerned. You are perfect...and I mean that." He smiled, showing his teeth and dimples.

"Yes, so you've implied. We should get one thing clear right now before it starts, Ted. I am a reporter doing a job. Think of me in that way rather than a girlfriend and treat me as such. Don't dwell on the male-female thing, because it might never happen between us. Even if it did, it might get in the way. Slow down, Ted."

Ted was listening but not looking at her while she spoke. His head slowly nodded, indicating that he took in what she had said. It wasn't agreement or rejection she saw in his reaction. What was he thinking?

The car swerved and turned briskly into a parking lot. Jill looked around seeing an attractive modern establishment, sparkling with glass, and perched on a small hill overlooking the broad river behind. The parking lot was flush with cars, most of them luxury models.

Once inside, Ted spoke confidentially into the ear of the hostess, and she happily agreed to whatever he had requested. In a moment, a beaming young woman offered to show them to their seats. She led the way toward the rear and opened a door, standing aside to allow them entrance. It was a private dining area which would seat four in a pinch but perfect for two. The dark water of the Potomac flowed silently below. Ted offered the seat facing the river to Jill and held the chair for her. The waitress patiently waited and took out her notebook. Jill looked around surprised at the lack of a menu.

Chuckling, Ted informed her, "No menu in this place. The will serve anything your heart desires. All you have to do is to tell her what you want."

Jill recovered quickly. "Then I'll have smoked salmon and a bagel. Cream cheese on the side and a small latte." The waitress scribbled it down and looked up at Ted.

He shrugged and displayed his attractive dimples. "Same for me," then turned his full attention on Jill as the waitress withdrew, closing the door. He noticed Jill's hands, which were clasped in front of her and resting on the table. Resisting the urge to touch her, instead he leaned back in his chair and studied her face before speaking.

"I've been appointed campaign manager for Ronald Reagan's bid for the White House. In my position, a lot of perks come into play. Such as organizing the team, supervising the public and private marketing of the candidate, raising money, planning events and so on. I'm picking you for a series of private interviews with him that will start the ball rolling. You know enough about politics to understand that the field will broaden over time, and you will lose exclusivity. But for now, and until we understand what we have on our hands, the job belongs to you and you alone. You, Jill Longley, can make or break this candidate, and because of that, you have to consent to some supervision."

"By supervision, you mean that you personally will edit my copy before I send it to the paper?"

"Not exactly. Don't get your back up now. I don't intend to tell you what to write, but I will give suggestions and reserve the right to censor if the need arises. You already understand the requirement for this, but if you don't, just watch the other newspersons act like barracudas."

"Surely I get it. But you have to remember the nature of a free press. We can't be told what to do. You have publicity people who already are one-sided. Don't tell me what to write, how to write or what I can't write. There's got to be some trust, or you can count me out."

"You are to be given exclusive access. Don't you realize what that means to you and your future? No matter what happens to Ronald Reagan, you will be propelled to the top of the press corps."

"That's a bribe, Ted. I won't accept the premise. You know how much this means to me to be able to write this story, but you cannot buy my copy for any price. Money and fame don't mean as much to me as to most people. I was happy being a nobody until yesterday, and I can go back to it again tomorrow with a clear conscience. You have to trust me."

Ted turned his head away from her and studied the moving river. They sat in impasse and silence until the waitress tapped on the door before coming in with a tray of food. She chatted non-stop about nearly everything inside and outside before focusing on the topic of the day. "You folks heard about the new Ronald Reagan?" she asked looking back and forth.

Ted roused himself and looked her in the eye. "Does that excite you? I mean, judging your age, you were born after President Reagan left office. Do you know anything about him?"

"Not him. The new one. He is so good-looking. I can't wait to see more of him." She finished her task and closed the door behind her.

"There you have it, Jill. The young ones will only go on what Reagan is at the moment. The old ones will think he is the same man as before. It's up to you to blend the two together."

"I'm ready and willing. My terms or no terms. What do you say?" she said.

Ted raised his latte toward her and waited for her cup to click against his. The bargain was sealed, and Jill felt like dancing around the room, but her eyes did it for her. Utter happiness, that's what she felt. The sky and the moon were hers for the taking. "Thanks, Ted. You won't be sorry."

"I know. I knew from the first moment I saw that little lost girl that you are special."

"Ted, finding you, or you finding me, has already been a great adventure. Something tells me that it's just the beginning." Relaxed and renewed, Jill stretched her arms outward toward Ted and the great river behind him. "I can't wait to get started!"

"About that Jill," Ted said seriously. "There's more to discuss." Before he could describe his new wrinkle, Jill's phone started to vibrate.

By reflex, she picked it up. "This is Jill," she said.

On the other end a voice excitedly crackled, "This is Jill Longley?" he asked.

"Sure is."

"This is Bob Severman, and I'll get right to the point. Your piece on Ronald Reagan caught our eye at NBC. Looks like you were the only reporter to get close. How would you like to share your story on a couple of our morning shows? I can schedule for tomorrow morning at our studios in New York. Of course, we will pick up all expenses. What do you say?"

"Not at the moment, Mr. Severman. I'm too busy to accommodate you. Perhaps later."

"Miss Longley, you should know that we pay well for airtime, and you are not only turning down a handsome paycheck but a lot of free publicity." Jill's phone started to buzz again with another incoming call.

"Sorry, Mr. Severman, but I've got another call. Back to you later if you don't mind." She switched to the incoming call by the press of a button.

"Hi."

"Am I speaking to Jill Longley, the reporter?" the voice inquired.

"That's me."

"Jill, this is Judy Johnson at the New York Times. My editor loved your piece about Reagan and asked me to recruit you to work at the Times. You can continue whatever your plans are and submit your work directly to the Times. I personally guarantee you a front page spot. This is an offer rarely given by the Times, Jill, and we would consider it an honor if you would agree."

"I'm absolutely thrilled, Judy, practically speechless. It's a great opportunity I realize, and I appreciate it deeply, but I owe something to my paper and my editor who have been loyal to me. I simply can't change employers at the moment, and I know as a newsperson you can respect that."

"That's admirable, Jill, but you also have to look after yourself in this world. Besides, the circulation of the Times will bring your story to vastly more people. Think what it would mean to the subject of your story. Ask him what he thinks before refusing. Please."

"I will do that. And thanks for the interest in me, Judy. I'll remember it whatever happens, and I'll be sure to let you know if I change my mind." Jill put her phone away and realized that Ted was intently watching from across the table, a small smile showed that he knew that he was right about something.

"How do they all acquire a private, unlisted cell phone number, Ted. How did you get it?

"The Internet, Jill. It's not hard. Let me guess, both of those calls were trying to hire you away from your little paper. Your answers were superb, by the way, and your editor would be proud of you for refusing." He frowned while thinking of how to phrase the next sentence.

"But. There's a 'but' coming, I can feel it."

"Sure is. From our point of view, your little newspaper isn't the best for exposure, you know. We would welcome a larger platform now that you are so accepted and proven. On the other hand, you will be subject to rigorous censorship from the very liberal editors of the mainstream press. You resisted my small efforts at gentle supervision, but you haven't seen anything yet until you get in bed with those outfits."

"You have an opinion then, I imagine?"

"Stay right where you are for the moment. They all will find your story anyway, and it will still get printed and reported by the big news outlets. Plus, it will make you even more sought after than now. It's a win-win for all of us. You are the loser in the short-term, because it's going to cost you a fabulous salary, but you'll make up for it later."

"I believe you, Ted, and that's what I was going to do anyway. But that's not what you started to say previously."

"No, another matter entirely. I'm hesitant to tell you because of your independent nature and how you will interpret what I want to say." He took a big sip of coffee and leaned back in the chair and rocked a little. "Here goes. There is a wealthy donor and supporter of our party who has a large estate over on the Eastern Shore. We have settled Ronald Reagan there for the moment so that he can be shielded from the storming press and protected from any real danger. It's a perfect situation for a series of interviews, very private interviews. You have been chosen to do the work for us."

Jill beamed her answer at him, but before she could say anything, Ted continued, "And the other, more delicate part. The facility is big, very big, and I want you to consider staying there as well for the time being. It will separate you from the rest of the press and allow you privacy, comfort, security and the freedom to do your best work. Will you consider it at least?"

"And you, Ted. Where will you be?"

"Not there, you can be assured, in case you are thinking what I'm thinking you are thinking." He laughed and showed his perfect teeth and dimples. "I'll have enough to do, but don't think I'm abandoning you, because I'll be a frequent visitor. Someone has to look after Jill Longley, and I am self-appointed."

"Well, thanks, Ted. You are a marvel of surprises. I agree, with reservations."

"What reservations?"

"A woman can change her mind. I'll have to see the setup first."

"Absolutely. Now turn off your phone so that we can finish breakfast in peace. By the way, there is a girl working at your hotel who will pack up for you and have your luggage at the front door in about twenty minutes. Should that be satisfactory to you, that is."

"And her name is Laura?"

2:15 PM   21 Pilmoure Place, Eastern Shore Maryland
Ted waited at the security gate as the uniformed guard phoned in for permission to enter. Jill noticed twin security cams on either side of the stone pillars, aimed directly at the car. In the near distance, the brick drive angled smoothly away from the entrance, the estate thereby hidden completely from view. Beyond a row of cultivated trees, shimmered the

open water of Chesapeake Bay. The far shore was completely out of sight, in spite of the blessings of a clear day. She rolled down her window and breathed the salted air, moist and fragrant from the nearby pines. Such wealth, she marveled. How is it possible that a single person can acquire so much? The thought troubled her in some vague way. It was one thing to see a movie representation of conspicuous wealth or even read about it. Firsthand, though, it was jaw-dropping, even at this distance.

"Cleared to enter, folks," the guard said, squatting down level with the driver's window. "Take the drive toward the house, and another guard will direct you from there. Have a good visit." The iron gates ponderously opened, and Ted rolled almost silently over the red stone drive. After a couple of gradual turns, the house came into view. It was, unsurprisingly, archetypal Georgian in design with a central building elegantly centered between two identical wings which took off at subtle angles, accentuating the taller structure in between, the driveway winding in grand fashion in a curve, its apogee the stately entrance, then continuing around toward a separate building which looked to be a multiple car garage. Another uniformed guard stood in the drive holding his hand up, signaling a stop, right in front of the short staircase to the front door.

As Ted shut the motor off, two young men appeared out of nowhere, positioning themselves at the trunk of the car, both dressed in identical white shirts, blue pressed pants over highly polished shoes. They seemed eager to claim any luggage and were relaxed but not talkative. After Jill's two small and tattered bags were withdrawn from the trunk, they seemed disappointed in some way. Without discussion, one seized the two bags and started for the door. The other smiled graciously and indicated with his arm motion that they were to follow him. He led them up the staircase toward the massive front door which was flanked by large stained glass panels on either side, topped with a curved glass window above, also in figured, clear glass. The door was finished in a glossy black and ornamented with highly polished brass hardware. Jill was rather expecting a reception desk and a register, but the door led into a high hallway encapsulating a double freestanding staircase, its first landing lit by another highly decorative window. The luggage started its way up the staircase, and when he reached the landing, he paused waiting for them to catch up.

"Jill, this is where I get off. I have a full afternoon so..." Ted explained.

"So, I am on my own from here on?" she questioned. "I was never even told the host's name, Ted. Don't you think an introduction is in order, at least, before you disappear?"

"You shouldn't worry about that at all. I assure you that you are expected and welcome, and the staff will see to your needs and even introductions when it becomes necessary."

"Meaning the host, whoever that is, isn't even here?"

"Correct. And is anonymous and prefers to remain that way. It's just you, the Candidate and the extensive house staff. He is quartered in the other wing, by the way, but I'm sure you will cross paths sometime today."

Jill turned toward Ted, wanting to touch him, kiss him, or in some manner show her gratitude but resisted, knowing that link would make her professionalism questioned. Ted seemed to understand what was in her mind and instead offered his hand to her.

"Told you that I had no expectations, Jill. And it's not that I don't find you attractive. I want you not to feel that I have a hold over you, but that you are free to write your story in any way you choose. Later, though, is a different matter, and even if I'm not by your side every day, you will be in my thoughts. I'll call you later this evening to see if there is anything you want and if you are happy with the circumstances."

Jill took his offered hand, and this time lingered before letting go. "Thanks, Ted. I won't let you down, and you can be sure that I will remember who was responsible for this break. You will be returning soon, won't you?"

"Truly, I don't know the answer."

With obvious reluctance, Ted headed for the entryway and his waiting car. Just before the door closed, he turned and gave her a wink and smile, then was gone.

Jill rushed to catch up with the waiting servant and followed him up the second and then third staircase and along a short corridor before stopping at a door marked "White." She wondered at the name until the door was opened for her and she saw the room and its furnishings. All white, the carpet, the walls, the linens...even the upholstery and drapes. The only color was from two Han blue Chinese vases flanking the double doors to the balcony. Both were full of red roses in full bloom. The boy opened the doors, allowing the fresh air and the view of the bay to stream in. Before excusing himself, he indicated the door to the bathroom, then politely left.

Jill went onto the balcony and looked out over the landscaped lawn, the stands of trees and the long dock extending into the Chesapeake. This place was as close to heaven as she had been. It was going to be an amazing adventure.

Chapter 4

Face to Face

At precisely 4:00, Jill heard a soft ring from the room telephone and picked it up. An accented female voice advised her that dinner would be served at 5:30 in the dining room and asked if she had any wants or special needs. She didn't and answered as such. The caller asked if she had appropriate evening wear with her for dinner. This question caught Jill by surprise. No, she didn't bring any evening wear. None at all. She didn't divulge it to the caller, but the truth was she didn't even own any evening gowns, and the last one she had used had been rented. She was told to expect an assistant soon who would be of service in this regard.

A soft knock at the door preceded it opening widely enough to allow entry of a small Asian woman who, without introduction or permission, commenced using her cloth tape to measure Jill's size. She gave a last up and down look at Jill, leaving without comment. Jill started to laugh. She felt as if she had stepped through the looking glass and was in another reality where things didn't go as expected. She took out her laptop and seated herself in a comfortable lounge chair on the deck and started organizing her thoughts. The events leading up to the present, while not printable as a news article, were still memorable enough to record. Later, they may be of some interest depending on future events. After typing and concentrating, she looked at her watch and realized that it was already past 5:00. She closed the computer and hurried to put on, at least, the best outfit she had with her. There on the bed was a lovely dress, spread out to show bands of sequins and the sheen of the soft fabric. Jill took a deep breath and touched the gown just to reassure herself that it wasn't imagination. It was real enough and visually appeared to be at least close to the correct size. It was obviously placed there for her to use at supper, so she started putting it on.

Try as she might, she could not pull the rear zipper high enough to close the back. Again she checked her watch. Five more minutes until supper. There was no other choice, she had to go the way she was and stepped into the hallway. There, beside the door, was the little Asian seamstress waiting on her to emerge. She seemed to already know that the rear zipper was a problem and, without asking, zipped it up and then nodded her approval of the entire effect.

The gown was nearly floor length with a partially open back and moderately plunging neckline. Jill passed a hall mirror and turned to inspect herself. It was a marvelous transformation indeed. She was beautiful even to herself, and she had no doubt that the newest candidate for election to the presidency was to be seated at the same table. Walking down the staircase, she felt like floating instead. This was a fairy tale that couldn't be imagined. She had to giggle when she realized that somewhere outside was a large pumpkin ready to take her back to her former existence.

At the foot of the stairs was one of the young men who had assisted at their arrival. He bowed slightly and grinned his approval at her appearance, then led the way toward the dining room. When the double door was opened for her, she saw Ronald Reagan on the other side of the room leaning against the wall, obviously waiting on her arrival. He put down his drink and moved toward her, smiling.

"I must say that this is a true honor, Miss Longley. If you don't mind me stating an obvious fact, you are remarkably beautiful. It sort of takes my breath away to look at you. I had no idea that my biographer would also be a stunning attraction." He politely offered his hand to her, and they shook lightly while keeping their eyes fixed on each other.

He pulled out a chair and stood behind it while she was seated, then chose for himself a chair right beside hers. The room was long and furnished with obviously valuable antiques, their mahogany red brown sheen speaking to ages of care and polishing. The dining room table was easily large enough to seat sixteen, and Reagan had chosen to use adjacent seats instead of the usual and expected choice of sitting across from each other. He was dressed in a black tuxedo complete with black tie and looked like he had one on since birth, mostly because he was so comfortable in it, like it was just another ordinary article of clothing.

After he was seated, he turned toward her, leaning nearly enough to touch her and said, "I already told you that I was excited that you and I might be together at some point. Now here it is...we are together after all." His smile was infectious, and she smiled back unsure of what to say.

"We may be in a formal place and dressed formally, Jill, but there is no reason we have to be formal. We'll be spending a lot of time together in the next few weeks and getting to know each other rather well, so, from this moment on, I'll call you Jill and you are to call me Ron. Do you agree?"

"Ron, I am happy to oblige. This is a privilege for me to have the opportunity to tell the world your story. It's going to be the most important thing I ever write."

"The first thing you should know, Jill, is that I think of myself as a very normal person, not as a prior president or a movie star or the governor of a large state. I only claim to be ordinary and just like everybody else except for one thing...I look like a famous person. So I want you to look past my appearance and try to see the real me, and when you do, I hope you find something of value."

"That's my job, I feel. To find and tell the truth. Are you willing to confide in me after such a brief introduction?" Jill asked.

"In this, I think Ted was correct in suggesting Jill Longley. You have the writing skill, and I can sense your sincerity and lack of malice, and you have already sent the right message that you are not here for the money. The fact topping it all is that you are entirely lovely and will be delightful to spend time with."

"To my ears, you didn't answer my question. Are you ready to have trust in me?"

"We have to work up to it, Jill. Told incorrectly, you may get confused with my story. There are things which have happened to me which are hard to accept unless you know all the facts. You and I will have to go slowly, because there is a lot to tell."

"Ron, you have to forgive me, but I want to know only two things tonight and then I promise not to ask any more until you are ready. Answer my questions and we can dine and enjoy each other's company in peace."

"I'm willing. Ask what you must."

"First, I have to know if you are actually related to President Ronald Reagan."

"In my heart, I'm positive that I am.

"The second question is about your name. Reagan wasn't your last name until recently, isn't that true?"

"We'll obviously spend some time with this question, Jill, but I'll answer it only briefly tonight. For most of my life, I had no idea that I was related to President Reagan. The truth is that I didn't really know anything about him for a long time. I grew up with an entirely different name and had absolutely no connection to the president or any of his relations."

"Thank you, Ron, for your honesty and for your compliments. Now I have an admission for you. I have never thought of myself as beautiful, not even once, but in your company, I truly feel beautiful. It's your presence which brings it out, and I am thankful for that."

The door at the rear opened with a snap and a steady stream of waiters and waitresses brought out the food and arrayed it near the center of the table. Two dapper individuals waited, ready to serve as requested. "Well, such a spread," Reagan joked. "We'll have to use the gym daily, I'm afraid." There was clearly too much to eat for two people. It was more a feast for a full table.

Reagan shook his head and summoned one of the servers to him. "I have a suggestion, and I know you will think it's irregular, but since I am the principle in this house at this time, you'll have to follow my instructions."

The man nodded with wild eyes, not knowing what to expect. He was only trained to serve, not make decisions.

"I want you and the other members of the staff to all come in, seat yourselves, and dine with us. I will not accept no for an answer. There is plenty of food, and we would enjoy your company."

"Well, if you insist, sir. But I've never seen that done before," he answered, unsure of what to do.

"I insist. Go round them up, and Jill and I will wait to eat until everyone is here." The man and his assistant quickly disappeared behind the rear door, and they could hear excited conversation on the other side. Reagan laughed aloud as he continued to watch the door and was quickly rewarded by a stream of cautious staff. Some of the women held their hands in front of their face and mouth in shyness. They filed in, mostly on the other side of the table and waited for someone to confirm the order to sit down.

Ronald Reagan looked up and said, "Please sit down, It's no mistake, and we welcome your company. While I'm in residence here, no man or woman is better than any other. We are all friends, you can be sure." He rose and went around the table, helping seat the women and patting the men affectionately on their backs. When everyone was in place, he returned to his chair. "My name is Ron, and this is Jill. Please allow us to call you by your first names. Now for introductions. Start with this fellow." He tapped the man seated beside him who seemed startled at being touched.

After a few minutes, the room was alive with conversation and questions. They all knew who their special guest was, and each had their own questions for him. Each time something sensitive was raised, he deflected the question with a joke or smile and returned with a question of his own. It was a skilled performance which could only be carried off by a unique and experienced individual. Reagan was at home with everybody, master of none, and his display of control amazed Jill. She got more understanding of the man at this event than anything she could have asked him. This was a person that the people would want as president, she was sure. She decided that her next report would be about this meal and how it was handled by the Candidate and that it would be typed and filed before the night was over.

When the food was consumed and several bottles of wine were enjoyed, Reagan again stood and looked around. "Thank you each and all for a very enjoyable dinner. I must say also that the food was superb but not nearly as wonderful as the company. Now I will allow you to get back to work so that I can spend a few moments alone with Jill before bedtime."

They all got up clapping, waving to him and Jill and thanking him again for the experience. All at once the commotion was over, and Jill and Ron were alone.

"That was simply marvelous, Ron. You are a very special person," she said.

"No, I am just like them. No better, nor worse, and I did that because I wanted to, not to make an impression. So if your plans are to scurry up to your room and file a story about it, I object in advance."

"Aw, come on, Ron. It's a great piece. People will love you for that," she protested.

"No, they won't. They will all think that it was staged or even untrue. You have to trust my intuition on this. The story will filter out in time, right out of the mouths of those folks we just entertained. That's the right way to tell it."

Jill felt crushed. She was expected to make or break the Candidate, but he wasn't going to make it easy for her. She visibly slumped in her chair.

"I have an idea, Jill. Instead of you slaving away on your computer trying to make a deadline, let's go out to the rear and sit in the dark and watch the bay. It's a perfect night for it." He got up and eased her out of her chair and folded her arm into his. "I think it's this way." It was, and he and Jill strolled through the big house and out into the night. The stars were out and, since there was no artificial light nearby, were very bright and clear. The bay was as calm as the bay could ever be, and moonlight danced over the small waves. They chose a white cast iron settee facing the bay and sat down together.

"I do have one more question that I'm burning to ask," Jill admitted.

"No. That's my answer, Jill. I have never been married." She could hear his chuckle and feel his body shake with laugher, because he had correctly anticipated her question.

"And you should answer the same question," he said.

"You know the answer already, I'm sure." she responded.

"Let me clear one thing up right now, Jill. I am not a candidate for romance at this time. You are exceedingly attractive, but I think it isn't a direction we should choose to go. There is much work to be done on behalf of the people of the United States, and we have been selected to do our duty. I want to be able to feel affectionate toward you, to look at you with admiration and even desire, but I won't ask you to go farther than that, even if you would. Right now, I need a friend, a very close friend. Could you feel that way toward me also?"

"I already do. You are the most interesting man I have ever met, and as yet, I know nothing about you. As far as I'm concerned, you are my very best friend, and I'm yours." He reached for her hand and held it affectionately as they both studied the dark moving water of the bay.

Chapter 5

Only In Daylight Might Truth Be Seen

Jill awakened and first noticed the ceiling. In the shadows of the long light of morning she could make out detail that she hadn't noticed yesterday. There was considerable ornamentation and depth, dramatic in tangential light but not seen clearly in the more direct light of nighttime artificial illumination. She allowed her eyes to play over the shapes, not thinking about anything in particular while drawing the covers up about her neck and chin. She was happy, incredibly happy, for the first time in her life. Was it the improbable luck of being chosen to be the companion of a remarkable man or was it the fulfillment of a desire to write something important, something bound to make her famous and wealthy? The curtains near the open door to the patio fluttered softly, making her look at them, halfway expecting to see the friendly face of Ronald Reagan. After a moment, she settled back down and forced herself to concentrate, instead of dream. In the short space of twenty-four hours, her world had been completely changed, her future path was aiming a different direction. New people had suddenly appeared who were important but unknown previously. Again, she wondered to herself if her fate had been preordained by some unknown force, coming to appreciate and understand the ancient world's explanation of such things.

A thought struck her with impact, elevating her pulse and widening her pupils. It wasn't possible, this string of good luck. It was all too perfect. She had been specifically chosen over thousands of better known writers of all kinds, some of them already famous. Why her, she wondered? Then the truth, or at least a possible truth, came rushing in. Did someone plan out this entire sequence? Was it all scheduled and pat? She took an inward look at herself, as seeing Jill Longley from afar for the first time. They, if there is a they, knew she would fall under the spell of Ronald Reagan and correctly guessed that he would be attracted to her. Were they cast together simply to intensify what and how she would report? And is Ronald Reagan part of the scheme, or is he simply a pawn like her?

Jill sat up, casting the covers aside, her focus introspective, looking at her knees but not seeing them. Who could have done this, she wondered. She remembered Ted, the resourceful and gifted schemer of the RNC. He never did say how and why he got his job, nor really anything about himself. Instead, he had made a rather obvious play for her, his intentions all but stated openly. Then, Ted placed her in this house, knowing that she would very likely have a serious affair with the Candidate. If Ted was genuinely attracted to her, why would he expose her to this predicament? He wouldn't, it dawned on her, not unless he was directing the entire little play. Ted, after all, was the one who had "found" her, and after that, things had moved awfully fast.

Jill dropped backward on the bed, assessing the ceiling again and thinking more clearly. There were only two possibilities, either what was happening was all arranged or she had the best luck on the planet. Which? Then, if she was to really get suspicious, she might consider the remote possibility that Ted could be working for the opposition by getting the new Candidate compromised in a seedy sexual dalliance with some unknown, fame-seeking reporter. It was clear from the way Ronald Reagan had spoken to her on the patio about avoidance of romance of a sexual nature, he could not be part of any scheme, if there is one. At least Ronald Reagan has morals and personal courage, she decided.

Jill stood for a moment in the center of the room looking toward the bay then realized the person ambling along the long dock was none other than the Candidate. She hurriedly changed, anxious to see him again. Perhaps more discussion would bring out hidden facts, and in spite of her paranoia, she was very ready for another encounter with him.

Ron looked up from the dock toward the big house and unexpectedly got a reward. Jill was coming toward him using purposeful, long strides. She had unpinned her long blonde hair which swung freely in the soft breeze off the bay. A simple cotton blouse over her white shorts and scuffed tennis shoes was the uniform of the relaxed Hollywood crowd, but he knew that it was real with Jill. What you saw was what she actually was, without pretense or deception. As she got closer, he could see the sparkle in her eyes, her expression of recognition of a valued friend, one whom she wanted to be with. Reagan knew that he had to resist her while keeping her close. A delicate task, to be sure. He realized that what he wanted was her love, but love without body contact, a sterile love.

"My, seeing you this morning is like a trip to the moon and back. Didn't Cole Porter write a song about doing that?" he remarked as Jill got close.

"You might be thinking of the phrase 'A trip to the moon on gossamer wings.' He did write that, but if you know the song well, it clearly does not fit us. It's more about a fling," she laughed and reminded him.

"Oh, that was before my time anyway. Pardon me, Jill, but you are a gift to mankind. However, I'm also grateful that I'm the only one seeing you."

"I spotted you walking alone as I was gazing at the bay. You should have company for your strolls, so when you remember anything interesting, I will be there to record it."

"You are reminding me that the party is over, and we are to get serious today, aren't you?"

"No pressure. I've got all the time in the world or at least as long as the owner allows us to stay in his glorious home."

"You and I are in agreement. There are real deadlines, though. A campaign for the presidency is about to begin, really has begun in some quarters, and if I am to be championed by anybody, I soon have to start opening up about my personal details."

"You don't really want to disclose the details of your life, even to me, do you?"

"It opens a lot of really dark and scary things, Jill. You won't understand that for a long time, and since I am transferring what the public thinks to what Jill Longley thinks, it's very important that I get it right."

"You mean to say that if you can make me understand and believe in you, then I'll make the public feel the same way. Is that what you are trying to say?"

"Very close. To me, the radiant Jill Longley *is* the face of the public. I need to think about you in that way to get through what is to be an ordeal for me."

"So some of your story isn't pleasant, or is it that some of it must remain secret?"

"There is both, and there is a period of my life that I want to keep hidden for as long as possible. You will begin to feel the edges of this space as we talk and be suspicious that I have either a hidden agenda, that I am controlled by some group, or that the public would be appalled if they knew. Trust me when I tell you that by the time you know me well enough, you will be given the entire story, but that knowledge will cause even you to doubt me."

"I can already tell you that the opposition party will do and say anything to stop you. They will make up facts, exaggerate any flaws and ignore any of your strengths. This morning, I got up and had suspicions that my presence here with you is no accident. Someone, or some designing group, set the entire thing up. But out here in the clear sunlight, I have put it in perspective. You and I are going to pull this off, no matter what schemes are at play. We are going to tell your story using the truth. If you are qualified to be president, then you should not worry. If you feel that the truth will out you in some way, you should withdraw while you have time."

"I have a desire to serve my country. Wealth and power are not interesting to me. I have managed to live without that all of my life and could do it again. Because of my appearance, I have a chance to be elected president where I can do the right thing. At this time, we, as a nation, are adrift, much as we were in the seventies, if not worse this time. I think I can make a difference, and that is why I must try."

"You sound exactly like the Ronald Reagan of old. It's what he would have said," Jill remarked. She had to resist the sudden urge to hug and embrace him, to find his lips with hers. She was in love for the first time in her life but could do nothing about it. Unless she could control her wants, she was in for a lot of frustration and pain being close to this man.

Reagan squinted into the distance toward the big house. "Looks like they are setting up breakfast on the patio for us. Juan is waving, wanting us to come." Reagan waved back and took Jill's arm in his. "Having you close to me with no demands other than being my friend means a lot, Jill. I won't let you down. We should begin after breakfast, and I have a private corner already picked out."

The Study

Ron was right, Jill mused as she looked around. The room labeled "The Study" was a rather compact room lined with books, walnut panels and tooled leather walls. It was entirely perfect for interviews. On the bay side, a stone fireplace was centered between two floor to ceiling windows overlooking a cultivated garden, behind which was the blue of the Chesapeake. With a little imagination, you could almost visualize D.C. just over the water horizon with its throbbing humanity, vanity and aggressive car traffic. Thankfully, since the Capital was out of sight, it was out of mind. Another world entirely. Today and for the next several days, even weeks...she hoped....was about the past. The specific past of the Candidate, Ronald Reagan. She chose one of the leather Chippendale chairs flanking the fireplace, Ron chose the other. He leaned back and clasped his hands as if he had committed to a scary and dangerous ride. On the small pie-shaped table between them sat two carafes, one contained coffee, the other tea. The location wasn't at all spartan, but there were no distractions. The staff was told not to interrupt unless necessary, but they were also invited to come in unannounced as needed just to quell any rumors of a sexual nature.

"First and foremost, Ron, we should start at the beginning. Your birth. Why don't you tell me what I would obviously need to ask and then I'll stop you for specific facts as necessary. I have a small recorder with me so I don't have to rely on my memory alone. Would that be where you would want to begin?"

"The first thing you will want to know is how, exactly, I am related to Ronald Reagan. I want to state clearly that I don't know. It doesn't even seem possible to me now that I think about it. My mother became pregnant, as far as I can tell, in April of

1981, and I was born that following December, just before Christmas. My parents were living together, as college students frequently do before marriage, but decided to have a baby and married several months prior to her pregnancy. When I was two or three, I'm not exactly sure of the date, they separated. Whether they were divorced at that time is another awkward mystery, but certainly later they were, and my mother changed her name back to her maiden name, mine also. I suspect out of spite or anger. I don't remember ever seeing my father, being too young while he was still in my life. My poor mother had a time of it...there was never enough money... and was saddled with a child to support and bring up. She worked as a lab assistant for a hospital in Maryland, being at least trained in something. It was a job, I was later told, that she loved, but it eventually caused her demise." He paused and poured some coffee for both of them, and while they sipped it, they both thought about what had just been recorded.

"Any chance that your mother could have come into contact with the president before you were born?" Jill asked.

"My mother wasn't a very attractive woman, Jill, and to my knowledge never ran in those circles, never visited the White House or the Capitol. There is no link imaginable."

"Sure there was. You are related to the president. There has to be a link, don't you agree?"

"Put that way, it seems clearly so. But for years, I've tried to think up a scenario but always came up blank. You must remember that President Reagan, unlike so many others, has never been accused of any infidelity after marrying Nancy, and certainly not in the White House. He had too much respect for the office for that. My mother had her faults, but she was no loose woman or prostitute."

"How did she die?" Jill asked cautiously.

"Lab accident, one not unheard of at that time. She became infected with Hepatitis B from a patient specimen and had a fulminant, rapid death in just two weeks."

"I'm sorry, Ron, but it's got to be part of your record. They would only dig it out anyway. You know, by the way, once you provide proof of your DNA relationship, they will accuse both your mother and the former president of infidelity."

"That will bring harm to both of their reputations, and it isn't deserved by either of them. That is one of the reasons I'm so reluctant to tell my story. There is even more coming that is equally painful." He stood and stretched, obviously wanting to stop for a moment. "Take a break?" he inquired.

"Of course. I can see now how distressing this is and why you dreaded it so. I've been thinking while you were talking. Once we start to divulge facts that can be traced, such as your mother's maiden name and where you were born, the press will rush out and start to gobble up the news and distort any facts with speculation. Tonight, I plan to write another fluff piece just discussing how you look and your gentle, considerate nature. I won't dare divulge our living conditions or where we are. That would be a big mistake, and I'm starting to be thankful for this location. If I write the bulk of the facts down and print them before the vultures get any wind of it, we may retain control of the news. And, with your permission, I want to fact check what you tell me with a responsible investigator, one we can trust."

"One who won't sell me out, I hope. How can you find an honest man any more? Frankly, just trusting anyone is difficult. I'm glad I have you. I couldn't do this without you beside me."

Jill couldn't reply because she abruptly flooded with tears and turned her head trying to hide them.

"Don't cry, dear. I can't stand the one woman in my life crying over me. Come, we are heading outside. I saw a speedboat in the boathouse, and I'm anxious to try it out."

Chapter 6

Collection of Clues

7:00 AM

Jill held the phone close to her ear, counting rings. Burns wasn't answering, and she wondered if anything had happened to him. This was the fourth time she had tried, and obviously, she wasn't going to connect. In a moment of clarity, she realized why. She was using the loaner phone Ted had given her. Burns would see her incoming call as an unknown number and, by now, was likely overwhelmed by calls regarding his star reporter. She clicked off and went to the closet and extracted her personal cell phone. She was somewhat afraid to activate it, but decided that following the call with Burns, she would be able to quickly turn it off again.

He picked up on the first ring. "Dammit! I have been trying for hours to get you. What is the problem, girl?"

"That long series of rings just now was me using another phone. I have been trying to call you, rather steadily."

"I get it. Like me, you are being pestered to death. Fine, I'll look up the other number and put it in my directory beside your name. Now to business."

"Me first, Chief. I hoped you'd like my story last night, but I already know it was a cheap little piece, so you don't have to remind me, but I have a reason, and I want your attention before you turn critical and start yelling again."

"Yes, a worthless little piece of nothing, but one which has already been printed and quoted around the world. I'm listening."

"There are facts, Mr. Burns, lots of them, and we need to check them out and run down a few other things, and we need to do it in near secrecy before the other newspersons get wind of where to start."

"Sure we do. This is a runaway car which will fling us off at the first turn. What do you expect from me?"

"Look, I know you have a long list of favors you can call in. My hope is that you know an investigator who will work for your paper and not double-cross us for money, one who will relentlessly pursue our leads and keep his mouth shut."

"It's a job which could become dangerous, Jill, given the political climate. Let me work on something which springs to mind, and I'll call you back. Meanwhile, you get busy and make me a list of facts you want checked out. In case I forget to tell you, Jill...."

"I know, Mr. Burns. I love you, too." And she did, of course, as a father figure. Burns was too old, too gruff and too long married to have any other thoughts. But he always looked out for her and gave her encouragement when she needed it, and for that she would always be grateful. Burns ran their small hometown newspaper like he would have a much larger one, and he managed to keep his readers happy, even though life had otherwise disappointed him. He was a man to count on though and very tough on those he disliked. There were rumors around the offices that Burns had seen a lot of action in Viet Nam, but it was something he never discussed, and there were no memorabilia in his small office to remind him of that violent period in his life.

The little recorder had done its job, and she started to review parts of the previous day's events. She laughed when she heard the boat's motor and recognized the sound of spray from the hull, because she had forgotten to turn it off, and the little thing had gone on recording the entire happy afternoon. Her shoulders had received more than a healthy amount of sunlight and would remind her for days of her carelessness. Listening, she realized that in his relaxed mood, Ron was remembering events and facts that she would have not otherwise recalled, and she started to listen closely. Almost inaudibly, because of the wind and waves, she heard him say that he was born at the "Medical School in Norfolk," and later mentioned that was the same place his mother worked when she became infected and died. As the afternoon progressed, they returned to the dock and private marina. Just as they were walking toward the main house, Reagan muttered, "Barbara," and added "poor thing, she tried so hard." Jill's conclusion was that Barbara was Ron's mother's name. There couldn't have been many Barbara's working for the Medical School Hospital that died from a work related illness during those years. She sat up and started making a list of so far gleaned facts for the investigator. Soon, she would try to confirm his mother's maiden name and her married name, if possible. Slowly, she would build enough information to put together a picture of Ronald Reagan's life. Only then, would she begin to write about the Candidate in detail. By then, the other press would be salivating and waiting for her next publication.

Breakfast was again served on the patio overlooking the water. A big orange umbrella fixed to the table provided shelter from the morning sun, mostly because Jill had quickly discovered that her skin wouldn't take any more radiation for a few days. As usual, Ron insisted on holding her chair while she sat down.

"A little sun is very becoming on you," Ron chuckled. "But, thankfully, we came back when we did."

He took his place across from her while the servants brought the food and coffee. By now, they were on a first name basis with the staff who were delighted to serve them and make small talk.

"Mr. Reagan, sorry, I mean Ron," Juan stammered while pouring the coffee. "I'm a veteran. When you get to be president, are you going to look after folks like me?"

"Well, Juan. You bet, because I'm a veteran myself. I know what you mean firsthand. Veterans' problems will be one of my first issues. You can count on that."

"No kidding! Where did you serve, or can I ask that question?" Juan blurted and smiled broadly at him, bristling his finely groomed goatee.

Jill perked up, listening while recording the entire conversation. "I was in one of the first batches of troops to be sent to Afghanistan after 911. For two tours," Ron stated and started pulling up his sleeve. On the inside of his left arm was a blurred blue tattoo which read "U.S. Army—Handle With Care." He and Juan shared a laugh, then Juan showed his "USMC" tattoo. They embraced and shook hands while slapping backs.

After Juan left them alone, Jill asked, "That's something I didn't know. Wow! What rank did you have? And were there any medals or honors given?"

"Since it came up, I guess there is no harm in telling you. I went there as a corporal and got promoted to sergeant before my tour ended. No, I was never wounded, but I saw a lot of action and lost several friends there."

"Can I ask you some questions, now that you are in a talking mood?" Jill pleaded.

"Of course. Isn't that why we are together? Of course, being with you is more like a partial honeymoon in some ways, and I forget about the real reason. Spending these wonderful days in your company is something I will remember the rest of my life."

"Ron, are you trying to make me fall in love with you? If you are, it's working."

"I thought about that last night at dinner. You were lit by candlelight, dressed in that marvelous white gown, and I couldn't take my eyes off of you. It's the way you move, the little change of expression around your eyes, the breathless way you speak. All of it. Sure, I'm trying. I can't help myself, and I guess I want you to share that emotion."

"You were serious when you mentioned that we weren't going to go any farther?"

"You can't imagine how painful that decision has become on my side. I'll say it again, though. We are not going to have a physical relationship, but the reasons are not what you might suppose. I am not infected with anything, have no physical limitations, no commitments with anyone else, and it's not because I don't find you appealing. It's entirely some other thing which remains, at the moment, private. Please be patient with me, the last thing I want is to lose your trust and affection."

"Can we at least kiss?"

"I couldn't stop with just that. Could you?"

"No."

There was a silence that descended under the orange umbrella, an awkward pause, an unexplained barrier. Jill was confused and couldn't look at Ron for the moment, instead picking at her food, but in a disinterested way, more like a child being forced to eat by her parent. The reappearance of the staff popped the somber bubble. They were delighted to be there and impressed by the Candidate, more all the time. He could not have made a larger impression on any party than he had made on the staff, who were more accustomed to being ignored than being made to feel as friends. Several younger women on the otherwise mostly male staff had become openly flirtatious with him and made every effort to gain his eye. Ron gently flirted back with them, laughing when they did something a bit outrageous but keeping proper decorum all the while. At such moments, Jill could feel a surge of jealousy, of possessiveness, come welling up without warning. A sideways glance from Ron always reassured her of the game he was playing, and the fact that he wanted her to know he realized her discomfort.

Once alone again, Ron spoke softly, "The question you had before our emotions ran rampant?"

Jill cleared her throat and tried to focus on her job instead of his handsome face. "Yes. Are you willing to tell me your mother's name and her married name?"

"Her name was Barbara McDaniels. My father was, or is, named Spence B. Jones. I don't know if he is still with us. I've never tried to find him. I would advise you or some sleuth your people might employ to run him down and get his story first. We have to assume that Spence is a man not to be trusted."

"Now the big question, and you know I have to ask it."

"You want to know what I was named before becoming Ronald Reagan." He had known this question would arise at some point. He wasn't ashamed of being what he had been, because his present existence seemed real, the former nearly a job of acting, nothing more. But he had made the best of that life, tried as hard as he could, and recalled the past with few regrets. "My previous name was Barns Trey McDaniels. Most of my friends will remember me as Trey, or at times, shortened to only Ray."

"Whom do you think you are? I mean in your head, your dreams, your memories?"

"We both know that I *am* Ronald Reagan. I have his voice, his face, and his personality. Why, I don't know, but there is no doubt in my mind who I am. I was only using the other name until I woke up."

"Want to tell me how you 'woke up'?"

"Not yet. You aren't ready for that."

Jill looked at the man she had fallen in love with and refused to believe that there was something dark in his past that he didn't want discovered, at least not yet. She was convinced that at the appropriate time he would tell her everything. It was a huge piece of a big puzzle, and the key one. His story would not hold up without it.

"Ron, I should go try to write something for the paper. I won't use any of the specific facts you divulged today or yesterday, but we have to keep the interest of the public up. Have you any plans for the afternoon?"

"Being with you is number one. Just a thought, Jill, but there are horse stables not far from here. Ever been riding?"

"Never. I've never even been close to a horse. Have you?"

"Once, in my other lifetime, I had an occasion to be around horses and people who know horses. I discovered a hidden talent in myself. Once on a horse, I suddenly realized that I intuitively knew what to do. They tell me that I ride rather well. Want to find out?"

"Only if you have patience with me and go really slow!" She got up to leave, then something occurred to her. "If you leave this place before we are ready, you'll be recognized and then our privacy will end."

"I've already got that figured out. Juan and Clarissa will go rent the horses and meet us out of sight of anyone. We will reverse that process when we are done. Think it will work?" He laughed that delightful routine he had when he elevated his shoulders in an exaggerated manner and covered his mouth with his hand.

"I don't know. Guess we'll find out. But, I don't own any riding outfits!" She brightened at the thought, because she could avoid the outing with horses using a perfect excuse.

"Oh, but you do. Madam Chang has your outfit already spread out on your bed, and my bet is that it will be a perfect fit." He chuckled again.

"You *are* pretty sneaky, aren't you?"

"It's not my fault. I was trained by the military, you know."

Once back in her room, Jill saw the riding pants, blouse and boots laid out in perfect order. A dapper helmet and riding crop were resting on the pillow. She grinned at the planning and the audacity, the lovey presumption. My god, how I love that man, she thought.

She threw herself into her pillow and reached for her phone. Before dialing, she held it up and stared at it. Was it possible that her call would be monitored using this gifted phone? If so, all the really important details of Ronald Reagan's life would be released before they were ready. She wasn't sure. Not at all sure. Instead, she resurrected her old trusted phone and headed out to the balcony, closing the double doors behind her.

"Hi, Mr. Burns, this is Jill," she said when she heard his voice. "Find a man yet?"

"I know your voice as well as my wife's, Jill. You don't need to tell me who it is."

"The man, Mr. Burns," she reiterated.

"I think so. It's a long connection but a good one, and I trust this fellow because of the people involved. You understand that we can't be more open on the phone, don't you?"

"Sure, and you don't even need to tell me any names. Better if I don't know. I do need to send you some clues though. How should I do it?"

"You should use the SMS. That's more secure than anything else we have."

"What?"

"Texting, Jill, or short messaging service. It's not perfect, but I don't see any way around it."

"Right then. Say, if I give you some names and dates, your man won't have to know why, will he?"

"I see your point, and it's a good one. If he's as smart as I've heard, then he will make the connection eventually, but by then he will understand the reasons we had for keeping him in the dark."

"You are quite sure about the trust issue then?"

"I can't say more. Don't worry, just send the info so we can get started, and, by the way, tonight I'm expecting a better column out of you."

Chapter 6

Chapter Seven

Beckman

Sentara Norfolk General Hospital, the sign above the entrance announced. Beckman glanced up at the towers of brick above. This was a large and active hospital, one likely to have excellent records but as well a staff of alert and suspicious professionals. He glanced at his reflection as he neared the glass door, grinning to himself at who looked back. Even he wouldn't recognize this fellow, he mused. He triggered the automatic door, and it opened noiselessly. Posted in the corner was a uniformed guard who was looking intently his way. Beckman detected him in his peripheral vision but avoided looking directly at the man. He stopped at the circular information kiosk as the foot traffic moved around and past. At the desk, he paused, placing his leather briefcase on the granite then pinning a moderate sized brass name plate on the breast pocket of his suit. From the briefcase he took another badge, this one on a chain, and put it over his head. His name, as embossed on the brass, was Herman Clousman, M.D. and below on the second line identified the dreaded organization, at least to hospitals. *"Joint Commission of Accreditation"* it read. The other, a typical plastic identification badge, had a recent photograph of Dr. Clousman with more information in smaller print. While this was going on, the three women behind the desk were watching him with interest. When he was ready, he signaled one of them and picked up his briefcase.

"Administration Office?" he inquired.

"Should I call ahead, Dr. Clousman, or are they expecting you?" she asked politely.

"Expecting? No. Perhaps anticipating would be more correct. The way?" he asked crisply. The clerk looked him over and inspected his identification more closely. The man before her had a hard look, weathered, but intense. Such a man usually has limited patience before anger arises. They all had been told, over and over, to give the Joint Commission investigators the utmost respect and consideration given that the entire hospital's reputation hinged on good reports.

"I'll escort you personally, if that is acceptable," she inquired. Beckman didn't approve or reject her proposal, he just stood there looking at her in an unnerving way. Without further comment, she came around the desk and motioned for him to follow. Along the way, she attempted small talk with the rather unpleasant fellow walking at her side, who looked around with interest but obviously without even being aware she was with him. Reaching the Administration hallway, she motioned toward a door then gratefully walked away, leaving him alone.

Beckman opened the door, finding a large woman behind a magnificent desk off to the right side. Ahead were several closed doors to various departments of administration. She smiled up at him and was obviously trying to read his tags.

"Ah, Dr. Clousman. Did you bring any staff with you this morning?" she asked, knowing the usual routine in unannounced inspections by the Joint Commission.

"If you recall from my letter, today's visit isn't unannounced and is not an inspection. There are no staff with me. I have allocated a morning to this visit, and it should be considered information gathering rather than anything more serious."

She did recall the letter which arrived only two days ago. It didn't state clearly the purpose of the visit other than to specify that they would be interested in data regarding fatal accidents, and more exactly, those occurring in the hospital laboratory facilities. Dates weren't specified. The letter had been treated with deliberate haste, and two staff had been assigned to gather any information possible. Rosa had been with the hospital for sixteen years herself and had yet to even hear of a fatal accident in the labs. To her knowledge, there were none. After two frantic days of searching, the Medical Records Department personnel had uncovered only four, and none of those were recent. Whatever the intent of the Joint Commission in this regard, the hospital had relaxed, no longer dreading the arrival of a formidable investigator from the JCAH.

"We have been diligently working on our files and are ready for you. Let me call our staff who led the search, and you can use our conference room for as long as you like." She stood with some effort and came around into the open space.

Beckman held up a finger, a indication for pause, "I will also need the medical records of any individuals who were both employed here, treated here and common to your list."

"Surely, Doctor. I'm quite sure that has already been done. This way, please." She ushered him into an impressive room both with a long stately table and a coffee bar at one end. The opposite end offered a dramatic view of the courtyard nestled behind the wings of the hospital complex. After she closed the door, leaving Beckman alone for a moment awaiting the excited arrival of assigned staff, he poured a cup of coffee and busied himself laying out papers, pens and a recording device. Enough to be entirely convincing of the seriousness of his visit.

After a brief pause, the door opened allowing entry of two women, one pulling a cart containing several thick charts on its lower shelf, the upper inhabited by a computer workstation. One of the women introduced herself as Gretchen Woodson, R.N., the other simply as Ruth, presumably a medical records librarian.

Nurse Woodson spoke first, "Dr. Clousman, isn't it? We haven't met previously I don't think. I'm always interested in the Joint Commission personnel. Do you have a specialty, if I may ask?"

Beckman realized that this sharp nurse was going to discover what he was capable of understanding before she divulged protected patient information. He decided to cooperate. "Of course...I'm trained in Infectious Diseases." He looked longingly at the stack of charts wanting to get his information and leave before his mask was pulled away.

"Oh!" she exclaimed. "Then you must know Dr. Rowlings at the center here. He is world-renowned, wouldn't you say?" It was a deliberate trap. Her Dr. Rowlings could be a nobody or even what she described. A erroneous response would set off this woman's internal alarms...then they would start to check him out.

"I'm on a schedule, Nurse. May we proceed?" Purposely, he was a bit gruff and looked her hard in the eyes. Seeing his response threw Nurse Woodson off her game. Should she continue or should she not anger this touchy investigator?

Nurse Woodson cleared her throat and pulled a thick and somewhat tattered chart from the bottom. "We should start with the oldest. This one is perhaps the saddest of all, but it happened many years ago. I assume you want to go back that far?"

"Since that is my directive, the answer is affirmative. Summarize first please."

"An employee of the hospital, trained in clinical laboratory testing, was inadvertently punctured by a sharp object while processing a blood specimen of a patient. She rapidly developed prostration, jaundice and eventually coma and death in the following days. She and the patient in question shared a diagnosis of Hepatitis B."

"A rapid course of only perhaps two weeks?" he reiterated, eyebrows raised, because this first patient was the very one he sought. "Then why is the medical record so thick?" he observed.

"She had also been a patient receiving previous medical care."

"Could her infection with the hepatitis virus be from an earlier date and not from the assumed exposure event?" he asked, carefully not getting too deep into medical terminology.

Nurse Woodson raised her eyebrows and pursed her lips. "I would have to read the chart, which I have not done. Since this occurred in 1985, I would ask the relevance."

"You are not the one who will determine relevance," he spat the offensive word back at her, then added, "I am." Beckman reached toward the record with his palm up and the heavy chart was placed in it. "What else do you have?" he said as he put the chart of Barbara McDaniels on his left and crossed his hands waiting for Nurse Woodson to continue.

"There are four in total. One died at work by jumping from the third story window. There were domestic issues." Beckman waved his hand. He wasn't interested in that one.

"The next one consumed a great quantity of laboratory denatured alcohol...he was on the janitorial night staff. He was found unconscious the next morning and unfortunately did not respond to treatment." That one was waved off as well.

"The last is recent enough to be on our digital system," she said and swiveled the screen toward him. "He was an experienced pathologist who acquired HIV, presumably from his work. We have not identified an exact moment of transmission, because he routinely handled that type of tissue."

"Are there lifestyle issues as well?" Beckman asked, catching a moment of hesitation in her speech.

"We are not legally able to answer that question. As you know, it is specifically forbidden by law to discuss those issues."

"Nurse, we are discussing a deceased person, are we not?" he asked.

"Still..." she responded.

"So, as an investigator, a representative of the Joint Commission, and a licensed physician, I cannot be allowed all the facts regarding a possible contamination in a medical institution?"

"I'm not sure. That's our policy, however."

"Here is what I insist you do, Nurse. While I review this first chart, you are to go to your superior, discuss this HIV case and bring me back a fax from your hospital appointed attorney indicating your legal position. Am I clear?"

"Very clear, Doctor." She left abruptly, anger darkening her face. This one was sure to cause a stink, he told himself, best to hurry. Centering himself and his small camera over the chart, he rapidly covered the various admissions, the next of kin, a copy of the birth record of the child she had delivered and various insurance papers. He ticked off the items he had to secure, one at a time. In a few moments, he had collected the social security numbers, the names and addresses of the three particulars as well as their places of employment.

Being thorough, he started tuning pages one at a time, finally coming to a discharge summary following Barbara McDaniels delivery. The obstetrician clearly stated that this was a case of successful artificial implantation of a fertilized egg derived from the legal mother and father of the child. The physician was most careful to document the entire record, likely because *in vitro* fertilization and implantation was a unique and not well accepted procedure at that time. Beckman was no expert on fertility disorders, but he wasn't aware that this procedure would have been done in what was, at that time, a smaller hospital. Interesting. Was this what he had been sent to find? Other than to confirm names and a few dates, he had no real idea what the interested parties were actually looking for.

Finished and satisfied, he closed the chart just as Nurse Woodson suddenly returned. One glance at her smug face told him that she had been proven correct. No personal information was to be provided on the patient in question. She slid the fax over to him without a word.

Beckman glanced at it, folded it away with his other papers and closed his briefcase. "We are done here. My thanks to you and the medical center for being as cooperative as you could be. Good day." With that last comment, Beckman disappeared down the long corridor walking slowly in a relaxed stroll.

Chapter Eight

Relevancy

Jill stared at her little screen gawking once again at the investigator's report. The facts he found supported what Ronald Reagan had told her; the baby of Barbara McDaniels had been born at that facility, just like he had said. Even the father's name was correct. The thing that jumped off the page was the small, passing mention that there had been both *in vitro* fertilization and clinical implantation of the egg. That opened up a new entire world of possibilities and had to be further illuminated. Once both the sperm and the egg had left the body of the donors, anything could have occurred. A simple lab error, a mix-up? Then the question arises about the president's sperm cells, and how they came to be in a lab in Norfolk. Her head spun with questions. First things first. She dialed Burns who answered almost instantly.

"Did you like that report?" he teased, knowing what the facts would do to Jill's imagination.

"Chief!" she blurted, then caught herself and looked around. She was in the far corner of the garden, and thankfully no one was in sight. "It sure is fascinating. Did your boy run into any trouble?"

"I wouldn't think so, but we are working through two intermediaries. He doesn't answer to me, but from what I surmise, this fellow can handle nearly anything."

"I have a couple of requests? Please, may I tell you over the phone?"

"Talk around it, Jill."

"I understand. The male parent. Can we look into him, find him, perhaps interview him? Another thing, your staff should conduct research on the interesting procedure used. That means finding out if it actually was done at that place and at that time. Do you know what I mean?"

"I think so. You don't want the trail of search terms on your system, correct?"

"It will not stand out on your end because of all the searches your people already do. On mine it will."

"We'll do that today. As for the other thing, I'll put out a request. It may take a few days...I'll get back to you when I can," Burns said, and abruptly the phone went dead.

Jill turned her phone off and put it away. She sat and looked around at nothing in particular while she thought things out. The investigator had uncovered something she had never considered. Was it still possible, after so many years, to illuminate how a mysterious, earthshaking, error had occurred? Or had it been intentional, with a motive, a deep and foreboding one. She shrugged. Speculation wasn't going to solve the riddle. It would be up to the investigator.

Footsteps were rapidly approaching her from behind, and she twisted to look, shielding her eyes with the palm of her hand. It was Peggy, one of the house staff.

"Thought I'd find you out here. Nice, isn't it?" She smiled and looked vacantly around as if she had forgotten why she sought Jill out.

"Did you or someone need me for something?" Jill prompted.

"Oh, yes. You have a visitor. I put him in the study," she said, then slowly wandered away, looking over the flowers and touching them lightly as she passed.

Jill stood, brushed herself off and hurried toward the big house. She found the door to the study closed when she arrived and hesitated, unsure of who could be waiting for her and fearful that whoever it was would bring an end to her enchanted existence. Pushing the door open without knocking, she saw Ted standing in the middle of the room. As soon as he saw her, he smiled and opened his arms toward her.

"Well, it's good to see you, too," he joked, referencing her restrained response.

"Gee, Ted, I thought you had forgotten your promise to check on me."

"Not at all. I have been in contact with the staff here, and they have assured me that you and Ron are getting along well. I've been busy, as you might guess, keeping my cool while being hounded and chased every time one of your columns appear. You, my dear Jill, are magnificent at stirring the kettle. I would imagine that you could ask for, and be rewarded, a salary as high as the moon, that is if you choose."

"No, thanks, I have other plans at the moment."

"Might I pry and ask about you and Ron. I mean, have you become friends or…"

"Close friends, Ted." She cut him off, not feeling obligated to light any dark corners of his imagination. Besides, somewhere deep in her was a growing feeling that Ted was more than he appeared to be.

"That's wonderful. Out in the world, things are progressing, thanks to you both. I am being pressed for details, though, by nearly everyone. Frankly, none of us have anything solid to release. How far have you come in nailing this down?"

"I have started, and he is being cooperative, but it is difficult for him. Plus, I want to honestly tell the story of his life so that the other news media can't invent a Ronald Reagan of their own, and I want it to be released all at once, backed up by details, every bit a substantiated truth."

"Want to venture a guess on how long that's going to take? I assume the public will lose interest if he continues to hide from them."

"You would want it done correctly, wouldn't you, and truthfully as well as in depth?" There was no answer to be given, the question answered itself.

"The RNC is pressuring me to have another press conference, another appearance for a hungry public. It's got to happen soon."

"It's not up to me, Ted, but any detailed news article authored by me is going to take at least several more days. I would guess that a really solid published report would nicely set the stage for a press conference."

"And you would be right about that. A compromise is needed. Give a little more depth on your next one, if you don't mind a subtle suggestion, and it will hold the dogs off a little longer."

"I plan to do just that." She continued to stand about five feet from Ted and made no sign of a willingness to get closer to him. Ted inspected her for a moment before abruptly moving in and lightly embracing her with his arms.

"Jill, I hope I didn't get you into something that is going to hurt you later. I would feel responsible."

"I don't see how my being happy can hurt me," Jill said, and gently pushed him away.

"That can be the worst kind of pain, I know because I've been through it. Promise me one thing, and I won't ever say another word." Jill looked at him blankly, not willing to give a blanket promise. Ted continued, "Don't let your heart get ahead of your brain. The world is cruel to the innocent." He paused, again letting his words soak in, then patted her affectionately on her shoulder. "I've got to go. Be sure and call me if you have any problems...any at all."

She watched him leave, unable to decide if Ted was actually the friend he wanted her to believe in. Every time she was with him, he was so convincing, really, so overpowering. She wanted to trust him and had no specific reason not to. There was her female intuition, however, and it was rarely in error.

Beckman slowed, watching the house numbers go by, getting closer by the block. The particular house, he calculated, had to be on this block and on the right side. He swung to the curb, turning off the car motor, planning to walk the remaining distance, partly to size up the neighborhood. It seemed safe enough, but Beckman never really worried about danger, only getting away after the gunfire started. He was not a large man, wiry by some descriptions, and no longer young, but he was experienced, trained by the best and willing to use deadly force in a split second. One look from his hard eyes was enough warning for anyone but the most foolhardy, and those who didn't see it in time paid the price.

The house was plain, small and nondescript. There were no children's toys or even ornamental lawn decorations. It was a house, not a home, and fit the stereotype for a retired male living alone. An orange glow from one side indicated occupancy, and Beckman ventured down that side of the house looking past the partially drawn drapes. An older, balding man, dressed in his underwear, was seen moving about in the kitchen. Beckman returned to the front of the house and rapped authoritatively on the door, then, by habit, stood to one side, his windbreaker open to allow quick access to his pistol. Listening, he could hear light footsteps approaching the door, then no sound as the occupant attempted to look through the peephole. Beckman stepped out in plain sight and looked back.

"What do you want?" the occupant demanded.

"Investigation. I want information, that's all. Open the door," Beckman demanded.

"Come back tomorrow. I won't see anyone tonight."

"You are advised to open the door. No harm will come to you, I give you my word."

"Are you with the police?" It was the question that should be asked by an intelligent person under the same circumstances but such a question expects honesty, not a Beckman.

"This is a federal matter, sir. You must talk with me tonight." Beckman held up an ID card that he knew could not be read through the little peephole. He heard the chain come loose, then the door open a crack and an eye looked him over.

"What's this about?" the occupant asked.

"Is your name Jones, Spence B. Jones?" Beckman inquired.

"What have I been accused of?" Jones asked, a slight tremble was starting to become audible.

"Just an interview, Jones, not an arrest. Open the door, please." This time the command was given with enough malice that the door opened, and Jones stood there in his underwear looking fearful.

"May I enter?" Beckman asked as he came in and looked around. The place was sad and had the odor of uncleanliness arising from the worn furniture and tattered rug. Beckman could smell a dog but hadn't seen or heard one. That could only mean one thing, the dog was no longer there. Beckman turned and nodded that Jones could shut the door. He took out a notebook and flipped some pages, mostly for show.

Then tapped on a page with his pencil. He took a good look at Jones before he spoke, noting that Jones was a slightly frail, stooped and unhealthy older man. His face only saw a razor once or twice a month, and his poor fitting underwear was grimy.

"You were married to a Barbara McDaniels at one time?"

"Many years ago. She's dead now. Caught an infection I heard. We were divorced by then."

"Did you have a child together?"

"Say, could I sit down while we talk? My knees won't take a lot of standing around." He ambled toward the couch and noisily seated himself without waiting for approval. Afterwards, he rubbed his chin as if thinking of a correct answer.

"Well, I'd say yes and no to that one. It was sort of the reason for our divorce."

"Want to explain?" Beckman asked.

"We tried and couldn't seem to connect, and Barbara really wanted one. She was working at the hospital lab, and they were doing this test-tube stuff, she told me. There was a guy working at her hospital, from Europe, Port-something, I forget. *He* convinced her, I do believe. She talked her head off at me, and finally I agreed. Making a long story short, she finally did get pregnant."

"But?"

"But after the baby was born, I could tell it wasn't mine. You can't see it now, but I was always a redhead, so was Barb. This kid was born with a head of dark hair and blue eyes. I'm no doctor, but it just wasn't possible, and I said so at the time. Barb didn't care a bit. A kid was a kid, and it was hers or so she thought. I took it for awhile and then left. After a couple of years, she filed papers on me. She never asked for any child support or really anything from me. Then I heard she died suddenly. That's for sure all I know."

"So you never tried to contact the child or offer any help?"

"No. As far as I was concerned, the damned hospital made a mistake, and they should have owned up to it. Not me, and I never felt guilty about it neither."

"What was the child named?"

"Barns, after my mother's people, and Trey, after hers. Say, can I ask why you want to know this stuff?"

"Ever hear any more about the child? What happened to him, how and where he was raised, anything?"

"Ain't my affair. No, I didn't. Perhaps you know and would like to tell me about him."

"I don't even know if the boy is alive or not so I have nothing to say to you about that."

"Kind of thought so. Then what's this all about?"

"It's a federal matter, that's all I am authorized to say. Further, I am officially warning you not to discuss this with anyone. You understand? I said anyone. If you do so without my personal authorization, you'll spend some time in a federal prison."

"I won't say a word, you can count on it."

"And we never had this conversation, and you never saw me."

"Well, that won't be too hard. You never did tell me your name."

Beckman smiled. No, he never did. "I'll be in touch as necessary. Remember my warning."

Back in his car, Beckman thought it over. There was no doubt now, the child was the person of interest. Wonder why?

Chapter 9

Finding The Needle

The report from the unnamed investigator lay on his desk in the usual manila envelope, and Jules Burns was trying to find time to open it and contemplate, even relish, the details. He admitted that, whoever the man was, he was quick and to the point. In Burns's imagination, the investigator looked a lot like one of the *film noir* movie stars, perhaps Powell or Mitchum, not Bogart however. It was a life he always thought he would have liked for himself. Action, conflict, living on the edge. No chance. What Burns had instead was the daily grind of turning out a newspaper, selling subscriptions, chasing reporters and trying to recruit advertisers. Not one moment of happiness happened any longer...except for Jill Longley, the little blonde who used to whine about doing mundane reports. "Training, look at it as training, Jill," he had said, sometimes too gruffly, to her. And it *was* training and now look at her. She had at least twenty or thirty news organizations who called daily, all desperate to talk with her. The SOBs were trying to hire her right under his nose, blatantly steal his best reporter. But little Jill, the peach that she is, has the only access to the hottest topic in America and the most sought after, and her columns were getting better and better.

Burns thought about his investigator and the willingness of his old pal Duffy to help out. He actually hadn't seen Duffy in person for years, and when he remembered Duffy, it was with an M16 in his hands, several grenades hanging from his belt, his skin brown from exposure, and wearing the constant sardonic grin he always carried. It was an old yellowed memory of Viet Nam that played over and over in his mind. Those times never changed for him, some of it good, most of it bad, but always frozen in time, suspended permanently in that fog which could never be altered, never relived. Somehow he had survived, but so many others didn't. Duffy stayed when the conflict ended and became a rising star in Army Intelligence. They talked once or twice a year for most years and always made the same promise, that they were going to meet during vacation someplace special and firm up ties. It never happened...at least so far, and probably never will. Duffy may have retired, but he still had his finger on the intelligence world and had many contacts with current or former people of his generic type.

The envelope contained several sheets of paper, all carefully typed and footnoted. The work of a disciplined professional and one who was not civilian trained. From what little Burns knew, this was spy stuff, high quality, and the best part was that he had not yet seen a bill for services. Another mystery. Why would these people work for free? He guessed that someone in the chain had already connected the dots and chosen sides. There was no other reason.

One piece of information was circled in red and caught Burns's eye: the partial name of the European who had apparently encouraged Reagan's mother, at least according to her estranged husband. Burns understood now that the chase was going to be down to solving the riddle about the transfer of the president's sperm into this little laboratory in Norfolk. The European had to be identified and interviewed, if possible. Not much to go on and he slumped, trying to think it through. He couldn't envision a return visit by the investigator to the same hospital, this time digging through employee records. The hospital would not permit such a thing short of a court order. No, this information had to be stolen, hacked directly from their computer. By 1981, they would have maintained electronic records for employees even while medical records of that type would not appear for several more years. This was an outside job and strictly illegal. Burns was going to be stretching and conspiring to break the law, but he could see no other way if he wanted to continue to scoop the competition as badly as they had been doing. He didn't want to use Duffy for this one, didn't want to admit a criminal act to his best friend.

Leaning back and looking at the uninteresting ceiling, Burns didn't even hear his phone ringing. His brain could ignore such distractions during moments of concentration. He rocked back to a sitting position and hit his intercom button. "Mabel, you remember the Pendergast boy?"

"The kid you personally saved from extinction?" she said sarcastically.

"Yeah, that one. Think you could find out how to get in touch with him?"

"What in the world...well, boss, I can try. Want to talk to him personally?"

"Sure do."

In about two hours, the intercom came on with Mabel's harsh voice, "Larry Pendergast, line 5."

"Hi Larry," Burns said smoothly. "Remember me?"

A voice distantly said, "Never forget you, Mr. Burns. You need my services, don't you; otherwise you wouldn't be calling me." Burns always had to admit that the skinny, asthmatic and pimpled kid was smart if not attractive. Hearing Larry's voice always made Burns want to ask about women in Larry's life, but he never had the nerve.

"It's a hush hush thing, Larry. Where are you these days?"

"Still in my Mom's basement, Mr. Burns, but not in jail like I would have been except for you."

"I need your services. Want to help?"

"Is it legal or..."

"Yes."

"Can I come over there and do it? I mean, they monitor my activity, you know." Burns remembered the terms of conviction but conviction with immediate parole. Monitoring for ten years instead of prison, thanks to the series he ran while the trial was in progress. Given the way Larry looked at the time, it might have been a lifetime sentence. Burns suspected that a smart kid like Larry had devised ways around being monitored, he just wouldn't admit it over the phone.

"Today?"

"I'm here."

After hanging up, he pushed the intercom again. "Larry's coming over. Show him in when he gets here. Did you have a chance to do the research on test-tube babies like I asked?"

"It's on your computer, you just have to look at it, or do I have to come in and read it to you?"

"I didn't see it. Oh, yes, right here…" he trailed off as his attention was focused on the screen.

"Say, there is a lot here. Want to come in and translate this stuff?" he asked on second thought. There was an audible sigh before the device clicked off.

Mable swiveled the screen around to face her and glanced at Burns with pique. "All right, now pay attention, it isn't that hard." Burns put his feet up on his desk and folded his arms behind his head, closing his eyes. She began, "The first time a test-tube fertilized egg was implanted was on a rabbit…who would have guessed…that was in 1959 in Massachusetts. Let's see…then it was first tried on a human in 1973…that failed…then an actual baby was born using in vitro, a Louise Brown, in the UK. Then another successful one in Glasgow in 1979. Oh, and I think this is the one you are looking for…14 pregnancies resulting in nine births in 1981 at the hands of Howard W. Jones and Georgeanna Seegar Jones at the Eastern Virginia Medical School in Norfolk, Virginia."

Burns opened his eyes. "Eastern Virginia Medical School? 1981? That's it! Who would have thought out there in Eastern Virginia...well, damn."

"Wait, there's more. The first one was born on December 28, 1981, and it wasn't a boy but a girl. Didn't you say that RR was born in late 1981? You don't get much later than December 28."

"I don't understand either, but what you just read is the proof that test-tube babies were being conceived and delivered about the same time and in the same place. It fits, don't you see?"

"Not exactly. There is still the problem, the very big problem, of the President of the United States having a link with some unknown lab assistant in Norfolk."

"Mable, the problem with you is that you have no imagination. Think. It's not that far between Washington and Norfolk, and we know for certain that there *was* a connection." The intercom sounded and Mable leaned forward and pushed the button.

"Mable, are you expecting a..." she could hear a muffled exchange in the background, "a Larry P., he won't give his last name. I think you should take a look at this one." Mable got up and straightened the screen.

"Your boy, Larry, has arrived. Want him back here?" she asked.

"Absolutely!"

She opened the door and motioned for Larry to enter, standing aside and inspecting him with contempt or distain as he passed by. "Hi, Mr. Burns. Long time."

"Yes, but not that long. You are looking unchanged, I see."

"And you, Mr. Burns, have put on a few more...."

Burns cut him off. "Larry, I need a job done and on the QT. Not legal but we need it. The paper needs it, the country might need it."

"Can you give me some idea before I answer? I mean, I've got to know if it can be done first."

"I want you to break into a hospital computer in Eastern Virginia and look through their employment records. I have a partial name, and that's all I have, but we need to know his actual name and, you know, everything they have on him."

Larry looked back through his thick glasses, pushing his limp hair from his forehead and, for a moment, didn't blink or even move. Burns was contemplating explaining it again for him when Larry said, "That's all you want?"

"Do you mean it can be done and that you agree to do it?"

Larry didn't answer but got up and seated himself at the keyboard and adjusted the screen then looked at Burns for instructions.

"We are interested in a man, I think it was a man, working at *Sentara* in Norfolk, Virginia around 1981. I only have the partial name of Port, and I don't even know if it's a first or last name. We were told that he was from Europe. That's all I've got."

Larry started clicking away. Burns watched him in wonder for a few moments. The kid was part of a different world, one that was vastly too intellectual to understand, and he found it hard to imagine that this skinny kid could manage to actually break the law from his mother's basement. After all, he looked frail and malnourished as well as unkempt. After a bit longer and more observation, Burns became aware that he was wrong. This boy was a master, a genius of sorts and a huge force of some new type. A thing which had grown up out of games and bits of code and become the size of an army and just as dangerous. Burns was looking at the future, and as a man of the past, it took his confidence and left it on the floor.

"Right," Larry said and turned the screen. "Here's your list." He pointed to the multiple column report starting at the upper left. "Here are matching names, in alphabetical order, next are the social security numbers...the ones blank are not citizens. The other columns are the local residence and then the permanent address. At the far right are the dates of employment and the wages paid per month."

Burns got up and bent over the screen, taking it all in. There were one hundred twenty-one names, all with social security numbers except two. One of those had an address in London as a home address. He read aloud, "Herman Manfred Porter, unmarried, born in 1946." He stood up. "I've got a feeling that this is the one. Can you print that page for me?"

"It's not a good idea, Mr. Burns. That's the kind of proof they look for."

"I see..." he paused thinking, not sure of how to proceed.

"Want more information about Herman Porter?" Larry inquired.

"Can you do that?"

"We have a name, a birthdate, a residence in two places. Of course. Wait just a moment."

Before Burns could organize his thoughts, the printer started making noise and ejecting copy, six pages of it.

"I think everything you need will be there. Anything else I can do?" Larry asked and pushed his thick glasses back up.

"No, I don't believe so. You have my gratitude, Larry. Thanks."

"I owe you, Mr. Burns. Anytime for any reason."

"Hi, brother," Duffy said dispassionately, using his artificial, thick drawl. Over the phone, Duffy couldn't be mistaken for any other human.

"Thanks for all the legwork. Don't I owe you something?" Burns asked.

There was a chuckle on the other end, "Why, Julius, my boy, you can pay me anything you can afford." He laughed again. Burns wasn't sure what that comment implied. With Duffy, you could never tell if he was kidding. The only time he was ever serious was bent over his M16 and firing at an unseen enemy in the woods.

"I've got something else," Burns mumbled.

"And I'll bet it has to do with the half-name our boy came up with."

"You knew?"

"I'm interested. Call it curiosity. Loose ends always have to be found."

"I've got a name. Might be out of the country though. Can you manage that?"

"Herman Porter? That the name?" Duffy laughed again.

"There's something you're not telling me, Duffy."

"Sure is sport. It's need to know. But when I get more on this Porter, you will be first in line. Or at least second."

"One last question, Duff. Were you going to tell me?" Burns could hear Duffy laughing when the phone went dead.

Chapter Ten

Capture

The shadows from the moving leaves overhead played on their faces, while a soft wind off the water puffed their hair. It was a scene from an old movie, complete with a handsome actor across from her, looking at her with longing in his eyes. There was even music drifting across the lawn from the open door to the house, wafting in and out, floating on the liquid sea of air. Jill was wearing a sunsuit with bare abdomen, skimpy, a bit more exposure than she was comfortable with, but the little outfit had been placed on her bed by an unseen party while she was in the shower, and she decided not to let the effort go to waste.

"And how was your latest report on me received?" he asked, not taking his eyes from her face.

"Burns said that it was the most quoted piece in memory, and the phone hasn't stopped ringing," she answered, looking back as intently.

"Well, that much is out there now. It was my first step, and it was a big one," he observed.

"You're positive that they can't trace you with what I've given them?" Jill wondered again, still not sure the timing was right.

"My name was changed twice. The court records were sealed after the first one...by our government." Jill noted that he pronounced it *Gummit*, something that always bothered her. "The press won't be able to find the second name, don't worry."

"Well, that's new. Do I get that part of your story next?"

"Today. But you won't be able to use it, and you will understand why shortly."

"We have a gap, you know, a big one. Even Burns wants to know what happened to you after you left the service," Jill reminded him. He shrugged and looked away. "I got a call from Ted. He wants you to appear someplace. Are you ready for that?" she asked.

"He called me also. I put him off for awhile yet. Something about being with you and how I didn't want it to end."

"You actually told him that?" Her question was put a bit sharper, something she didn't intend.

"Any reason that I shouldn't?" he asked with raised brows.

"If I were him, I would *assume,* given that response."

"Let him. It's true anyway, even if it's only in my heart."

Jill sighed, twirling the drinking straw in her fingers before letting it drape from her lips while she studied his face. This relationship was getting harder every day, and she, for sure, didn't understand the reasons. It all came down to his past and something back there that was so well insulated that even she couldn't be told the truth. She sighed again. "Now is a good time," she offered.

Ron shook his head slightly, glancing back at the house, then holding his finger to his lips briefly. That was it. This part of his story was not to be overheard, even by a friendly house staff. Jill realized that whatever it was, Ron would never allow it to be printed in black and white on newsprint.

"Care to go on a short boat ride after lunch?" he asked. She could read something, some playfulness on his face that was meant for her to see. Was this boat trip going to turn into a romantic encounter, she wondered, a very private one on the floor of a bobbing speedboat?

"I'd likely go down into a volcano with you if you wanted. Of course."

They rode the waves, heading north, until the estate was nearly out of sight. The Chesapeake was not smooth this time, and Jill felt the exhilaration of being carried up the steep side of a wave, then descending the other, dropping toward the trough like an elevator out of control, and bracing for the inevitable wash of spray cascading over the bow, rushing over the windshield and around the side enclosure. She was intermittently watching Ron, who chose to stand for the ride and was using both muscular arms to control the circular steering wheel guiding the rudder. The wind, the taste of the salt in the air, the plaintive cry of the gulls mixed with the sudden roar of the engine as the rear of the craft was hoisted out of the water while cresting a wave, the experience was hypnotic, glorious, and yet she strangely felt no fear, no apprehension while Ron was there. He was enjoying himself, she could tell by the smile and the twinkling glances he threw toward her, making sure she was still there and hanging on.

He made for the shore and quieter water, turning smoothly toward a small estuary flanked by tall sea grass. "You watch that side for oyster banks under the surface," he ordered. "It's high tide right now, and you can't see them well, but they're there."

Jill had never been told about oyster banks and had no clear idea of what they would look like. She studied the water carefully, but all she saw was the sheen of calmer water seemingly arising between tall stands of brown and green grass. She stopped looking abruptly, turning when the motor stopped, and a comparative quiet came rushing in. All that furious noise had been replaced by the gentle slapping of little waves against the sides of the boat. Ron threw an anchor over with a splash and tied it off to a cleat on his side. Together they pulled up the canopy, and in the shade, sat down together, nearly touching along the length of their arms.

"True privacy, at last," he said, looking surprisingly somber. Jill's heart sank. This was not going to be physical after all.

"After my return to the States following the second tour, we all returned to Fort Bragg, right where most of us had come from. A few weeks were spent without much going on, for the Army, that is. We still had to train and march on occasion but mostly spent time learning new skills and going to classes."

Jill interrupted, "Did you visit your adoptive parents when you returned?"

"The Townsend family," he remembered, then shook his head. "No. Truthfully, we were never much of a family, especially for me. There were other children of their own, and I always felt like an outsider. Still, they looked after me, fed me and spanked me when I needed it. I did call and talk to them when I got back..." he trailed off for a moment, thinking and remembering, "but that was our last contact I'm afraid." Ron stopped talking as if there was some guilt he was repressing.

"And after the tour?" Jill prompted.

"A voluntary posting came across. One of those little pearls the military puts out now and then. You see, the Army Attaché Management Division handles this business. Usually they require officers, but there is an occasional opening for an enlisted man, like I was. To make a long story short, I was paired with an officer who was assigned to liaison with the Polish Army for a short tour of six months. I jumped at the chance. Anything to get off base and do something new. This was not a combat assignment for a change, and I needed a break." He stopped talking and opened the cooler, then handed Jill a frosty bottled pop.

"Captain Billings and I were quartered at the Polish Second Recon Regiment near their eastern border. The facility was drab, left over from the communist era, but I must say that the poles we encountered were friendly and fit for combat. They take their role as allies of the U.S. very seriously." Ron paused again, thinking over those times. It was hard to determine if he had nostalgia or that some part of the story had become personal.

"I became close with one of the fellows there, a man named Izajasz Bujnowski. I couldn't pronounce it then any better than now," he laughed at the effort. "But we called him Bud, and he answered to it. One day, Bud and I hopped a train on a five-day pass so he could show me Warsaw, his hometown. I never made it there. One minute I was sharing a bottle of schnapps with Bud, and the next thing I knew, I woke up in the dark, locked in a very small room."

"You mean you were arrested? For what?" she asked.

"No, not arrested. Abducted would be more descriptive. I had no idea who or what organization I was dealing with nor did I know where I was at the time. After an interminable imprisonment in the dark, someone finally opened the door, an American, a friendly open-faced fellow countryman. I thought I had been rescued and was thankful to see him. He slapped me on the back and escorted me down the hall, his arm across my shoulder. We turned into a large room which was full of people seated around a big table. I was given the seat at the end. Some were dressed in suits, some in casual wear, and several in the uniform of the U.S. Army. I was made to feel welcome, and several asked about my health and wondered if I needed anything."

The first thing out of my mouth was the question, "Where am I, and who are you people?" They laughed. Finally someone quieted the room and directed a question at me. "Who is your father?" he asked pointedly. They all were looking at me, and no one was laughing.

"Why are you asking me that? Surely you have my records."

"Your real father. Have you ever thought about it?" the man asked.

"My real father left my mother and me alone when I was very young. I never remember seeing him."

A photograph was placed in front of me. The man in the photo was balding with red hair and a thin face. It was a face I had never seen before.

"That is the picture of Spence B. Jones, your father of record. Think he looks anything like you?"

"No," I admitted.

"To us, your face looks like the face of President Ronald Reagan. Ever heard that before?" the man persisted.

"We all look like someone, I'm told. Sure, I was kidded about it once or twice," I answered.

"No, my friend, you look exactly like him," an older fellow stated. I looked at the photograph of Spence Jones again and suddenly beside it appeared a photo of President Reagan. Before I had a chance to comment, another photo was given to me. This time it was my face I was looking at. I was astonished. There was no doubt that I was at least a facsimile.

"So, what does this mean and what do you want?" I asked.

"They call you Ray, don't they?" the first man asked.

"Only my friends do, and I don't recall you as one of them." The response brought a laugh as well as some hard looks.

"Look, Ray. It's clear to us that there is something wrong with your history, or what you knew as your history. You are not what you thought you were, and we are here to rectify that."

"And just what does that mean," I asked.

"We want you to become President of the United States. And you can, with our help."

"I'm a sergeant in the U.S. Army. That's who I am and where I belong. What you are saying is foolishness."

"That's who you are right now, but in two or three years, you'll be a different person. You will be him." He made his point by tapping forcefully on the face of Ronald Reagan.

"Frankly, I'd rather return to my post. Being president is not something I want to do."

"Your army has listed you as deserted, my friend, and a murderer. You will return to prison if they get their hands on you."

"Not a chance. I have a perfect record of service and many will vouch for me. Say, who are you people?"

"We represent the future, Mr. Reagan, and you represent our best hopes of achieving it."

Chapter Eleven

Dilemma

The next day I was, once again, allowed out of my cell. This time I was ushered into a different area, also with no windows. Outside a door was a guard, a U.S. Army Pfc., holding an M16 loosely across his chest. I glared at him on the way past, wondering how he could be so casual about the false imprisonment of a fellow soldier. I was seated at a table, and the door was closed behind me."

"I didn't have long to wait, because a smiling fellow in a suit, a thick sheaf of papers under his arm, suddenly came bustling in. He was middle-aged, thin and wore a well-groomed beard sprinkled with grey. The eyes weren't middle-aged at all, they were clear and penetratingly hard."

"Greetings, Mr. Reagan," he said, sitting down and getting comfortable.

"Get this, whoever you are. That is not my name, and you know it."

"I know and so do you, but you have to accustom your mind to that name, because from here forward, that's who you actually are. We have to lay our cards on the table, my young friend. You have a tremendous future, and we are going to help you achieve it. It's not an easy thing, running for president, and being one is even harder. You have to know and understand finance, politics, current and past events and the intricate operations of the American Congress. You currently don't know anything about these topics, wouldn't you agree?"

"And why should I? I'm only a sergeant."

"Exactly. That's why you are to start lessons this morning. Your education has begun."

"I'm not willing to play this game. Just take me back to my base, or better, just let me walk out the door."

"Your comrade, whom you addressed as Bud, was murdered. Your fingerprints are on the knife which killed him. The Polish press reports that there was a rumored love triangle, and Izajasz Bujnowski was eliminated because of it. The U.S. Army has declared you AWOL and issued a worldwide alert. By the way, your burned body will soon be found in an automobile, and the hunt for you will cease. Save yourself the effort, you cannot return to your former life."

"Why me?"

"It's clearly obvious. You are a match for one of the most respected presidents. With your voice, your face and your presence, odds are that the public will fall in love with you. Mr. Reagan, you are a sure bet."

"And what do you people get out of it, and who the hell are you, and where is this place?"

"Can't you tell? We are your people, doing the country as well as the world a favor by finding you and bringing you to the forefront."

"I'm not buying that. In this life, you get nothing for free."

"Not true, at least in your case. We are offering you a trade. Your previous life spent in the sands of Afghanistan versus power, money, fame and all that comes with it. It's free, Mr. Reagan, how could you possibly refuse?"

"So far, there hasn't been any trappings of what you suggest. I have been sleeping in a cold dark cell, in case you weren't informed, and I am deprived of my freedom. How can I possibly believe anything you say?"

"That has all changed. From here forward, your life will be pleasant indeed. All you have to do on your end is to study the lessons and topics we will present to you. In a short time, you will begin to see things differently." He stood and opened the door without another comment. Waiting outside with the guard was a stunningly beautiful woman beckoning toward me to join her. I got up and willingly followed her down the long hallway, not looking back.

"My name is Joanne, Mr. Reagan. Could I please call you Ron?"

"Where are we going, can you at least tell me that?" I asked.

"To your new quarters, and I think you will be surprised." Joanne smiled mysteriously as we turned down several more corridors until at last we came to a large door. She opened it and stood aside, her arm indicating I was to go in first.

Ron looked over the side of the boat suddenly and stood up. "Tides going out. We've got to leave or stay here until the next one." He started pulling up the anchor as Jill peered over the side and immediately understood. There was a grey indistinct mass under them that wasn't there before, and there were traces of other grey mounds just breaking the surface of small swells only feet from the boat.

"At least the bay is calmer," he said reassuringly. "The trip back should be a little less wild." The motor started on the first try, and he pivoted the prow back toward the open water, but instead of gathering speed, he crept along while watching the water closely. "If we hit one, the sharp shells will rip the bottom off," he explained. Slowly he gathered speed as they headed south. Wind whipped about the boat violently, creating more spray than before. "A southern breeze," Ron yelled his explanation to her. Jill hung her head low and held on to her hat, wishing for the trip to end.

She looked up when the motor was cut back to an idle, noting the dock coming rapidly toward them at an angle. Ron cut the motor at the perfect moment, allowing the boat to naturally edge up to the dock and bump lightly against the rubber sides. Jill didn't get up at first, but continued sitting there, looking back at the bay and absentmindedly holding on to her hat.

"Want to go back out?" Ron asked with a laugh, "or something wrong?" He sat back down beside her, waiting on her response.

"I understand a lot more about you than I did. But just as many questions have arisen. No wonder that you don't want to tell this story, I get that, but Ron…"

"But, I didn't finish, did I?"

"Not even close. Come on…what happened, where were you, who were they?"

"Even I don't have those answers. Wish I did."

"How long were you there, can you at least tell me that?"

"I didn't have a watch, calendar or even sunlight to go by. Every day was the same. Endless classwork, lectures and reading. I also watched every old movie and newscast about Ronald Reagan that exists…several times. The movie scripts are burned into my memory."

"And, surely, you have at least an estimate," Jill persisted.

"Two years at least, perhaps more."

Jill nodded her understanding but was obviously burning with more questions.

"Are you wondering about the woman named Joanne? Frankly, I'd hoped you would ask."

"You can tell me, if you're willing."

"There were several like her, all attractive, intelligent and attentive to me. That's what they were supposed to do…keep me prisoner because I wanted to be there. I'd say that it didn't work the way it was planned. First of all, it was too obvious. One day I'd had enough, and I decided to make Joanne talk, really make her, by using force. I nearly killed her, but it still didn't matter. Either she really didn't know anything or she was masterfully trained. She wouldn't divulge the smallest fact of where she came from, her purpose or exactly where we were. I had earlier tried to see what she knew about America, you know, the common things we all know about this wonderful land. She would just smile at me in a harmless, affectionate way until I gave up."

"How did you get away, or did they just turn you loose?"

"I broke out...escaped." Just then, they looked up to see Juan coming toward the boat, grinning as usual. Jill wondered if Juan imagined they were out for a dalliance in private. It no longer mattered to her what Juan or anyone else thought, because....well, just because.

They walked together, but without physical contact, back toward the big house. The puffs of cold wind coming off the bay was nature's message that they had returned just in time. A storm was brewing over Virginia and was about to churn the dark water of the bay into a frightening froth. Jill became lost in thought while they were walking. Any telling of Ron's capture and indoctrination would make the public think a true Manchurian candidate was running for office. Leaving it out would leave a huge gap in his life story leading to speculation and endless fabrication. It was a true dilemma.

At the door, Ron held it open as usual, allowing Jill to pass close by him. She paused in the doorway and looked up into his face, holding his eyes in hers, her face void of expression. Now and forever she would no longer think of him as Ronald Reagan, but another man who only looked like Reagan. This man was not the movie star, or the president, but someone she loved deeply for just being himself and for trusting her above any other person.

Jill headed upstairs for a shower to wash away all the salt from the bay. Before bathing, she picked up her phone and headed for the balcony. Jules Burns picked it up on the first ring.

"Jill!" he said excitedly, "I've been wanting to talk with you all day. Your name is all over the news, because our paper had the facts before anyone! If you haven't already, turn on the television and see for yourself. One thing most interesting...the man you identified as the biological father of Ronald Reagan, or Barns Trey McDaniels-Jones, or whoever he is, has gone missing. There is a mess down there around where they thought he was living. The media is beating this story to death, and it's all because you dragged it out, a little morsel at a time, until *whammy*, you hit them with some hard facts. I am dying to see what you write tonight."

"I'm going to disappoint you, Chief. There won't be a report tonight."

"Why not? Your column has been responsible for us selling out every copy we can print. Please don't stop now!" Burns was back at shouting and becoming angry in spite of himself.

"Listen, Mr. Burns. We have a problem with some of the new information, and that's all I can tell you over the phone. I'm working on it, and you and the world will have to be patient."

There was a long silence, then Burns started talking lowly, "I have an observation on this end also. There are things going on and people involved...well, let me put it this way. You better be careful and alert. Things may not be what they seem."

"I agree. Thanks, Mr. Burns." She turned the device off before it could ring and headed for the shower.

Chapter Twelve

Hunting Manfred Porter

10:35 AM   Manchester, England

Bobby Zuba unfolded the worn scrap of paper and checked the number before knocking. The address was indeed correct. He buttoned his jacket, partly to hide the automatic tucked into his waistband and partly to make himself more presentable. It was always an issue, his looks, and one that mostly was a disadvantage, only rarely the other way around. He bounced the metal knocker hard against the door and, by habit, stood slightly to one side.

When the door partially opened, all he could see was the top of her head...grey hair under a coarse hairnet. Her curved bony nose gave her a birdlike appearance, as did her sharp voice.

"What?" she croaked, then the nose disappeared from view while she awaited the correct answer. Bobby discretely and noiselessly placed the toe of his shoe in the crack to prevent the door from closing.

"Top of the morning, Mum. Nothing to fear. I'm no *bill* collector. In fact, I may be able to pay *you* a few quid instead." This morning, his accent was heavily Irish, a facile talent which allowed him to switch dialects as easily as taking a breath. The door opened halfway, and the older woman expectantly searched his face.

"Here...what do you mean sticking your foot in my door like that?" She was looking at his foot which was withdrawn.

"No harm, Mum. I just want a bit of information, then I'll be on me way."

"Let me see the color of your money first," she croaked, her faded blue eyes fixing his face.

Bobby held up a five pounder and waved it around while she watched, then extended it toward her. It was snatched away, disappearing behind the door. His foot quickly blocked the swinging door before it closed. She took another look and saw a thickset man with longer reddish hair and a three-day growth on his chin. The scowl on his face said it all, a man not to trifle with.

"You took me money, now you answer me questions." His voice was stronger and less accented this time. The door swung fully open. She was still in her full-length nightgown, a wrinkled, faded, soiled one. He could tell that she was going to be more cooperative this time.

"Your name is Rebecca Porter, is that a fact?" he asked. Without looking away or waiting for a response, he came right to the point, "I'm trying to locate Manfred and not having a bit of luck. Suppose you can be helpful?"

"Manfred?" she laughed. "My brother's own. Can't say I've seen Manfred for years. What would you want with the likes of him?"

"Me? Nothing at all. I'm just hired to find 'im. They tell me he's due some money for some odd thing."

"Really?" Rebecca mused. Could be that Manfred would be generous in gratitude for being found. "Last I saw of Manfred, he was working over in Cambridge, in the lab. He had a lass that he fancied who went off to America. He quit his job and followed like a lovesick puppy. Last I ever heard of Manfred. Do I get to keep the quid?"

"Do you know what he did over in Cambridge?"

"That was thirty-five years ago...something to do with frogs is all I know." She started to close the door, but Bobby pushed back.

"The lass. Recall *her* name?"

"Like the ringing of a bell. One of those hippie types in fashion at the time. Saw her once or twice. You know the hippies, don't you? Free long hair, no bra and an empty head. Pretty though, if you could look past her bell bottoms. She was called Sommerlyn. ...Crosby, I'm pretty sure. Course, you can't be positive that was her given name." She stopped talking, because the investigator had his back to her as he walked away.

Near Free School Lane, Cambridge

Bobby thought he was going to go mad. This rat's nest of addresses was incomprehensible. This was the third time around, on foot. By now, he recognized structures along Pembroke, Downing and Corn Exchange. Not to mention that Wheeler became Bene't leading back to where he was again. This time he would ask. The first group of obvious students that happened his way looked as if they had been around for a while.

"Cuse me, Lads," Bobby said, trying hard not to look threatening. The group stopped and inspected him closely. "Looking for the Registrar's office. It's on Free School Lane, but I'm damned if I can find it."

A couple laughed, mischievously mocking him. Bobby could feel the blood rushing to his head, the anger rising. "Look, my good fellow," one pointed. Bobby could see an entry way roughly thirty feet away. "That's the door. My advice is to take it."

Bobby nodded thanks, unable to trust his voice at the moment. One of the group called out to him as they walked away. "We all have had that problem. Hope we don't see you in class though." The group left tittering amusement at his expense.

"The impudent little bastards were right," Bobby muttered to himself when he saw the lettering. He stopped and flipped through his various identity cards, selecting one which would get what he wanted by implied threat. This time old Bobby would be a proper Robert representing none other than MI5. That would do the trick, he knew.

It took a few exasperating moments belly up to the tall counter before one of the older women took notice of him. By then, his pent-up anger was showing.

"Yes?" she asked, in a manner that told him that she didn't really want to know.

"I'm tasked with finding out about a student or employee, I'm not sure which. Worked in a lab experimenting on frogs, I'm told. About 1980 or thereabouts."

"And you are?" she pierced him like a specimen, eyes over the top of her glasses. Bobby, at this moment Robert, slid the badge toward her but retained hold of the edge. She carefully studied the badge and him a couple of times before responding.

"Well, which is it, student or employee, and could I at least have a name?" she demanded, not intimidated in the slightest by his identity card.

"Oh, excuse me," Bobby blurted, then passed a paper over to her with the name Manfred Porter written in pencil. "Could be either," he added.

She turned away holding the paper between her finger tips as though it was smoldering. Bobby watched as she disappeared through a door without markings. He drummed his fingers on the mahogany desktop. Short of this source, there was no trace of this Manfred anywhere. He was at a dead end. Bobby sighed, he hated to report that he, of all people, simply couldn't find the subject. Now it would be up to the IT people. He looked up to see the secretary returning and was relieved to see that she was holding a paper.

"There was a Herman Manfred Porter registered that year as a graduate student in Zoology. Could that be your man?" she asked, still not offering the paper.

"Exactly correct. Have an address?"

"Nothing since his departure. He didn't finish his studies, you see."

"Great," Bobby fumed, then remembered, "Another name if you will. He found the other paper, the one with Manfred's supposed consort. He handed it over.

"Sommerlyn Crosby," she read. "Unusual," she added. With a roll of her eyes, she once again disappeared, leaving Bobby frustratingly looking around the large room. This time the secretary returned promptly.

"Found it, Mr. Zuba, or do you have another title you would prefer?" she asked, still unsmiling.

Bobby was staring at the paper she was holding in anticipation. "Tell me you have an address on this one, please."

"Not exactly, but I feel sure that you will find it somehow. Crosby graduated with honors as a Bachelor of Science, minoring in laboratory technology. The last contact was a request for her grade transcripts to be sent to George Washington University Hospital in Washington. That's all we have. Anything else I can help you with?"

"Not a thing, thank you,"

8:20 PM   Arlington, Virginia

Beckman flipped his still burning cigarette into the street, watching as fleeting little sparks bounced along with it. He stepped out from the dark and leaned against the streetlight pole, intentionally making himself plainly visible as she walked toward him. He didn't want any surprises that might make her call out in alarm. He gauged her progress for a moment, then started walking directly toward her as she moved in his direction. She was carrying two paper shopping bags, and he knew she could not afford to drop them, running away in panic. No, she would just seek to avoid his eyes as they passed. After all, what man would want a frail woman approaching old age. She no longer was attractive, owned little of worth and had spent most of her current cash on the pitiful groceries she was carrying. Just as they passed, her on the outermost edge of the sidewalk, he reached out and touched her arm.

"I mean no harm, don't be alarmed, I just want some information," he said, as she expectantly jumped away from his touch and stood looking at him in fear, an obvious tremor just beginning.

"Your name is Sommerlyn, correct?" he ventured. At first she didn't answer, just stood there in wide-eyed startle trying to think how to flee.

"Yes. What do you want?" she managed.

"I am an investigator, and I'm not interested in you, just a former boyfriend of yours. I'll even pay you for any information you have. Could I accompany you to your door while we talk?" Beckman put on his reasonable, comforting voice and demeanor, a chameleon like transformation. Sommerlyn started slowly moving forward, occasionally glancing at Beckman, still not convinced of his good intentions.

Beckman always had found it useful to present himself as only one part of a larger more mysterious group by emphasizing the plural. "*We* were told that you once had an acquaintance by the name of Herman Manfred Porter. Would that be correct?"

Sommerlyn nodded that she did.

"Know where he is?"

Sommerlyn nodded that she didn't. The next question was delayed, giving her time to collect her thoughts.

"He followed you from Cambridge, did he not?"

Sommerlyn nodded, nearly imperceptibly this time. A weak acknowledgement meaning that there was much she didn't want to discuss. Beckman didn't know the reason but could sense the bone of the issue would be harder to extract.

"I could pay you fifty bucks or drag you downtown for interrogation," he informed her in a casual voice, the implied threat not hidden by his smooth delivery.

"Yes, we were a thing then. But we parted ways long ago, and I don't know where he is or even if he is still alive. I have managed not to think about Manfred for years."

"You worked at George Washington University Hospital from 1980 to 1985. What did you do there?" His question implied that he already knew the answer. He didn't.

"I was a laboratory technician. Just that, at first, then I was raised to supervisor level."

"You quit or were fired?" The question impelled her to look directly at his face, nearly halting their forward progress. Did he already know the answer?

"I was fired."

"Let me guess. Smoking too much weed?" he postulated.

"That was the start," she admitted.

"Manfred part of that scene?"

"Not at the time I was let go. He was gone by then. Didn't even say goodbye when he took off. I always had a notion he had to flee, but the reason, I never knew. We all smoked pot at that time...everyone I knew did. After Manfred left, I went downhill fast. The wrong crowd you know."

"You mean more and different drugs and lots of men in your life?"

"Sure. Didn't stop to think then."

"Where did Manfred work when you were with him?"

"Oh, he was over in Norfolk at the time. We only saw each other once a week, sometimes not that. He loved what he was doing over there, talked about it endlessly."

"Can you give me a summary of what he was involved with?"

"It was the start of a big thing, IVF they called it. He was in the lab, and from what he said, if it was true, he was the one actually doing the main job."

"You mean 'test-tube babies'?" Beckman asked.

"That's what the press called them. The story Manfred told sounded like petri dish work. It was similar to what he had been doing while in his degree program in Cambridge. He was devoted to it, nearly reverent when he spoke of it."

"Anything else, Sommerlyn?"

"No," she said too quickly, then looked forward, wanting to shed herself of questions for some inner reason.

"Here is your fifty," Beckman said, offering her a folded note. "I know where you work, in fact, everything about you. You can't run away from me. I want you to understand that fact, but once again, you are not whom I am interested in, and you have nothing to fear as long as you don't have anything to hide."

Sommerlyn took the cash without eye contact. She did have a secret indeed, but it was something no one could ever know and could never discover, even if she was tortured for it. Manfred was the only one who knew, and he was the cause, damn him to hell.

Beckman stopped and watched as Sommerlyn Crosby walked away without looking back. He felt sorry for her in some distant way. He had seen photographs taken when she was young and full of dreams. A nice little package with puffy lips and long gorgeous blonde hair, innocent and wild, a thing of dreams for a young man. Beckman lit up a cigarette as she slowly disappeared into the night, wishing when he was young he could have known what he now knew. A dish like Sommerlyn should have been put on a pedestal, worshiped, respected and given the world. Instead she was used and thrown aside, just like he himself had carelessly done to girls just like her. He blew a long puff into the night air. What in hell was he investigating? In this business, you were never told the big picture, and unless you managed to grasp the meaning yourself, you only saw the little parts. How did two hospital centers, miles apart, have connection, one so important that it would link continents? He took one last drag and flipped the remainder of his smoke into the street. While walking slowly back to his car, he absentmindedly picked some scraps of tobacco from his lip, remnants from his choice of unfiltered cigarettes, then stopped suddenly. His question had a simple answer, an obvious one, and he felt like slapping his forehead. The child of Spence and Barbara Jones had become Ronald Reagan. He was conceived by artificial means, and it was obvious that Spence was not the provider of the sperm. Little Sommerlyn was not only a link to the mysterious and unfindable Manfred Porter, she was the obvious link to the male parent of the Jones child. He looked back again in the direction she had disappeared, the shadows of the descending night enveloping her and removing all traces. She could be found again, but first he had more work to do.

Chapter 12

Chapter Thirteen

Discovery

The ceiling was being bathed in soft fluttering light, some of it reflected from the bay, the rest from the indirect light of the morning sky filtered through trees, an occasional bright puffy cloud of summer briefly increasing the ambient light as it passed slowly overhead. Jill's eyes wandered about the edges of the intricate ceiling, not seeing anything but her imagination and her memory. This was an important morning in both her and Ron's life, and the event was going to happen exactly at 11:00 AM. Everybody with a television and even a remote interest in politics would be tuned in for the interview and guest appearance on a popular Sunday morning live broadcast. She had been invited also, as Ronald Reagan's principal and, so far, only confidant. The opportunity had been graciously declined. She didn't want or deserve any spotlight on herself. Thus far, the press had not even displayed a photograph of her, but that didn't stop them from writing about her and openly speculating on her relationship with the new star attraction in politics. What they were implying was indeed true: they loved each other, had said so and even looked like they did. The physical part was something else entirely, and in that implication, the gossip monsters were flat wrong.

She stood and stretched, glancing at the time. Two hours left before the broadcast, enough for dressing and breakfast. This would be the first meal without the presence of Ron, his laughing eyes, soft caressing voice, his unexpected humor and above all his tenderness toward her. After spending days extending to weeks with him, immersed in his personality and history, captivated by his charms, his natural manliness, she was feeling the void. He and Ted had left before dawn to prepare and to be at the studio at the precise moment he was needed. They had talked openly about the precision required to avoid any prying chitchat from the television press followed by an immediate departure after the interview. Ted wanted Ron to stick to the political imperatives of the moment and to avoid his personal history, which retained a big dark hiatus, unknowable and secretive. The time would come, Ted explained to both of them, for the rest of the story, but first the public should only be allowed to see the person who will solve the country's problems, right its wrongs. After all, Ted noted, many historical and religious figures had parts of their lives remain unknown, and yet they continue to be honored and worshiped by the public. Ron seemed unconvinced and noncommittal. Jill wasn't sure Ron would obey political advice, instead trusting his instinct and relying on the obvious attraction the public felt for him.

The plan called for Ron's return to the estate in the early afternoon, and later, they planned to watch the newscasts together as well as the usual army of political pundits pontificating on the impact of his appearance. Jill's stomach flipped as the importance of this interview sank in. She felt like pacing or biting her nails, but instead kept control on the outside while churning on the inside. The question being raised, especially by the hostile press, was the now notorious "ten-year gap." Where was he, what was he doing, what was he named at the time? There were no answers, just questions, and the DNC was making the most of it. Jill fully understood the impossibility of her describing his capture and indoctrination during part of that time. Here, the truth would absolute condemn any bid for the presidency. Amazingly, the press had not zeroed in on the details of his birth, his parentage, his connection to the man he resembled so closely. Was it still coming? The disappearance of Spence Jones was, apparently, not all that interesting to the public.

Jill's reporting was at a standstill. Not yet fully explaining his capture and "education," Ron also omitted details of his escape, his return to normalcy. Nothing at all, until he returned to college under an assumed name with the apparent cooperation and permission of the U.S. Army. She was told that he was "assisted and encouraged" by the Army, whatever that meant. Ron described how he grew a beard, let his hair grow long and attended Yale, even achieving a degree in political science. She was hazy on details, and until he disclosed the name he was using, there was no way to verify his story. Jill resolved that now that the first big onscreen interview was going to be behind him, she would start to press for details.

She sat anxiously watching the big television screen, nearly holding her breath as the announcer spoke his name and the camera followed his familiar face across the floor. It had started. Ron looked at home on the screen, and his face showed no stress. Jill was again struck by the fact that she was looking at Ronald Reagan, either the one she knew or the other one that she had only known by pictures. No wonder the public is lathering to see more of this man, she realized. Even Jill could hardly believe it was true... Ronald Reagan lives again.

The moderator, a man of distinction himself, rose out of his chair and shook Reagan's hand. "Welcome, Mr. Reagan, and thank you for allowing the American people this opportunity to see you and to understand more about you." They both sat down, and Reagan folded his arms on the table top and studied his interviewer. The gracious smile was gone, replaced by a serious, intense look.

"And it's my privilege to be here, Mr. Ramon," he responded.

"My first question, sir, is...where in the heck did you come from?" Ramon smirked as though he had smitten the giant, delivered a blow for those who had doubts.

"I think that information has been printed, discussed and digested already. What I want to speak to instead is the sorry condition of your, my and their country. I want to point out the immense national debt, the high rate of unemployment, the attacks by hostile forces on us and our allies. There should be no need to remind the public of the disgrace of our public schools, the crime in our poor neighborhoods, the high tax rate. Those are the issues which need to be discussed, Mr. Ramon."

"And I suppose you have all the answers in spite of the fact that you have had no political experience or ever been elected to public office?"

"Perhaps you should include in your diatribe facts about serving my country in war, something you have never done, Mr. Ramon. For your viewers, I will state that I have attended one of the more prestigious universities and become educated in an effort to improve my understanding of what ails the country and what needs to be done. More than that, much more, is that I have been paying attention to the blight all around us, the state of corruption of our government and the need for urgent action before the scale is permanently tipped and disaster follows."

"Well, we haven't heard that part previously, Mr. Reagan. Care to enlighten us with details?"

"In good time. Speaking of time, I want the viewers, the entire political class, to know that change in our system is long overdue. We need to return to a system of law and values where people are treated the same. First, I would advocate removing any questions of race from any and all government forms immediately. My thinking is that we are all equal under the law and many of us have a mixed racial background. Which race should those people choose under the law? They could pick from one of the few provided boxes, but it would be in error...or a lie. Mr. Ramon, those individuals are Americans and that is all that matters."

"That, sir, is a rather radical idea and would take an act of Congress, something very unlikely."

"And that is exactly the problem. We are crippled by our inactivity, our political correctness. The public cry for action and that is exactly what I am going to give them."

Jill's hands were over her mouth, an attempt to keep herself from crying out. Ron was handling himself and fighting back in a way she could not have imagined. If the public are seeing what she is seeing they will erupt with approval, of that she had no doubt. While Ron and the moderator went back and forth, Jill started pacing, the nervous energy coming out, her desire to be there in a supportive role was overwhelming. Obviously, there was nothing at this moment she could do but watch and hope he didn't make a slip they would use against him.

"The question remains, Mr. Reagan, regarding events surrounding your birth. We are all smitten with the physical similarity between you and your namesake. Can you clarify your origins for us?"

"As your viewers know, I had parents who separated early in my life. My mother did her best for me but prematurely was lost. After that, I was raised in foster care like so many of my fellow citizens have been. Starting out in life with several strikes against you is very character building, and history is replete with examples. Hard knocks make you tough and strong, Mr. Ramon, and that would describe me."

"Your military record does indeed prove that, Mr. Reagan, but I fail to see how that qualifies you to run for president."

"Because I am like my fellow citizens, not different, not special, not privileged. I am one of them, in my heart and soul, and I won't let them down."

"The question of the day, Mr. Reagan, is: *are* you the son of the president?"

"And my answer is, Mr. Ramon, to you and the watching public: I am Ronald Reagan from my toes to the top of my head. I have no doubts who I am, and I think most of the American people do not either. My sole purpose in life is to lead this nation back to success and power. Along the way, I will not forget those of us in need, in poverty or in hopelessness. This country was founded with respect for all people, giving all equality under the law and equality of opportunity. We are not doing that presently. Our large cities are brimming with people who daily fear for their lives, remaining hopeless about changing their situation or bettering themselves. I will change that, they can be sure. Under my administration we will concentrate on improving the lives of ordinary citizens, of U.S. citizens. Foreign wars will be fought only to win, and our goal will be to reduce our enemies to cinders, yet we will seek no wars, only peace for the world. Men like me have seen war firsthand, and we know that killing only breeds more killing in the end, accomplishing nothing. I promise that if I bring this country to war, it will be a war that our enemies will not survive, and it will be a war fought strictly to protect our own country. A war of absolute necessity, but a war of absolute destruction on those foolish enough to attack us."

Steve Ramon was nearly struck dumb by the powerful delivery of his guest. He had hoped to disable the man, expose him or make him stumble, but instead he had sat there and watched Reagan dominate the screen, the room, and likely the political opposition of both parties. It was a masterful performance more fitting to a well-rehearsed script of an old movie where some unknown rides out of the mist and takes life by the throat. Ramon knew he had just been party to a tidal wave, had watched it form, then break and flood into the televisions all across the country and probably the world. Steve Ramon's reputation for a savage interviewer, a reputation buster, was ended, over, and this apparition calling himself Ronald Reagan was the instrument which had openly slit his throat while millions watched it happen.

Ramon stood humbly and, for a notable moment, just looked at his guest not only in awe but certainly in a different light. This man was not only going to become president, he was to become a great one. "Sir, I thank you for being here with me, and I want to tell you and everyone watching that I for one am convinced that your motives are pure and your cause noble. Congratulations and the best wishes for your campaign." He stuck his hand out for a shake, and Ronald Reagan took it between his two hands with warmth and sincerity, then he turned to the camera and his smile returned.

"And thank you, my people, for granting me this chance to serve you. I will never let you down."

Jill switched off the set and collapsed into the couch, streaming tears of happiness. Like everyone watching, she was overwhelmed by the presentation, the competence and the strength he had displayed. Her doubts were over about his ability to lead, now the necessity of making it happen was laid out before her. She couldn't allow his detractors to keep him out of the White House. There was a way to tell his story and to complete his record, she just had to find it, but first she needed all the facts.

The door creaked and murmuring voices drifted into the study where Jill had curled up and fallen asleep waiting on Ron's return. She wanted to be the first to tell him how wonderfully he had done, how utterly presidential his image came across. She sat up and listened carefully. There were two male voices, one belonging to Ted, the other Ron. She pulled on her shoes and ran across the room toward the hall when the door opened in front of her. Both were there, and both were grinning at her. There was no way to stop her forward progress, and she ran toward him, throwing her body against his and wrapping her arms around his chest.

"You did it! You were marvelous!" she gushed looking up at his face with obvious love. Ron hugged her in return and lifted her off of her feet, twirling her around and smiling his love back at her.

"A lot if it, I owe to you, Jill. It's mainly your idea that I should completely ignore the questions that I wasn't ready to address. You've made it your job to figure out how to tell that part of my story, and I have no doubt that you will." He put her down on the floor right in front of Ted.

"On that subject, Jill and I agreed without even discussing it in advance. To my mind and to the rest of the RNC, we are ready to accept you as a candidate for president. You will still have to gain the votes you need at the convention to secure the party's nomination, but after tonight, I no longer have doubts you will." Ted seemed happy and relieved that this day was behind him. Still, Jill saw something in his eyes that puzzled her. Ted was holding something back. There was a slight, nearly imperceptible lack of sincerity in his face, even though his words were positive enough.

"What, if anything, do you have planned for tomorrow, Ted?" Ron asked, glancing between him and Jill.

"I can see that you two need to continue the interviews and that will be enough for me. There is going to be a lot of discussion about today's appearance, and I should be around to put the record straight. So...you both have the day to yourselves, but I must warn you that the public will demand more and more frequent looks at the Ronald Reagan they have fallen in love with, thanks to Jill, and your time together from now on will be limited."

At that moment, they were interrupted by a guard entering the house in a hurry, a concerned look on his face. "We have a problem," the man said urgently. There are several cars full of reporters in front of the gate, and they are demanding to be let in. I don't think they can be stopped short of gunfire, and I'm not willing to do that."

"Call the cops, get some help. Now get to it!" Ted snapped. He went to the front door, opened it and looked out at the night while listening to the rising commotion at the gate. He shook his head. "It's my fault. I should have guessed that some smart ass would follow our car. Now getting rid of them may be impossible. They will form a permanent watch on the gate from now on. I guess your privacy is at an end. Hope you enjoyed it while it lasted."

"To me, Ted, my privacy is not as important as Jill's. Finding her here, the press will speculate about our relationship and then try to demean her work because of it. I'm not aware that they even have her photograph thus far, are you?" Ron asked while keeping his eyes focused on Jill.

"It would appear they don't or they would have published it by now." Ted thought for a moment, trying to ignore the ruckus coming from the gate, then perked up. "I have a plan to distract them, and it may or may not work. They followed the limo here and may follow it away from here. Perhaps not all of them will fall for it, but the few who remain will be no match for the local constabulary. I was leaving anyway, but I'll make a big show of it and try to pull them off. Tomorrow is a different matter, and we have to take one step at a time."

Ron put his left arm over Jill's shoulder and offered the other hand to Ted. "You've been masterful just as I was told your are, Ted, but this time I have my own plan, and I'll let you know tomorrow if it worked."

Ted's eyes rolled and jumped back and forth between their faces. "You aren't going to do something rash, I hope. Remember, you are the leading candidate for President of the United States. Don't go cowboy on us, Ron."

"The way I see it, Ted, Jill and I need just a little more time to go over my story. Then it's got to be a separation for us, even if it's a bit painful for awhile," Ron addressed Ted, while looking down at the girl under his arm. Her tears were already streaming down her uplifted face, and she made no effort to wipe them away.

Chapter Fourteen

Night Voyage

In the commotion created by Ted's departure through the gates, Jill had suddenly become aware that Ron had disappeared. She started through the big house looking for him and listening for his voice. She was certain that he had not gotten into the limo so had to be around some place. She peeked into the kitchen, usually the domain of the house staff, and there he was bent over some papers spread out on the preparation table in the center of the room. He glanced up absently as she entered, then returned his attention to the paperwork.

"I think we have a solution, Jill. Ready for an adventure you will remember?" Ron looked up at her, while pointing to a position on a large nautical chart. He tapped the spot with satisfaction.

"Look at this location…it has a marina as well as a large resort, and there are innumerable places to tie up."

"I don't understand," Jill said and started trying to orient herself with the strange markings on the map.

"Here we are right now," he said, circling a location with a fine red marker. "This is the resort…our destination." It was clearly on the other shore of the big bay and somewhat south of their location. He drew a loose line in red which crossed the bay in a straight westerly direction then turned south following the ragged western shore.

"Destination?" she questioned.

"Yes. You and I are going there tonight. Juan is gassing up the boat right now."

"You mean cross Chesapeake Bay at night?" Just saying the words out loud was terrifying. Her recent experience in the big swells and wind of the bay had taught her that the dark moving water was powerful and capricious. Crossing at night...

"It's the only way, Jill. There are still a good number of reporters out there, and they are camped permanently. The ones foolish enough to follow Ted will only return shortly. Crossing the bay will get us to the Virginia side by dawn and then Ted or someone can pick us up at the marina in the morning."

"It sounds so simple, but isn't it really dangerous to do this anytime but especially in the dark?" She could hear her own voice speaking like she was an outsider listening in. Her mind was racing with objections but unable to bring any into focus. She was petrified with fear. Water was not one of those things she was comfortable with, even in a heated pool. The Chesapeake...at night. It was more than she could even imagine.

"I've checked the weather. There's a bit of wind from the north, and it's overcast. One moment when we will need to keep an eye open is when we cross the shipping lanes, out in the middle. We don't need to fear the shallows and exposed oyster shell beds there, just waves and other ships. The tide is coming in right about now and will be full before we make it to the other side. It's going to make a bit of a chop out there because the wind and tide are contrary."

"What do you mean about shipping lanes?"

"Oh, the bay is frequented by freighters heading to and from the Baltimore docks just north of here. Large ships keep more or less in the deep water channel in the middle of the bay, but we have to cross at some point. It's just a matter of timing."

"Ron, have you ever done anything like this before?"

"No. And I never ran for president before either. Don't fret now because it's only twelve miles across, and the bay is well marked with buoys. It's going to give us the time we need together, and it's going to be just the two of us out there. We can talk about anything and everything." He stood and started rolling the maps, satisfied with his plan.

Jill didn't want to go, that was certain, but neither did she want Ron to go without her. She had developed a possessiveness toward him, a sort of ownership in some vague way. It was just that she had no previous encounters with real danger and risk in her life. She didn't know how she would handle herself, what she would do other than cower and simper like the coward she suspected must be living just under her skin.

"What do I need to take with me?" she asked, trying to persuade herself to actually go while mentally rejecting it in no uncertain terms.

"Juan is getting the squall jackets from the sailboat. You will need a dry set of clothes for when you arrive. Just put them in a big plastic garbage bag and tie it up really tight. At night, the bay can get chilly, so dress warmly for the crossing. One other thing, Jill. You need to wear your life preserver at all times while we are on the water."

Juan came bustling in, bright yellow rubber coats protruding from under his arm, and wearing his patent smile over burning bright dark eyes. "Got them, Boss!" he exclaimed.

"Gas topped off?" Ron inquired.

"Sure, Boss. Ninety-eight gallons. She's ready." He smiled at Jill who didn't want to smile at anything or anyone at the moment. Juan studied Ron for a moment before adding, "One thing, Boss...the wind." Juan paused, wondering if Ron had heard his note of caution. When Ron looked at him, waiting on more explanation, Juan continued, "Blowing a bit out there and right down the channel. Might get a little bumpy." Jill's blood ran cold. Just what she didn't want to hear. At first they wondered if Reagan had heard any of it, but when he nodded slightly at Juan, they knew he had. Juan caught Jill's eye and briefly raised his eyebrows and shoulders at her. It was all he could do.

Ron took one of the jackets from Juan and started unfolding it carefully. He held it open at Jill's height and smiled at her. "Ready, Jill?" he asked.

"In a minute. First I have to gather my things. I'm assuming that we aren't coming back here?" Jill answered.

"No, this is goodbye to a memorable time and a magical place to have spent it. At least we have a few more hours together and even after that our separation won't be forever. We'll find a way to get back to each other, because I'm not about to let you get away from me."

"In many ways, I still don't know you, Ron. My mind gets caught up with memories of Ronald Reagan's old movies, and after seeing you in the flesh, I run the two thoughts together. Being around you has been nearly hypnotic for me; I can think of nothing but you, and I even dream about you. You are a part of me, yet we have hardly even touched."

"I know what you feel about me, Jill, I can see it in your eyes. At first they showed your wonderment of me, then as you became accustomed to being close, your eyes mirrored your affection and trust. I'll tell you again as I've told the American people, I'll never let you down."

"I know that, Ron. And you can count on me, for as much as that is worth. I don't have much to offer you but...."

"Don't say that, Jill. You have given your friendship, and I count that a bigger gift than anything I have ever had. Now you'd better go collect your belongings, and I'll wait right here until you return."

Jill returned shortly holding two large plastic bags by the neck and letting them bump down the stairs behind her. Juan rushed up to help and hefted them up to his shoulder. Ron was waiting, as he had said, and held up the storm jacket again, and this time she turned and allowed him to put it on her. She pivoted back toward him, her face uplifted, her eyes on his, her mood calm and deliberate. Ron hesitated, looking into her eyes and thoughts made him mindful of how precious she had become to him and how irresponsible it might be to take her out at night to cross the Chesapeake bay.

"You should know that I left my fear upstairs. I'm not taking it with me tonight," she said.

"And you should know that I will not allow anything to go wrong tonight."

She almost could hear the words come out of his mouth, the words that said "I love you," but the thought never made it to his lips, only his eyes. He carefully placed his arm over her shoulder, and together they walked down the long hall toward the back of the house and the waiting power boat bobbing at the dock.

In the dim light, Jill took another look at the boat before stepping aboard. It was a husky twenty-one footer, twin hulls up front, two gleaming outboard motors at the rear. A small three-sided glass cabin enclosed the minimal electronics and controls. Juan had turned the running lights on, and they reassuringly glowed at the four corners of the craft. She silently took a deep breath and was about to step on the gunnel as an unexpected blast of wind pushed her back onto the dock. A steady wind, strong enough to flap her jacket open, was accompanied by occasional strong puffs coming from the north and the black waters of the bay. She looked at Ron, wondering if he actually had enough experience to attempt a crossing under these conditions.

"I know what you are thinking, Jill, and yes, it's going to be a bit rough going while this wind is pushing along. But the water out there is warm this time of year, and my guesstimate is that the waves we will encounter will not be higher than three or four feet. That's no problem for a sturdy boat like this, and the waves are similar to your experience on our first outing. Because of the tide and the north wind, the waves will be a little steeper and with more chop and spray. We'll get wet but stay safe enough."

With one glance, Jill could read Juan's face. He didn't think this trip was at all safe or even a reasonable idea. Getting aboard the rocking craft made her recall thrilling rides at the amusement park. You knew that the ride was designed to be frightening, yet somehow forced yourself to believe that it was safe. After Ron climbed aboard, Juan tossed the bags to him, and they were made fast in the stern. The twin motors started with a rumble and, with a little wave and the toss of the line, Juan slowly slid away as the boat bumped across the little waves of the inlet. The trip had started, and Jill clutched her seat with both hands, her terror just under the surface.

Ron's plan to cross almost directly west was immediately in question. Once into open water, the boat was rocked back and forth across the crest and troughs of steep breaking waves until Jill actually feared the boat was about to roll. Ron slowly changed directions, heading more in a northerly direction, trying to cross the waves more perpendicular to their travel. The rocking diminished, but the spray coming from the cresting waves was like a salt infused rainstorm.

"We have to head northwest for awhile. It'll make for a longer trip, but we have plenty of fuel. Try and keep a watch for larger vessels on your side," he shouted at her, still barely audible because of the confusion of other noise. The boat slowed to match the oncoming waves, rolling over one, crashing into the next with a shudder and spray. Jill tried to shield her face from spray and watch for ships, but she didn't have a clear idea of what she was supposed to see.

"I can see the center channel markers coming up toward the port, so we are in the commercial lanes right now," he warned at the top of his voice. Jill strained her eyes looking into the black water, then she saw something moving.

"Ron!" she shouted, pulling on his jacket. When he turned, she pointed out the lights. There were green and white lights visible, and they were slowly moving toward their position.

"Good work! That's a large ship coming from the sea. The green light is on its starboard side, and that's where we need to be." He turned their boat nearly due north, and the result was a harder hit against the oncoming waves. "We'll pass by its stern, but hang on when we do because the waves will come at us from a different direction and be bigger," he warned. "One thing you will notice, big ships move faster than they appear to. There's one on the western channel moving toward us from the north right now. We may be able to cross in front of it..." he trailed off, suddenly seeming to lose his footing, but catching himself in time.

As he said, the big ship came at them all of a sudden and, when closer, appeared immense. Under its deck lighting, Jill could make out the big containers, stacked one on the other like wooden building blocks. It just kept sliding by in the dark until, at last, the white lights on its stern came into view. Ron turned toward the center of the channel as the freighter's stern appeared, and just as he had warned, they encountered big swells coming at them from the west.

"Can they see us?" Jill shouted, pointing at the ship.

"I doubt it. We may not show on their radar, and a freighter like that carries a very small crew."

On passing the stern, the waves diminished somewhat. In the distance, approaching from the ocean, was another ship, this time, a red light was visible. Ron studied the ship carefully, trying to determine the distance and speed before committing to crossing in front of it.

"Hang on, I'm going to pick up speed!" he shouted, and the motors responded with increased RPM. As they crossed the channel, the big ship grew ever larger as they started to hit the waves again, this time violently rolling the boat as they headed due west. Jill was concentrating on the oncoming ship and bracing herself when she noticed that Ron had fallen. He had been thrown into the left side and was weakly trying to get back up.

"Take the wheel!" he yelled. Everything was confused as the boat was being tossed from side to side, and the wind continued to bring a dense spray of water onboard with it. Jill struggled from her seat and pulled herself behind the wheel, grasping it with both hands. She glanced down at Ron but was surprised to see him curled up, as if in pain. A huge dark shadow was rapidly closing from the north as their boat was tossed and rolled by the larger waves in the channel. Forgetting her fear for the moment, she held on and determinedly kept the boat pointed west.

A series of five blasts of a horn was heard from the approaching ship, which grew ever larger by the second. The warning was repeated several times as the shape became more distinct. Jill was struggling to keep their boat from rolling and wondering if she should try and make a turn.

"Stay on course," Ron shouted from the floor. "Pick up speed if you can." Jill carefully pushed the throttle handle forward and braced herself. A huge grey shape lumbered menacingly toward them as twin spotlights from the ship lit them up. Jill could tell that they were going to miss, but not by very much. The warning horn continued, and she could make out the sound of the big ship's motors. At last, the great ship started sliding by behind them as they were propelled along by its bow waves.

"Try and turn south now," Ron suggested from the floor. Jill complied, and the rocking from the waves diminished a bit. When the stern of the ship was showing, Jill saw that Ron was again trying to get up while holding his abdomen with the other hand.

"Are you injured?" she shouted.

"No. I'll be up in a minute. You saved us just then, you know." He struggled, using one arm, and managed to sit in the passenger seat. "Keep heading south but move a bit to the west. When you see the green buoys, keep them on our starboard."

Jill realized that he meant on the right. Her heart was still racing and her mouth dry in spite of the continued spray soaking her face and hair. Ron was leaning back and watching her, and when she looked directly at him, he held up his thumb at her. She slowed the motor a bit and relaxed, there was nothing left to fear, and she realized that she had never felt so much alive.

"What's wrong?" she asked.

"It's an old injury. Comes back sometimes. I'll tell you all about it when we stop."

Jill navigated as directed, and they edged closer to the line of green buoys and closer to the western shore. The waves and wind diminished on this side, and the boat's rocking became less and less. She managed to look up to see a massive array of stars visible in the night above Virginia. Any fear she had was now gone, replaced by a sense of satisfaction and well-being as smooth rhythmic sounds of the water slapping the hull, in harmony with the deep hum of the twin motors, crept into her soul. She glimpsed the lure of the sea, of boats, and the night air that had been in the blood of so many sailors throughout the centuries.

"You can slow down, because we are navigating by sight alone. The Patuxent mouth should be just ahead, and in the dawn light, we'll just follow the coast right to our destination."

Jill sat down and leaned back into the seat, studying Ron's face under the starlight and the glow of the small dash light. She could see the strain as well as wrinkles, making him look suddenly much older.

"Want to talk things over?" she murmured, wanting badly to bring him into her arms instead of talking.

"Yes. It's time for you to know more about me."

Chapter Fifteen

Escape

collapsed back there at the wrong moment, didn't I?" he asked, the little sideways smile returning to his face.

"Were you in pain? It looked like you were holding your stomach?" Jill asked.

"Yes, pain. It comes back to me at odd times, but that was not a welcome visit to be sure. It's part of my history that you haven't been told...up until now. I mentioned that I escaped from the group who were attempting to indoctrinate me. It was after two or more years, and I finally got an opportunity as they became accustomed to me. The army trained me well, and my captors slipped up. I took out two guards on the way, but once outside, I realized it was night, and I still had no idea of where on the planet I was being held. I started running in a direction chosen at random. The terrain was flat and dry with no trees or shrubs to hide behind. I decided distance was my main asset, that and the M16 I had taken from the guard. After several miles in the dark, I stopped to rest, hoping for dawn so I could see landmarks in the distance and determine where I should go. I had no identification, no money, and I was fearful that my English was shortly to become a liability."

Ron paused, obviously thinking about the past and how to relate his story. The boat progressed slowly along, making a comfortable and pleasant journey beside the shore. The eastern sky was still dark across the water, the only artificial light was from the intermittent markers of the channels. Jill sat silently, listening both to Ron's story and the now reassuring sounds of the water world they were gliding over.

"There was no water, no food, and I never saw another living thing. After I caught my breath, I headed out again, this time at a steady jog in the same direction I had originally chosen. My tracks must have been easy to follow, but I reasoned that distance between me and them was the most important consideration. It wasn't the best choice, I realized, when I saw two sets of vehicle lights in the distance, and they were headed directly for my position. There wasn't even a large rock to hide behind, only dirt, sand and pebbles. My army training came back to me, and I took a firing position on the ground, waiting for them to get into range. The clip should have held twenty rounds, enough for a nasty surprise, as they were about to find out."

Not far away, the lights of a large ship steadily moved forward, seemingly floating over the water, the sounds of its laboring motors drifting toward them in intermittent batches. The wind steadily diminished and the temperature of the air rose, returning the peace and solitude of a timeless world to them. Jill unfastened her life preserver and removed her wet jacket.

"At about one hundred meters or so, I opened up with the rifle, letting go a burst of ten rounds then moved to the next vehicle. Both stopped in their tracks, and the lights went out. My gun was empty, and I left it behind as I started running at a diagonal to my original course, hoping that they would not return fire. After a half hour, I stopped to listen and couldn't hear any sounds of pursuit. By then, a sliver of dawn was hovering in the distance. It was good I would finally be able to see but bad in that I was unable to find shelter to hide. There was no doubt that someone was going to run me down eventually. And they did exactly that. When I started running again, I heard a sound coming at me too late to avoid. Something big and heavy hit me and everything went dark."

He stopped and pointed east. A slender line of pink had made its appearance on the surface of the black water. Morning had at last arrived.

"We should have brought a few sandwiches. I'm hungry," he joked.

"I thought you were taking me to breakfast at the resort. Don't you think after that harrowing ordeal that you at least owe me a coffee and donut?" Jill replied.

"Indeed I do and grateful I am to do it. You were magnificent back there, and after I had assured you that I would protect you, you turned around and saved both of us."

"You should know that I've never been so scared in my life," she added.

"I couldn't tell. You were calm and deliberate through the entire thing. You reminded me of my old tough drill sergeant." He laughed out loud at the thought.

"Thanks for the compliment. Did he look as good in a bathing suit?"

"Never had the pleasure but, of course, no one does."

"Compliments won't finish your story. I'm anxious to know how this ended."

"I opened my eyes before I realized how much pain I was in. The ceiling was plain and painted with a flat white, and my leg was in a cast and elevated. My left arm was held by a restraint of some sort and when I turned to see why I couldn't move it, I saw the IV. Looking around, I understood that I was in a drab room lying on a hospital orthopedic bed. A young orderly happened by and saw that I was awake."

"Hey, Sergeant! I see you finally opened your eyes. Welcome back!" he exclaimed. I looked at his name tag and saw a PVT HOSP under the name *Hoffman*.

"Where am I private?" I asked.

"Landstuhl, Sergeant," he answered quickly.

It was impossible, I was still confused. "You mean I am in Germany?"

"Sure, Sergeant."

"Well, how did I get here?"

"Donno. You just appeared one day about three weeks ago. I assume you were medevaced from wherever you were injured."

"I need to talk to someone," I blurted, remembering the possible murder charge and my listing for AWOL.

"Yeah, they'll be making rounds in an hour or so. Want anything to eat?"

"No. Just go tell somebody that I'm awake, Hoffman, and I mean right now."

Hoffman shrugged and sauntered out of the room in no particular hurry, closing the door to the hall behind him. I listened for conversation, for footsteps, for the sound of a guard on the other side of the door, but there were only typical hospital sounds. After Hoffman left, I tried to assess the extent of my injuries by feeling around and trying to move. Clearly, my leg was fractured and in traction, and when I shifted, the pain from my hips made it obvious that there were deeper injuries. My hand found a long bumpy incisional scar across my left temporal area which explained my unconsciousness for an extended time. I wondered what had hit me and how I came to be found and treated by the Army.

The door to my room abruptly opened, and an officer came in. I could tell by his demeanor and physicality that he was not medical personnel. I guessed regular Army. Now I was going to get both barrels.

"Sergeant McDaniels," the captain began. "You had us worried for some time that you weren't going to make it. Glad to see you conscious."

"Am I under arrest?" I asked bluntly.

"For what?" he wondered.

"I was told that a Polish officer was murdered, and I was to be blamed. Plus there is the AWOL."

"Nonsense. As far as I know, there's been nothing of the kind. Our information is that you were captured and held by forces hostile to the United States. You were brought in unconscious with multiple injuries, and we are glad to have you back again."

"Who imprisoned me for all that time?" I asked and added, "and where was I being held?"

"It's under investigation, that's all I can tell you. When you are up to it, we need a debriefing from you, and by that time, we may have more answers."

"The man named Izajasz Bujnowski... he was a Polish junior officer. What happened to him?"

"Yes, I remember that name. He is the one who reported that you had been abducted. As far as I know, he is still with his unit."

"After the Captain left, I was in a state of near collapse from the stress I had put myself under. No charges for being AWOL, no death by murder. My captors had lied to me. But other than that, thinking back, I could see no ulterior motive. They appeared to be simply training me to become president, giving me the education and the awareness of my potential. Before my capture, I was only dimly cognizant how much like Ronald Reagan I looked. With the right hair styling, facial expressions and above all, the right attitude, I began to realize that they were right. I was a dead ringer. How surprised they must have been when I killed two guards and more in the vehicles sent to bring me back. Running me over was no accident, they had meant to kill me and, in all probability, were going to try again."

Dawn was rapidly approaching, the sky brightening in the promise of a clear warm day ahead. There was enough light for Ron to study his charts, and after closely observing the landmarks, he directed Jill to turn slightly west, following marsh grass in a sweeping gentle curve.

"Soon you are going to see rows of boats tied to their moorings. We will continue nearly west for three or four more miles before looking for a free slot. I'll take it in from here, if you'd rather."

"Not a chance, big boy. I like running the boat, especially right now when we don't have to dodge big killer ships. You sit down and finish your story and let me drive." Ron had to laugh at her new found skill as a captain and her cute way of expressing herself. He even loved the little pucker she formed, appearing during periods of concentration. She was standing, holding on to the wheel with both hands, and squinting at the horizon, her long hair fluttering behind her in the breeze of forward motion. It was one of those moments which freeze themselves in our memory forever, and when it is remembered, will return accompanied by all the sounds, smells and emotions deliciously and fleetingly present.

"What happened to the life preserver I demanded that you wear while on the water?" he asked, waiting for her moment of surprise and fluster as she discovered that the life preserver in question was lying on the deck behind her. Her response was even more amusing.

"That old thing? I didn't think the color went well with my wardrobe this morning." She never glanced his way or broke into a smile. "Will you quit teasing me and continue your story? Please?" she asked and looked directly at him.

"Let's see...I think I stopped on the day I awakened from a long coma. Well, eventually the surgeons and their acolytes came in for evening rounds, all of them, and were obviously delighted that their worrisome patient was going to pull through."

"Ah, McDaniels...I was informed that you had suddenly become conscious," the older one said, looking over his bifocals at me. His name tag just said "Pierce" on the first line and "Major" on the second. He and his colleagues bent over me, probing, listening and consulting my chart with looks back and forth between them.

"Yes," the Major summated. "By now you realize that you came to us with severe trauma. Repair entailed surgery, which has been accomplished, and traction, which is ongoing. Were you aware of any medical problems prior to your injury?"

"Not specifically. I'm sure you know better than me that fighting fanatics in a near desert environment for two years does generate a few aches and pains."

"Indeed it does. I had in mind more the issue of unexplained aches and pains, particularly in the flank area." The Major demonstrated by using his understudy and pointing to the kidney area of the man's back. He looked at me for confirmation of his theory.

"Sure. I have pain there rather constantly. Doesn't everybody who lies prone for hours looking through a scope?" I answered.

"That tells me what I wanted to know, Sergeant. We studied your internals rather well during your lengthy stay and discovered some unexpected findings." He stopped short of explaining his comment and just stood there looking at me for some reason.

"And?" I prompted, deliberately not addressing him by his rank.

"And, at the moment, your body is functioning normally, and you are obviously mending. The other is just of scientific interest to us."

"As it might be to me if I had the slightest idea of what you are talking about," I quipped.

"There are morphology changes apparent on your CT exams. I have no treatment recommendations for your findings."

This time one of the other physicians piped up, "You will come out of traction tomorrow and will be moved to a rehabilitation area. I am given to understand that your debriefing process will start soon after." It was not a statement with which to take issue. The Army has an organic nature to it and things proceed with a certain rhythm. Yours is not to argue futilely with a process which seems beyond anyone's control.

Ahead, the first signs of the yachting world started gleaming in the distance. Rows of white shimmering hulls were lined up like little children's toys, not equal or even, but simply put away for the night. Jill cut the motor to an idle, and they made slow progress toward the playgrounds of adults. Just past the shore could be seen glimpses of stately homes just being lit along their roof line by scarlet beams of the morning sun. Jill's heart sank a little when she realized that they had just come from a similar world but were heading for the real one where the rough and tumble of life would quickly come crashing back in front of her. Ron was partially right, it was a honeymoon, but without the full body contact that Jill had desperately, and expectantly, wanted to be immersed in. Right there was the missing, unexplained, biggest mystery of all. Why would Ron avoid what he obviously wanted as much as she did?

"My physician was right. They got right to it the very next day. I was placed in a wheelchair, my cast and leg sticking straight out in front of me, and wheeled into a small grey room where two officers were waiting, pen and paper at hand. There were no smiles or welcome or even pity from those two. I guessed that neither of them had ever seen combat, being more of the many paper-pusher types the Army keeps well behind the action. They outranked me, but I had the edge in experience, and we all knew it."

"Today we are fact-finding about your capture and imprisonment, Sergeant. You can start at the beginning and leave out no detail." Lieutenant Crosby was talking and the more senior, Major Leggre, was listening.

"I hope you have a lot of ink, Lieutenant, because we're talking two years or more," I began, then I asked an important question, at least to me. "Have you any idea of why and by whom I was taken?"

The Major did have a voice after all and answered curtly. "We are asking, you are telling...remember that." I remembered, all right, and decided then and there that I was going to drag this and every other session out as long as possible. If I could make them sit there on their hard chairs until my leg and other injuries healed, then that was to be my goal.

Ron quickly consulted his nautical chart once again, then pointed. "Up there on the right there is an inlet and the resort's marina. We should be able to find a space to tie up. I'll give Ted a call, and he can meet us for breakfast. A big cup of coffee sounds good, doesn't it?"

"Don't forget the donut, Ron. You promised, didn't you?" Jill reminded him.

Just as Ron predicted, another large array of boats peeked around the next bend. For every taste and wallet size, there is a yacht made, and it seemed that every variety was there bobbing softly in the calm water and lit by the morning sunlight. A couple were large enough to be positioned alongside their own dock and gleamed with polished bronze and mahogany, their owners still sleeping in some distant abode. In her life, Jill had been spared this ridiculous display of conspicuous consumption, and it was a shock to see all this money and human labor floating uselessly in wait for occasional occupancy. In her family, they fought for the single bathroom and were driven around in a small older car, and none of them ever even knew this lifestyle existed. She felt as though she was from a distant, poorer planet, where her fellow creatures were judged by hard work and accomplishment, not by extravagance.

Ron seemed to divine her thoughts and patted her knee in an affectionate way. "Impressive, isn't it? Remember that all this hardware is created by people who earn their living that way. The money changes hands again and again and is how our or any economy works. It's simply capitalism. Many owners of these impressive yachts rightfully earned the money to spend it as they choose. Most will tell you that owning a big boat is next to flushing cash down a toilet. Besides, as you can relate, being out on the water in a boat is a wonderful experience. Don't let yourself envy anyone for what they own. Often, the possession owns the possessor, and no, they can't take it with them." He laughed while looking around and shaking his head. "That's what they promised me, what they wanted me to desire if I became

Ronald Reagan. Wealth, prestige and power. Anything I wanted I could have, they said. Now I am Ronald Reagan and what I want is not material things or power. I want our country to be safe, to prosper and to progress. If possible, our people should be able to acquire and own anything they desire...but I don't want any of it. My only wish is for America, not for me. I don't want anything at all."

Jill was quiet and looked straight ahead. Ron had left any desire for her off of his list. Without wanting to, her tears started their journey down the sides of her face, and she made no effort to wipe them away or even hide them. Her display of emotion wasn't missed by Ron though, and he stood up and moved alongside her, his shoulder against hers. "You, Jill. I haven't forgotten you. You deserve better than me, and I have no right to you. If only things were different..."

"I don't understand, Ron. I know you love me, I can feel it every time you look at me. Why?"

"Someday you will understand, I promise. Don't be hurt or angry with me, because I need you, your friendship, your smile and the vision of your loveliness. You have become the most important person in my life, also the one I dream about. When we separate today, I'll shed some tears about it, but I also know we will come back together at some point."

Chapter Sixteen

Ted?

A vacant spot beckoned them, and at Ron's direction, Jill cut the motor at the perfect moment, allowing the boat to expertly drift into position just inches from the rubber tires hanging from the dock. The quiet descended like a blanket, leaving only the soft slapping of the harbor waves and the occasional deep thump of a craft hitting the bumpers alongside. There was always the sound of gulls anywhere near the bay, and they silently appeared overhead, washed in bright sunlight, studiously inspecting the boat below for any edible morsel which could be stolen in a flash of wings. Ron dialed Ted's number while he looked directly at Jill's face. Yes, it's true...he loves me, she knew. She could see and feel it in his eyes.

"Want to come to breakfast?" Ron asked when Ted answered. "No, not the estate...closer. We crossed the bay last night and just arrived." He listened as the voice crackled in his ear. He winked at Jill and rolled his eyes. "Now listen, Ted," he said sternly. "We came through just fine and had a good time. You can find us in the restaurant having coffee. Just look for the last resort on the north bank of the Patuxent, and you will find us waiting." He chuckled and put away the phone.

"Ready to go eat?" he asked.

"There's no rush. It's going to take Ted an hour to arrive so you have time to finish your story, and that's more important than food right now."

Ron took a deep breath and settled into his seat, letting one arm comfortably dangle over the side. "I told them every little thing I could remember, and the telling of it took days and days. The revelation that I was being coached to become Ronald Reagan didn't seem to jar them or even be unexpected. They listened without a flinch. When they were satisfied that they knew every last detail, the sessions were suddenly at an end. My physical therapy appointments grew more intense, and I was nearly able to walk on my own once more, when I got another summons to the little grey room. This time I was unexpectedly greeted by two men in civvies, accompanied by a middle-aged woman. They were friendly and gracious and immediately put me at ease. After I awkwardly sat down, and with no introductions from these mysterious people who wore no identifying name tags, they began.

"You were intentionally hit by a truck, Sergeant, and nearly killed. You can't be discharged and reassume your life, you must realize that. If they find you, and they will, anything could happen. We are here to offer you an entirely new identity. You will be listed as deceased, and the former part of your life will be permanently over. With a new name, new paperwork, and some monetary assistance, you can resume your place in the world without anyone being able to find you," she said as the others nodded agreement.

"Just a moment," I ventured. "You would acknowledge that I do resemble the former president, and this group, whoever they are, were training me to run for public office. Do you have any explanation as regards their motives?" The question was both a fundamental one and necessary to discuss. For myself, I had no glimmer of the answer.

"We believe we do, Pete," one of the men responded. "Yes, that is to be your new name, Pete Evans. We are sure that your training and indoctrination was not yet complete. First, they had to be sure that you could act, talk and even think like Ronald Reagan. Then, we feel sure, they were going to start swaying your opinions to correspond to theirs. It's a technique which has proven effective. In the beginning, they encourage trust, then slowly mold a person to their way of seeing life, to their political and religious beliefs. They never got that far with you. You made an escape and killed some of them while doing so. Your contract was spoiled, and they had no choice but to immediately eliminate you before you managed to return to us and tell your story. There may have been some anger and revenge in it since you had cost them time and money as well as a few lives."

"Now what? What do I do now that I really look like and think like Ronald Reagan?" I asked.

"You have to change back, Pete. Grow a beard, even change your hair color, but return to the man you were prior to your abduction. You are free now, and you can do whatever you want in life. Isn't that all anyone can expect?" she said bluntly.

"I suppose so," I answered. "Do you just let me go now?" I asked.

"Soon. We have a place for you back in the States along with a well-funded bank account. We owe you that. For a period, we will keep an eye on you just to be sure you are adapting well," the other man interjected.

"So, I am to go into hiding, just as if I had testified against the Mob. Name change, appearance change, no friends and put down in a strange place. That's just great."

"We studied you, Pete. You have no friends, no family that you interact with. It's a new, wonderful experience with no worries. How can you be depressed about it?"

"They were right. It was sounding like a good deal after all. I could do anything I wanted and would have the money to do it."

"What did you do when you returned?" Jill asked. Her tears had dried, and she was listening carefully, sifting through his story, subconsciously writing it down for later publication.

"I changed outside but not inside. At first, I was still Barns Trey McDaniels. After they got me into Yale, I majored in my new interests: Political Science and Philosophy. No one there ever looked at me twice. Not a single person was aware that I was a roughed-up copy of Ronald Reagan. That college-aged bunch had never seen one of his movies, and most were born after his death. They wouldn't have noticed even if I had looked exactly like I do right now."

Jill relaxed, listening to Ron and his unfolding story, one that no person had ever heard before now. His voice was masculine and yet caring, soft and still unique. It was the voice of Ronald Reagan, either one of them, and a voice she had been attracted to long ago in her childhood, while lying on her bed, watching his films and wishing it was her in his embrace instead of the beautiful actress shimmering in black and white. She had been in love with Ronald Reagan for as long as she could remember, and there he was only two feet away, but in some ways just as distant as an old long-forgotten movie. When she was younger, she had looked up the screen idol's career, his history. It was very different from the Ronald Reagan's she was close enough to touch. No matter how similar they were, her Ron was not the original. There had been no time warp or trick of nature bringing back the deceased. Jill had learned something important from watching the old movies made in the thirties and forties. Humans have, on occasion, amazing similarity to people past or present, at times breathtakingly close. She recalled Ingrid Bergman, her stunning celebrated beauty was matched by her skill as an actress and enhanced by a delightful accent. Who could think that any woman could ever again duplicate Ingrid, but along came her daughter, Isabella Rossellini, who could have doubled for her mother. Her mind snapped back to the present when Ron hesitated.

"What did you just say?" she asked.

"I was trying to tell you what a failure I was teaching college. Weren't you listening?" he asked.

"Ron, I'm so sorry. Being up all night and all that adrenaline...I missed something."

"That part, I'm surprised you didn't hear. I was just saying that my biggest concern was that the co-eds wouldn't stay away from me. Not that I ever got involved, you understand, they were just so available that the other faculty decided that I would slip and fall eventually, if I hadn't already done so. I was asked to go elsewhere."

"And did you...teach elsewhere?" Jill asked.

"No. I had had enough. It was going to be the same anywhere I went. After a couple weeks of introspective thought, I took a position at an investment firm. I thought college would have prepared me for high finance, but I learned more in six weeks than college can teach in four years. After my preparation in Political Science and my more real-world immersion, I woke up and understood how the economy of the country works. Not only that, I understood the politics as well. In one moment of intense epiphany, I discovered the truth...I was the one destined to save our country from itself. There was a reason I happened to be born looking like Ronald Reagan as well as thinking like him. I *was* him. No matter how or why, the fact was and is inescapable. At that instant, I decided to change my name back to what it should have been all along. This time, no one was going to stop me from attaining my destiny."

"That day I first met you, you remember, was your first foray into politics. How did it happen? Did you just walk in at the RNC office and announce that you wanted to be president?"

"They found me...after I shaved my beard, styled my hair and hired an attorney who assisted me by filling the petition for my name change. One week after my new name was approved, he was at my door."

"He?"

"Sure, you know. It was Ted."

No, Jill didn't know that little fact, because Ted had pretended not to know even who was being introduced, pretended that meeting Ronald Reagan was a complete surprise. "Ron, do you know the name of the wealthy donor who provided his estate on the Eastern Shore for our use?"

"Of course. That place belongs to Ted. Thought you knew."

"No, Ron. That was kept from me. I don't think I would have agreed to go if I had known."

"Well, I'm glad then. It has meant a lot to me having you there, and I hope that you feel that way about me. Whatever Ted's reason, it worked out just fine. You and I are very close, and you have established yourself as a reporter in the view of a grateful nation. Plus, you got my story out in a nearly perfect way by keeping interest in me alive week after week. See, we have a lot to thank Ted for, don't we?"

Jill didn't answer. She focused on Ted, every detail, every word he had spoken, hovering in her memory. Ted was not what he wanted you to see. From the first, she had worried that when Ted "accidentally" found her at the convention center, it had instead been planned to the last detail. She had been chosen for this role by Ted or by someone controlling Ted. They, or he, knew what would happen. She was expected to become a romantic partner to Ron, even a passionate lover, who would never betray the man she cared so much for, all orchestrated to happen on a remote, lavish estate away from snooping eyes and camera lenses. A lowly unknown female reporter would be the first to give details about the hot, handsome candidate, and her reporting would be favorable, if not glowing. She had been used.

"I believe that I am a victim of a large plot, Ron. Someone knew enough about me to feel sure that I would fall in love with you. They wanted a favorable press, and they used my female weakness to get it. The fact that you encouraged my affection then refused to act on it makes me believe that you have only been acting. You don't really care about me, or you would have found an opportunity to demonstrate your love and attraction with at least an embrace and kiss. God knows I let you know my willingness, my passion for you." Her soliloquy was accompanied by another flood of tears, and she suddenly stood and moved toward the end of the boat, trying to put some distance between them.

She felt his hand on her shoulder gently turning her toward him. "You are right about everything but me. I had no part in any of it and, like you, I also suspected someone of manipulation by providing a pretty little reporter to win my heart and soul. And so you have. As much as I have resisted physical contact with you, I want to tell you again that it has been in your best interest. I don't feel worthy of you, and I'm simply trying to protect you." He spoke softly, his eyes sparkling with moisture. The moment she thought would never occur had arrived as he pulled her closer and closer until they met with lips and bodies. After a very long time, he pulled away and whispered, "I love you, and you should have realized that."

"I thought I did, there were doubts for a moment, but now I know it's true. I love you also, but I'm sure you always knew."

"I did. There were moments when I felt guilty about your feelings for me but couldn't undo anything I had said or done and really, down deep, didn't want to."

"And we are lovers, aching for each other, who will separate shortly, going our separate way?"

"In distance, but not in our hearts."

"If we don't get out of this boat immediately, something is going to happen," Jill predicted.

Ron laughed and looked around. "Yes, we have to go, don't we? Breakfast then. And you promise not to eat more than one donut?" he teased.

"Jill no longer promises anything. My head is spinning, and I can't think straight other than to fantasize about you."

Ron stepped onto the dock and pulled her and two bags of clothing up beside him. "Do you need to bring all those clothes to breakfast? he joked.

"You're kidding! I'm soaking wet from salt water and the perspiration of total fear. My hair looks like a rat's nest, and my clothes are ridiculous. Yes! On this matter, a woman's instincts are not to be disputed."

Chapter Seventeen

"Gone, and a cloud in my heart"

Jill left the ladies room and felt his presence before she saw him. Ron was watching, his eyes never leaving her as she walked toward him across the crowded, noisy room. She felt at least a little clean and certainly better dressed than when she came in. Other eyes appraised her, cat eyes and hungry male ones, their owners dissecting her, inspecting her and placing her into some niche of their own creation. Jill ignored anyone but Ron, smiling just for him on her way toward their table.

"Hello, stranger!" he said, nodding approval. "Looks like you were right again. A blue crab transformed into a princess by fifteen minutes in the ladies room."

"Like crab, do you?" she wondered, amused by his choice of words.

"Some will try to hurt you, if they can, and you can hardly blame them. So far, my experience with crabs has been delightful, but *you* are no crab, my pretty. Did you see all the men with envy and lust on their faces watching you walk toward me, and all that before coffee?"

"And the women were thinking something else," Jill observed. She looked around discreetly, not wanting to call attention to the arrival of a newsworthy person sitting right in public view.

"Anyone spot you yet?" she asked, trying not to be overheard.

"Our waitress, a few others, who are right now deciding if I am who I appear to be. Don't worry, I can handle a crowd, friendly or hostile."

"Are you ready for what's about to happen?" Jill asked.

"As much as anyone can be. I am convinced of my purpose, and my intent is honorable. It's what I want to happen, and I won't be swayed by adulation or criticism. The country needs a leader whose interest is what is good for its people and not for himself or his party. I have no other motive, no other ambition in life, so let them come at me or be with me."

Before Jill could respond, the waitress appeared, notebook in hand. She had obviously noticed her famous diner and had put a name to his face. "You are much better looking in person," she confided.

"Thank you, Tonja," Ron remarked, reading her name tag. "You should see me when I'm clean." He laughed a bewitching laugh making it sound like it was meant just for her.

"This your wife?" she asked, pointing with the end of the notebook toward Jill.

"You are looking at the most sought after reporter in the United States. Meet Jill Longley," he said and motioned for Tonja to look at his dining partner rather than at him.

"No kidding!" Tonja remarked. "So that's you!" she said, surprised, indicating that Jill's name was indeed becoming widely known. "Wondered what you looked like."

"Just a plain jane reporter, that's all," Jill admitted.

"Not from the eyeballs I see giving you the twice over. Wish some of those rich guys would pay attention to me like that," Tonja observed, glancing defiantly around at the offenders.

"Two coffees for now," Ron requested. "We have a guest coming, and we'll all order food after he is seated."

"Another celebrity?" Tonja wondered.

"Very handsome and very unattached...you'll see," Jill promised, sending Tonja off to speculate and watch for the newcomer.

"We're both famous," Ron grinned.

"One question before Ted arrives," Jill asked, leaning forward to make it private. "Can I put in print the rest of your history after your discharge from the Army, and may I disclose the name you were using?"

"Now you see my problem, don't you. We can't tell anyone, even Ted, about my abduction and reeducation. You know they will think I was brainwashed."

"They would for sure. No, I'll never breathe a word of any of that. The rest, though, is clearly important. You obtained a degree in Political Science from one of the world's leading universities, and you worked in finance and investments. The public needs to know that."

"I don't see any reason not to use that. Go ahead, with my blessing," Ron agreed.

"One more and it's highly personal, and I'll understand if you don't want to tell me." Jill watched his face closely wondering how he would react to her question. "It's about your lady friends. I can see how attractive you are to the opposite sex. I just wonder..."

"If I got physical with any or became enamored or even in love with one or two? That's what you meant to ask, isn't it?"

"It is. Do you mind me asking?"

"Not at all, but you won't believe my answer. There were none, Jill. Absolutely none."

"Not even the beautiful companions who hung on your every word and glance during your captivity?"

"Especially not them. That's what I was expected to do, and by now, you know that I don't follow rules easily."

"I'm a good example of that, and it's the only reason I would believe you. But, I'm still mystified about it."

The waitress, Tonja, returned with the coffee and positioned herself as close to Ron as she could while she sat the cups down. "Anything you need, just wave at me because I'm watching you." She looked back once or twice over her shoulder as she left the table.

"You could have that one in a minute and experience no guilt about it," Jill observed.

"No thanks. I have you, and that's all I'll ever need."

"Keep at it and you'll make me cry again."

They both looked up in time to see Tonja leading Ted toward them, beaming a smile and wink at Jill.

"One look and I knew he was your expected party," Tonja confided. "Coffee for you also, sir?" she asked him.

"Sure," Ted said, "and a menu, please." Without a pause, he acknowledged Jill and Ron. "Good morning and welcome to shore. Hope it was an adventure last night." He glanced disapprovingly at Tonja who had lingered, hoping to eavesdrop their discussions.

"For sure it was, Ted," Jill said and watched as Tonja reluctantly walked away.

"First things first, lady and candidate. We have a full schedule coming up. You are rested and ready, I presume?"

"Ready for action," Ron said. "Jill isn't coming with us," he added.

"Yes, about that Jill," Ted said turning to her. "When can we expect another blockbuster from you?"

"About tomorrow morning. That's suitable?"

"High time. Also, I've had it up to here with inquiries about you and Ron and your relationship. The question comes to mind...what about it?" Ted wasn't smiling this time. He really wanted to know.

Ron cleared his throat and laid one hand across Ted's arm. "Jill and I are close friends, Ted. Nothing more has happened, if it's any of your business."

"It isn't my business, but everyone is making it theirs. Sorry, I had to ask, don't take it the wrong way."

"Didn't your loyal staff tell you everything you want to know?" Jill asked.

"So you know. I thought you would refuse if you knew, that's why."

"Well, did they report to you or not?" she persisted.

"They said that nothing happened," he admitted. "And I'm kind of glad. We all didn't need any more to worry about at the moment. Things are going to get nasty from here on and salacious stories get around, you know."

Jill studied Ted closely, wanting to catch a slip of any kind that would fit into the narrative she was starting to form. Either he was being truthful or a master of deception, because she could detect nothing amiss in his voice or face.

"Jill, do you have an idea of what you are going to write about now that you two will be separated?" Ted asked casually.

"I have some ideas I'd like to follow up on, but I am also at the beck and call of my editor. He may have plans."

"Normally, I would avoid discussing our political strategy with the press sitting at the same table, but in your case, you've proven yourself, and we all trust you. However, much of this conversation will be off-limits for your newspaper. It's one thing to tell the life story of a candidate, even to discuss his political views, but our strategy for the election is confidential. You do understand?"

"I consider myself part of the independent press, and I don't want you to include me in matters that I should not be party to. This particular candidate has become very important to me so you can depend on me to continue to put him in the very best light I can, but your version of politics is often messy and deceitful, and I don't want to even hear that stuff. Better if I don't know some things."

Ron lightly slapped the table and looked for the nosy waitress. "I think Jill has it correct. Let's enjoy a nice breakfast and leave politics and romance off the table for the moment. Ted, you and I have the rest of the day after we drop Jill off. We'll resume this discussion later."

The rest of the meal was uneventful, even pleasant. The larger room displayed an extensive view of the marina, and beyond that the bay itself, hovering as a thin blue line on the horizon. Eyes from various corners lingered on the three of them trying to make connections, and puzzling on the unexpected appearance of the most talked about presidential candidate in recent memory. Finally, one diner had worked up the nerve to approach their table, and they looked up surprised to see him standing there smiling down at them.

"I just had to say hello," he blurted. His portly belly hung over his trousers and was made more manifest by his inappropriate bow tie and seersucker jacket. "You are going to be my favorite. I just wanted to tell you," he boasted. Afterwards he seemed to run out of words and just stood there looking back and forth at them.

"And, I am most happy to receive your support, my friend," Reagan answered with his famous smile.

A moment of silence nearly convinced the unwanted guest to turn away but another thought popped into his mind. "I voted for Ronald Reagan, our greatest president, and I'll vote for him again." A thought engaged his mind, and he couldn't help but express it. "You look so much like him it's spooky. Are you his son...or something?"

Ted spoke up quickly, "That thought is one we hear all the time, and you are not the first to express it. Now, if you don't mind, we would love to finish our breakfast, but thank you for your support." They turned their attention away from the interloper, trying to encourage him to leave, but he continued to stand there, obsessed with the image of Ronald Reagan and trying to decide for himself what it meant. Eventually getting the message, he slowly ambled away back to his waiting table.

"That's the question you have to address. It's the one everybody will want answered and until you do, it will dog your campaign," Ted stated.

"Let them speculate," Ron said. "The extra attention will keep the news people busy and keep my name on the front page. Isn't that what's important?"

"True, but there are, at the moment, two schools of thought. One has it that you were simply born lucky enough to resemble the president, and you are making every attempt to make your fans believe that you, magically, have assumed all the former president's attributes and political motives. The other, which is really more forgiving, believes that you were born to a woman who had a personal relationship with the president, no matter the improbability of that. Want to give us your view, Ron?" Ted asked.

"To you and everyone who will ask, I shall state what I feel in my heart. I am Ronald Reagan, and I want to become president because the country needs me."

Ted smiled, "That's simple as well as eloquent. We'll see if it's enough in due time. What does his biographer say, Jill?"

"I know that Ron believes what he says, and I've never met a more honest person. In my writing, I've tried to avoid that issue as much as possible, because people will believe what they want and facts or logic don't matter anyway. Ronald Reagan is real and is no phony. I'd advise just letting speculators go wild and ignoring them. Run the campaign on what he will do as president and not what the former president did or said. Treat him like what he is...an idealist, not a populist, and let the fact of his existence speak for itself."

"I can see that you were a lucky find for all of us. Nicely put, Jill," Ted observed.

"Lucky, Ted? Didn't you research me before you found me and knew more or less for certain how I would feel and how I would react?"

"Not at all, Jill. To me you were and are a fresh face. I simply reasoned that a small town reporter with no ax to grind and no permanent bias would be a good voice for us. And I was correct."

"And part of that assumption was that Mr. Reagan and I would fall for each other and cement the bond?"

"You have developed your own theory, unsupported by the facts, Jill. It's quite the opposite from what you think. The truth is that I am attracted to you, and I hoped you could tell. Granting you this position was a way for me to...hell, isn't it obvious or am I that bad at it?"

"It worked until I woke up and realized that you are more complex, more manipulative than you wanted me to believe. Catching you in a lie, or perhaps more than one, made me see the real Ted."

Ron patted her hand, trying to keep her from becoming the center of the dining room's attention. "Jill," he said in a fatherly way, "Ted lives in a world that is often evil and Machiavellian. He has to do what he must and simple people like us can't forgive him for being good at it. Please remember that Ted is on our side, yours and mine. Look at his results, not his methods." He removed his hand from hers and turned toward Ted. "Whatever you wanted to happen on your estate wasn't up to you to determine. Jill and I feel very affectionate for one another, it's true, but it's also true that we will never compromise the political campaign. We three agree on one thing which is the important one: we want to win. Everything else has to be put aside for now."

Jill listened as he spoke and a light turned on. What Ron said was the real reason that he had so avoided romance with her. He was not going to be compromised. It had nothing to do with his morals, or his physical ability, or his expressed love. Ronald Reagan was determined to become president and sex with Jill was not part of his plan. She suddenly felt crushed. In her mind, love was the ultimate achievement in life, no amount of power or money or fame should be in competition. Obviously not true with Mr. Reagan. His love could be postponed until a more suitable time. She suddenly wanted to leave, to get away from both men, to breath air not contaminated by politics. Her thoughts were scrambled, all her assumptions were shaken. Home and Mom sounded like what she most needed at the moment.

Jill's inner voice was telling her to get out of there, and she realized she just might have a way. "Ted, doesn't Juan have to come get the boat?" she asked.

"I've already told him, and he should be around at any time. Did you leave some belongings in there?"

"No, but if you don't mind, I would like him to drive me into town."

Ron looked concerned. "Did we say something to make you want to rush away, Jill? I thought we had a few more hours together before parting."

"I have a few things to get caught up on, and I also know that the campaign needs a good headliner out of me. We have to say goodbye at some point." She was dry-eyed and calm. Too calm, too deliberate. It was obvious that something had changed. Ron studied her face and tried to recall all the words which had been used. His feeling for her was unchanged, and he meant it when he had expressed his love for her on the boat. He wondered if she had not been attracted to Ted all along and seeing him again rekindled something in her. It was otherwise unfathomable.

"I'll call him and find out just when he'll get here," Ted said and dug out his phone. Juan must have been waiting for a call because the connection was immediate. A mumbled conversation followed and Ted clicked off. "He's just arrived and parking right now. He will be delighted to drive you anywhere you desire. Sure you want to leave us this quickly?"

Jill stood and retrieved her plastic bags from under the table. Ron rose also and stood there helpless and silent. One glance at him told Jill that, if given the chance, Rod would again embrace and kiss her, because his heart clearly yearned for her. His look softened her, as did the thought of being in his arms, because she had not changed her mind nor her feelings for him. She was his, if he wanted her, but of course, as he had plainly stated, the campaign was uppermost. People were watching and a kiss or affectionate embrace was out of the question. Instead she stuck out her hand and waited for him to take it. She hoped that no one but her could see the glistening in his eyes as he finally accepted her handshake while keeping her eyes fixed with his. Ted stood also and quickly offered her his hand, a big professional smile on his face for everyone watching to see. Always the politician, she thought. Ted was what he had to be full-time, never a glimpse of the man hiding inside, if there was one.

She left them standing while everyone watched, dragging her plastic sacks of belongings behind and not looking back. She hoped the tears forming would wait to run down her face until she got outside.

Chapter Eighteen

Stranger in Shadow

After Juan dropped her off at her hotel and wished her well, the first thing she did was shower. Wiping down using a restroom sink wasn't nearly clean enough for her. A long hot shower always made her think, and she stood under the hot water until her skin glowed pink. Separation from Ron was very painful. She had become accustomed to his warm smile and, at times his awkward jokes, but not being able to hear his voice or stare into his face was withdrawal provoking. In spite of his somewhat ridiculous claim that she was too good for him, she wondered if the opposite was true. What if he became president? Would they marry, or would she simply be an occasional mistress? How would it feel being first lady? Could she do that, carry that burden? All the questions swirled around like the water and ended in the same place. Down the drain. There were no answers, only questions.

After she toweled off, she put on her cushy, old cotton robe and pulled a chair up to the little desk where her laptop sat ready. This was to be, had to be, a great one. All the new information would be there, and she would put the events out of sequence to hide the more than two year gap during his capture and indoctrination. She stopped typing suddenly and stared at the wall. The indoctrination...it wasn't completed, there was no indoctrination, as Ron had told it. But...the length of time...two years. What if Ron was indoctrinated after all but won't or can't remember it? She could be helping to install the greatest Manchurian candidate of all time, one whom the public remembers and instinctively trusts. No one in America would believe that this man, the single man they feel they know so completely, could be something else entirely, a plant of an enemy power, a Trojan horse with intent unknown.

She got up and went to the little refrigerated high-priced bar and took out a small bottle of Scotch. She needed this drink, she thought, and tossed it down, then nearly wretched on the harsh effect it had on her unaccustomed mucosa.

On the other hand, she had spent hours and hours with him, looked into his eyes and felt his touch. She would have given herself to him a dozen times, but he was too honorable to accept her. That kind of man simply could not be a traitor, she concluded. His story just had to be true.

At 6:00 PM on the dot, she pushed the button and uploaded her file. Burns would be more than pleased to see it come in early instead of her usual near midnight, seconds before the filing deadline. She stretched and realized that she was unusually hungry, that she had missed lunch and the rest of a nearly perfect weather day trying to get the article down flawlessly. And she felt happy about this one. It was one of the most anticipated reports since she began, and it would cement her name in the news world. Gathering her purse, she headed out for the restaurant situated off the lobby of the hotel. Dining alone was always trying and usually made her feel like some kind of outcast with no friend or even relatives who could provide conversation during a meal.

She asked for, and was given, a small table along one wall, not far from the entrance to the kitchen. Her waitress provided a small candle, but her table was not often chosen because it was so isolated. Exactly what she wanted. Ordering was done swiftly, because she was eating to live and not the other way around. A simple meal rapidly prepared and rapidly consumed. She consulted her watch and realized that if she left right after eating she could make it to her mother's home just after midnight. That would allow for some sleep before surprising Mr. Burns by showing up in his office about the time he arrived. She needed to sit with him and seriously discuss the direction of any more articles about Ronald Reagan. She knew that he was conducting some research of his own, supplied by some shady characters from his old days. It didn't matter to her where the info came from as long as it was accurate. Anyway, if she stayed in this room for long, the other press would hunt her down and use her as their news story of the day. Being a celebrity or star had its downside for sure.

She hurriedly packed her bags, not intending to return to this hotel when and if she was in need. Glancing out the shaded window, she could see darkness descending quickly. It was going to be a drive through the night, something she hated more than finding spiders in her slippers. The room had been charged to the newspaper so time of check out was not an issue, but parking her rental car had been. There was no parking attendant at this level hotel, a feature, next time, that would be on her checklist. An adjacent parking deck used an unattended toll exit gate. If her memory served, the facility was dimly lit, unguarded, and mostly vacant.

Bumping her suitcase up the stairs with one hand and trying to balance her backpack full of photo gear in the other, she finally found the second floor entry door. She pushed it open and paused to listen. The level was quiet as a graveyard and only scattered parked cars were in view. She breathed a sigh of relief, quickly spotting her nondescript car parked by itself. Someone had once told her that single women could be attacked by someone lying under a car, waiting on an opportunity just like this one, with no one to observe or come to the aid of a defenseless woman alone. Jill stooped down and studied the underside of her car from a distance. It was a useless thing to do, because there was only darkness visible which could have contained several villains or none. She started walking toward the car, hyperalert to any extraneous noise. At last, the trunk popped open, and she hurriedly tossed the bags inside. All she had to do now was to get in and start the motor.

"You are Jill Longley," a man's voice stated. Curiously, it was not a question, just a definitive statement. Jill instinctively turned in fear, placing her back against the unopened car door. She could just make out a man's shape emerging from the shadows of a large vertical concrete column. He was not much taller than her, but his shadow was still massive, made more so by the large brimmed fedora hat he wore. She felt for the door handle at her back, contemplating a mad rush inside and a quick exit.

"I know that is your name. You have nothing to fear from me. I have some information that might prove useful to you, and I wanted privacy when we met."

"Don't come any closer," Jill warned. What she would do about it if he did was another matter.

"This is close enough. If I wanted to harm you I could have done so by now. You can relax."

"What do you want?" Jill asked, her voice rising against her will, making her answer sound more like a plea.

"You are the one writing about the Candidate...the Copy Candidate. I am an investigator and have been pursuing leads about persons who are of interest to you. First, I have a warning to give you. The birth certificate father of Trey Jones was alive when I found him about a month ago....name of Spence B. Jones. Since then, he has gone missing. I wouldn't be surprised if he is dead by now. You are being warned that there are interested parties in this matter who don't follow the law."

"Are you the one who killed Spence Jones?" Jill asked.

"Not me. That's not my department. My tip is about a girlfriend of another party. She knows something. Better find her while she's still walking and talking, if you catch my meaning."

"Is there a risk to me when I find her?" Jill asked, sure that his answer would be positive, but hoping not.

"I don't know if she is in the spotlight yet. Maybe. You should be careful."

"Just what do you think she knows?"

"It's a hunch. She's the one."

"She have a name and address?" Jill asked.

"Sommerlyn Crosby. I found her over in Arlington, but if I were her, I would have fled by now. She lives on the edge, and I expect that she won't have the resources to run very far away."

"Why are you telling me all this?" Jill asked, suspicious by now that she was being set up for some nefarious reason.

"If they had let me, I would have put all the pieces together by now. Someone doesn't want all the facts in one place. Perhaps you can do it for me. Watch your back and whom you confide in. It's a dangerous game from here on."

His shadow disappeared from view, indicating that the clandestine meeting was at an end. Jill threw herself into the car and made sure it was locked all the way around. She had a notebook handy and scrawled the girlfriend's name down. Exactly whose girlfriend was never mentioned. She hit the starter and was never so glad to have a car motor throbbing just in front of her.

Jules Burns briefly acknowledged his staff as he

came in, as usual in a hurry, plus he was still fatigued from the previous late night getting the paper ready to start printing shortly after midnight. His little newspaper was able to sell more than they could print, and he was already coming under pressure from the owners to diversify the process. They were convinced that the paper was about to hit the big time...national distribution, printing facilities in multiple sites, all that fluff. No one wanted to hear the truth...that if Jill Longley was hired away, their precious small town newspaper would fold flat like an old cardboard box. He chuckled, recalling that not that long ago, Jill had been griping about all the petty articles she was required to produce. Hell, he thought, the entire paper is just useless and local stuff. Until now. Jill was a star, a household name, a rocket, and all the talent scouts were itching to sit down with her and bargain. The stark truth was that if her inside position as the single reporter allowed to interview Ronald Reagan was lost, she would disappear like a ice cube in summer. But at the moment, Jill Longley was a hot item.

Absentmindedly, he turned the handle to his office door, hardly noticing that the light was already on. "Greetings, Boss," she said, and handed him a cup of steaming coffee using his favorite old stained and chipped cup.

"Jill!" he said, startled. "Is there a problem? Have you been kicked out of the loop? Damn, I was afraid this would happen eventually." He bustled over to his desk letting his body down in a near fall to the chair.

"That's it? You aren't glad to see me? Just worried about your paper?" Jill said indignantly. She put her hands on her hips and squared off, her lower lip protruding in a pout.

"Hi, Jill. Now tell me why you are here."

"Burns, I've only been gone a whole month, but I can see that you wouldn't care if I never came back."

Burns got up with some effort from his chair and stood before her. "Jill, baby, I worship the ground you walk on. You are the greatest reporter in the history of the western hemisphere and the best looking also. Thank you for gracing this shit hole office with your magnificent presence. I am honored that you are standing here for these old aching eyes to linger on. Thank you, Jill, for being Jill." He returned to his chair and fell into it then pulled a folded newspaper from the top of the stack and tossed to her. "Here's your piece right on the front page. The AP has it and is printing it all over the place as we speak. Congratulations...it's your best work."

"You old dog. You never change, do you." Jill said.

"Would you like Jules Burns to be a nice guy? Come on, the thought alone will give you indigestion. Now, really, why are you here?" He leaned back and ran his hand absentmindedly over his bald head as if smoothing down his long missing locks. Sturdy half-glasses were perched on his nose, and he looked over them defiantly waiting for her answer.

"Ron and I split for now. He's started his campaign, and I guess his handlers didn't want Jill

Longley, best reporter in the western hemisphere, to take any attention from their boy.”

“Ron, huh. That mean something that you wouldn’t want me to really know about?”

“I didn’t sleep with him. He and I kissed once and other than that never touched skin to skin. Surprised?”

“The entire world wondered. Nobody but me would believe you though.”

“It was his choice. There is something in that man that I don’t...well, I don’t even believe it.”

“Do you ever think he just didn’t find you attractive enough?”

“Just the opposite, Burns. Something else. I may understand it someday, at least I hope so.”

“You know the saying: Be careful of what you wish for.”

Jill pulled up a chair and found her notebook. “Something happened last night that almost made me think I was in an old movie. A man came out of the shadows in the parking garage. I was scared to death and thought he had me, but all he wanted was to pass me some information then he was gone. I never got a look at his face, and he never said his name. He intimated that there were some really bad people who were interested in Ronald Reagan. Even mentioned a possible homicide and warned me that it was dangerous to go snooping around.”

“What information?” Burns asked.

“A girlfriend of an individual that he didn’t name. I have no idea of how she connects. He mentioned that she was in Arlington but might have left. Should have left, actually."

"And her name," Burns asked patiently.

"Sommerlyn Crosby. Ever hear of that one?"

"Nope. Who do you imagine your friend was?"

"He said that he was an investigator working the case, but someone didn't want him or others to have the entire picture."

"Well, isn't that a familiar story. My old buddy, Duffy, has gone silent. I know he has more information that he has not told me about. 'Need to know,' he said. All I know is that Duffy was or is highly placed. He may still be active, you never know with those types. He runs investigators, professional ones, perhaps even your boy." Burns leaned back in his squeaky chair and sipped his coffee.

"I came up with a name that Duffy already knew. That's when he went silent. Girlfriend, huh? The name we found, and don't ask how, was a Brit who was working at the hospital in Norfolk where your candidate was born. Sommerlyn Crosby could be his girlfriend, or an old one. She may be the link to finding this Porter fellow, and if Duffy's people want him, I would think that they don't want us finding him first."

"My leak told me that Spence Jones was missing, likely dead. That could happen to Porter or Crosby...or me!" Jill exclaimed as it hit her that the danger to her was real, not just words on paper.

"One thing for sure, we can't let old Duff in on anything we know from now on. He may be the bad guy you fear. Back in Nam, Duff was well-known for pulling the trigger...anyone for any reason. I excused it then, given our circumstances, but the memory of those deaths gave me pause over the years. I figured he'd changed, but maybe not."

"What's next, Boss. Have you any suggestions for me."

"You've done enough for me, for your Ron and for the public. I don't want anything to happen to you, so go take a break, go home, get a real boyfriend or something."

"That's not what I want to hear from a fighting editor like you, Burns. We can't walk away from this one. The public is eager to learn the truth about their politicians, and they obviously trust us."

"You are telling me that, regardless of the risk, Jill Longley wants to stick her innocent long nose back into this brew?"

"I am going to with or without your help, Burns. Just so you should know, there is a lot I heard and can't talk about, perhaps never, not even to you."

"More intrigue?" he correctly guessed.

"Big time," she answered. "I want the truth even if it never gets printed. It's emotional...and personal."

"I get it, Jill. You are in love with the Candidate and want to figure him out. He's still something of a mystery, and there is just that thing hanging out there that you just can't see yet."

"Exactly."

"If you would take my advice, I'd tell you to find a sweet loyal boy, marry him and live happy with three kids, mortgage and dog included. But you won't...I can see that. You are in love and desperate for your love to be returned. It's an old story, older than human wisdom, if there is any." Burns sat up and took his glasses off. "I'm with you if that's where you want to go, but it's not for the paper and not for fame or profit, but just for you."

"Now that we have that settled, where do you suggest I start?"

"We...notice that I said 'We'...should start in the phone book and find the address of Sommerlyn Crosby in Arlington. Go to that address and start sniffing. You'll eventually get on her trail. People will often tell the press things that they won't tell cops or some hard-assed stranger. And a pretty young girl has all that more of an edge. If you find Sommerlyn, ask her about Manfred Porter. I'm sure that they are connected. He is the one you are actually looking for, but if old Duff and his people couldn't find him, then it may be impossible."

"The paper going to fund my expense account?" Jill asked.

"With all the money the paper has made from your stories, I will allow you to shoot the works. Sure, you are funded. Another person worth finding is Spence Jones. Nobody has printed a word about him. It would be another scoop."

"He's the one I was told may be dead. At least missing."

"Your task is twofold, then. First, uncover facts we can print and, second, satisfy yourself regarding Ronald Reagan and who he actually is."

"I can tell you that he says the same thing in private that he does in public. He believes he is

Ronald Reagan, but what that means isn't really clear. Up close, he is the most sincere and honest person you could ever know. He's able to win anyone over to his side, because people are swept away by him. I think that with Ted's help, there is no doubt that he will become president."

"From the point of view of an editor, the most interesting story is not what he says or believes, but where he came from, who he actually is. What you have written about his two name changes has led to a lot of confusion. On one hand, the physical similarity between him and the former president is uncanny, on the other arises questions about his origin. Does he just happen to look like the president or is there truly a genetic link?" Burns took the last of his coffee in a big swallow and leaned back again.

"I was told that he presented a DNA study to the RNC which proves his genetic identity. They have not released the test results so far but stand by it."

"Such a comparison would have to be confirmed by an independent lab for the public and me to be convinced," Burns noted.

"I don't think they need to do that. It's visually obvious that there is a connection, and besides, the press and the public want a politician, not a pedigree."

Chapter 18

Chapter Nineteen

Tracking Sommerlyn

Jill followed the voice coming from her dash, warning her that a right turn was approaching in two hundred feet. She slowed and carefully made the turn onto Vine, glancing back and forth between the navigation screen and the street ahead. It was an unexpected place to find an apartment building because all she could see were industrial big trucks and dirt. In the distance was a modest sign advertising auto repair. She came to a stop when the machine announced that she had arrived at her destination. And there it was, nestled between two rectangular commercial buildings, a narrow, dilapidated structure with minimal parking. There were three cars positioned at skewed angles, all older and rusting. A rudimentary sidewalk led to the outside stairs, constructed of unpainted steel, now succumbing to the elements.

"Well," Jill grumbled to herself before exiting, "Jules Burns had tried to warn me." At this moment, she could be sitting on her mother's back porch and tossing the dog's toy. She got out and surveyed her surroundings. Seedy at best, dangerous at worst. At least the nearby workshops were still running and busy, and a scream from a threatened woman should at least bring a few to her rescue. Perhaps. She checked Sommerlyn Crosby's listed address one more time, then headed up the stairs, careful not to get rust on her palms.

The door was marked by the once bronzed numerals "16," now partially covered by hurried paint jobs from the past. She knocked softly, then, after a pause, more deliberately. No one answered, and there was no noise from inside. She looked around, trying to decide her next move but without seeing a solution. Sommerlyn Crosby was the link to Porter who was the primary interest. He might or might not know how Ronald Reagan had been created, but unless he was found, the information would be lost forever. She knocked louder and listened.

A creak signaled her to turn toward the noise. The adjacent apartment door was opening enough to allow motion on the other side to be seen. A partial face appearing in the slit was unnerving, and Jill backed up a bit.

"Did you try the handle?" the same voice asked. Jill couldn't decide if the voice was male or female but intuitively felt that its owner was older. "Go on...try it," the voice commanded.

Jill tentatively reached for the handle, finding it would turn, and pushed the door open. The apartment was obviously vacant and a hollow sound returned from inside. She just stood there looking at the dust on the floor and in the air, trying to think what to do next.

"You trying to get the rent money, aren't you?" the voice asked harshly. It opened more allowing the entire head to show. It was an older woman with thin grey hair looking her way with something other than hospitality.

"No. Nothing like that," Jill answered.

"Cop then? Were those cops by here yesterday friends of yours?"

"I'm not from the police. My name is Jill Longley. I'm a reporter."

"Did Sommerlyn break the law or sumthin?" she asked. "Why is everyone after her all of a sudden. What did she do?"

"Far as I know, she hasn't done anything. I just want to know about a friend of hers from way back."

"Yeah, I heard that tune before. You got any ID?" With that, the woman emerged onto the walkway. She was dressed in an old housecoat and barefooted. A glance implied that her teeth had been missing for years, allowing her nose tip to line up with her smile line. Jill found a press card and held it up. The woman inspected it closely then looked her in the eye. "What do you really want?" she asked.

"Do you know where she is or how I can talk to her or not?" Jill asked.

"Maybe. You do something for me, I do something for you. Sounds fair, don't it?"

"Maybe. What do you know and what do you want in return?" Jill asked.

"I'll tell you what I know for a fifth of Jim Beam. You go get it and come back, then we'll talk."

"You have to tell me something of interest before I will trust you," Jill retorted.

"I'll tell you right now that I don't know where Sommerlyn went or how to contact her. But I do know who helped her pack up and leave just before dawn late last week. Deal?"

"All right. Where do I go to get your bottle?"

"Right up the street, turn right and then two blocks. You'll see the sign." She closed the door behind her, finished for now with the conversation, leaving Jill alone on the rusting balcony walkway.

It took fifteen minutes, and they were not the best minutes of Jill's short life. She felt like an old alcoholic buying a fifth of whiskey, an item that she had rarely even tasted. Paying cash, she slunk out holding an obvious quart sized bottle wrapped tightly in brown paper.

At last she arrived before the door of a possible source of information, while holding the bottle out from her as if to avoid chemical contamination. She knocked softly on the door.

The first thing the woman did was to say, "Let's see," requiring Jill to open the paper bag for inspection. "That'll do," she said. "Sommerlyn worked at the McCoy Bar and Grill. Waitress there. The barkeep occasionally slept over here. He drove a red truck and parked it right there." Jill turned to inspect the very spot which was being pointed to. "Same truck as came and got her early in the morning before the sun come up. I saw it." She quickly took the bottle before Jill changed her mind.

"You know his name?" Jill asked.

"Sommerlyn called him Bubba." With that short answer, the bottle and the old woman disappeared behind the closed door, the deal completed.

Jill drove by the McCoy bar, slowly, while looking in the adjoining parking lot for a red pickup truck. Sure enough, it was sitting there and, by the looks of it, had been slowly losing paint and parts for more than a few years. The sign on the bar door announced happy hour, and the parking lot was full of patrons' cars and trucks who were inside becoming happy. Jill was not about to go inside and get happy also. She parked about a block away and made her way back to the bar parking lot on foot. She gave the red truck a cursory look over, not really expecting to find Sommerlyn Crosby hiding in the cab. Her cell phone camera focused on the license plate, and she snapped the photo. The smart money finds out all it can before placing a bet. Jill had thought over what the neighbor had said. Bubba and Sommerlyn were not only working in the same joint, they occasionally slept together. Jill would bet that wherever Bubba was staying, Sommerlyn Crosby would be there also. Moving out of the apartment had occurred at an hour early enough to prevent observation. They wanted it to be a secret. Jill would bet that no amount of persuasion, short of torture, would extract any information from a bubba. She would just go around him.

"Jill," Burns answered. "What news?"

"Nice to talk with you too, Burns. I'm fine, if you wanted to know. How are *you* this fine day?"

"OK, OK, I'm rude and a bore. How are you, Jill, and how exciting it is to talk with you. Now, what do you want?"

"I need you or someone to look up a residence from a vehicle plate number. Can do?"

"Probably. Are you on to something?"

"I don't know for sure. You'll get the photo in a few moments. Send what you find back to me by text. I'll be waiting."

"First thing in the morning. That soon enough?" Burns inquired. He had to get the boy wonder back down for that. Well, the kid had volunteered.

"Sure. I don't want to go over there in the dark anyhow."

She kicked her shoes off and plopped down on the big double bed. The window overlooked not only the parking lot of the Inn but was backed up to the golf course which was itself backed up to the Potomac. The location was a nice one in Arlington, just fifteen miles south of the Capital. She studied the sparkling Potomac and remembered that it drained into the Chesapeake just a bit south of where she and Ron were only days ago. The memory welled something unpleasant into her mind, back in the spot where you can't tell if it is good or bad, just powerful. It made his face come into her mind, the little wrinkles around his eyes when he smiled, the voice he could make so soft and appealing. That's what she was experiencing, it was the misery of separation. Just seeing his face in her mind brought it up.

She turned on the obligatory television across the room and started switching channels while thinking vacantly. Suddenly, there he was, full face and in full color, talking in that familiar way like he was in the room, just in reach.

"Of course, I believe in trade with other countries. We can't go back to isolation. This world is interdependent and interconnected, like it or not. But…we have to be sure that any deal we sign is a good one, one backed by verification and one with adequate provisions for punitive actions should they become necessary."

The camera flashed back to the room, showing a vast crowd of people of all kinds, some holding signs or flags emblazoned with the name Ronald Reagan. They applauded enthusiastically, some standing with their arms over their heads. The screen shifted back to a panel of political analysts, their smiling, smug faces indicating to the home audience that answers were apparent, the Candidate transparent.

"Reagan talks a good game, but does he actually know anything that didn't come from a book. You have only look at his record to understand that Reagan hasn't had any actual political experience." He was interrupted by the female expert on his right.

"Gee, I mean, the man has charisma, that we have to acknowledge, and he does appear sincere, at least to me."

"Thanks for that female insight, Christina," the fellow on the end said with sarcasm. *"But good looks does not a mature president make. My opinion is that he will fade as soon as his initial novelty declines."*

The first one looked into the camera and took on a serious face, *"You know the single interviewer responsible for all this adulation, don't you?"* Without waiting for the obvious answer, he continued without a pause, *"everyone assumes that this previous unknown and minimally published small town reporter has gotten too close to Reagan to be considered responsible. The rumor is that their relationship is indeed not entirely professional. Excuse me, but that's what people are saying."*

"You can't prove that allegation, Frank," Christina snapped. *"Your people are just jealous that Longley got there first."*

"Yes, Frank, Christina, we have to move on…"

Jill clicked the screen off and tossed the remote control toward the foot of the bed. The anger welling up inside of her was just short of rage. She had been warned, and intuitively knew, that this sort of spite reporting was going to happen. At one time, perhaps, reporters at least made an effort to appear non-partisan. Those days are gone, she saw. From now forward, one side wins and the other tries to prevent it. An intellectual war fought with lies, exaggeration and misconception, the dumb herbivore public trailing along behind, feeding on the scraps, believing only what their party told them to believe. Whatever the pundits say could never change her impression of Ronald Reagan. He means what he says and wants nothing in return, neither money nor power. A true American, he only wants what would be for the benefit of his countrymen and women. The thought brought tears to her eyes and her lip trembled. He had trusted her with his most closely guarded secret, and his love. She owed him the effort to find the truth about him, even if some of it never made it to print, and whatever the risks to her.

Chapter Twenty

Found and Lost

Jill parked a block away and sat there sipping her coffee while watching her rear view mirror. The red truck was parked in the driveway, motionless for the moment, but as soon as it left, she resolved to find out if Sommerlyn Crosby was hiding inside Bubba's home. This sort of espionage was thrilling but stressful. Jill realized that the underarm deodorant she had used this morning wasn't enough for this kind of activity. She gripped the steering wheel and tried to make herself believe that she was a detective or an agent assigned to a case. Furtive, intelligent and dangerous. Problem was that she didn't have either a badge or gun and certainly no backup.

A movement caught her eye causing her to put down her coffee, her attention focused on the little rear view mirror. She could hear the truck door slam shut followed by a motor roaring to life. In a blink, the truck jerked backward into the street and, thankfully, headed the opposite direction. She watched as the image got smaller and smaller, finally turning out of view. Her turn. She really didn't want to open the car door and, most of all, didn't want to knock on the door of an unknown address just based on a hunch, a supposition. Mostly, she wanted to drive away and try to put it all out of her mind.

Jill walked robotically toward the address, alert but trying to blend into the surroundings, just as she had read how to do numerous times in the cheap detective stories her father had been so addicted to. The nearby homes were mostly in need of repair as well as painting, and weeds were prolific. Even the sidewalk wasn't maintained and forced her to watch her footing. A scattered brick walk lead to the front door, and she made the turn to it while watching the windows for anyone looking out at her approach.

Jill drew up her nerve and knocked on the door, hesitantly then more forcefully as she presumed that being polite would never work. There was no answer, but she could detect muffled sounds as if someone inside was moving around trying to see who was knocking.

"Sommerlyn Crosby, I know you are in there. Open the door," Jill surprised herself with her strong command which arose spontaneously. Listening again, she only heard the passing traffic. Inside was quiet.

"Look, Sommerlyn, you have nothing to fear. I am a reporter, not a cop or a bill collector. Open the door."

"What do you want?" came weakly from the other side. Jill could picture an older woman crouched in fear.

"I'll tell you face to face if you let me," Jill answered.

"Go away," the voice said.

"Remember, if I can find you, others can also. You only have to talk to me, and all I want from you is information."

The door chain was dropped and a crack was formed, an eye appeared, a faded blue one. "What's your name?" Sommerlyn asked.

"Jill Longley."

"You the one? The Jill Longley?"

"The very one. Can we talk now?"

"Not here. Go around to the back, and I'll let you inside." The door closed, and the chain rattled. Jill looked back and forth and decided it wouldn't make any difference. Either way around the house she had to thread her path through tall weeds. Picking her way along, past weeds and scattered refuse, she finally made it to the back door. Sommerlyn was waiting and opened the door as soon as Jill arrived. "Come in quickly. I don't want anyone to see," she said as she nervously looked back and forth. Jill entered into the kitchen and paused to look around. It was in disarray with dirty dishes stacked alongside a crusted sink which at one time had been stark white but no longer was. A small dinette table and two chairs were crammed into the corner, and Sommerlyn pointed to one of them. "Sit, please, and excuse the mess. It's not usually like this."

"You know my name, and I assume you know that I've been producing stories about a presidential candidate," Jill began. Sommerlyn sat down opposite her and nodded that she knew that fact. "Your name is linked with that of a person I'd like to speak with...a certain Manfred Porter. You know this man, am I correct?"

"I knew him long ago, more than thirty years. Haven't heard from him or about him until recently. I have no information for you," Sommerlyn said, becoming more relaxed talking to a young female reporter rather than a burly agent of something.

"At one time, Manfred worked at a hospital in Norfolk," Jill stated. "Did you work with him there?"

"No, I never set foot in the place."

"How did you meet Manfred then?"

"We were a thing back in Cambridge. I graduated and came here to work and Manfred followed, giving up his degree and his research on frogs. It lasted a few years until Manfred left abruptly."

"Where did you work?"

"George Washington University Hospital."

"Doing what?"

"I was a lab tech, then later a supervisor."

"That was not very close together for lovers, was it?"

"He got a position in research over there and loved it more than me. I was happy where I was."

"What research?"

"Oh, you don't know. It was the first test-tube babies, you might call it IVF now. Manfred was in the lab while that was going on."

"Did you see him often?"

"When he needed a warm body...we met for that."

"So none of this tells me why you are in hiding. Want to explain?"

"I'm not responsible for anything Manfred did, you have to believe that."

"I'll buy that, but it still doesn't answer why you are so frightened."

"A man tracked me down recently. He was harsh...threatened me. I don't want to see him or his kind again."

"I assume that you told him everything you knew about Manfred. Is that all he wanted to know?"

"With that kind, you can never be sure of anything. I don't want to get hurt or go to jail."

"But, for what possible reason would anyone want to do that?" Jill questioned.

"If Manfred did something bad, they might want to blame me also."

"Did Manfred do something wrong?"

"No." Her answer was final and definitive, but her face and her eyes betrayed her. Manfred certainly did do something outrageous, and Sommerlyn Crosby knew what it was. Jill took a deep breath, wondering how to coax some deep secret out of her that had been locked away for more than thirty years. Perhaps fear would work.

"I've got to level with you, Sommerlyn. There's something you should know," Jill said in a soft voice. She noticed that Sommerlyn perked up, studying her face for clues. "I was paid a visit from a man in a parking garage. He wouldn't show his face but said he was an investigator and wanted to give me a tip. It was about you, Sommerlyn. This man said you knew...that you were the key. He wanted me to hurry up and find you before something bad happened."

Hearing that, Sommerlyn sat bolt upright, clasping her face with her hands. It was exactly like she feared. They were coming for her.

"Oh, no!" Sommerlyn exclaimed. Her eyes rolled around as if looking for an immediate escape, but as the agony of realization hit, she sagged back nearly lifeless into the chair. There was no way to escape, she had run out of options.

Jill placed her hand on Sommerlyn's arm, "Listen to me. It's not you they want, it's only information. If you give to me what you know, and especially if I print it, the pressure will be off of you forever. There would be no reason to hunt you any longer. Don't you see how telling me will set you free?"

Sommerlyn put her face down against the table top and started to sob. "No...that won't work," she managed to get out the words between breaths. It hit Jill that her tactic had backfired. Sommerlyn Crosby had also done something illegal and so despicable that even after thirty years, she could not bring herself to tell the truth about it. Jill wondered if this single act was the turning point in her promising career working in a famous big city hospital. Sommerlyn had to have a reason to have ended up the kept woman of a tavern bartender with nothing to show for a long life.

"I promise that whatever you tell me will go no farther. I'll never repeat it to the police or anyone else. That I swear."

"If you knew, you wouldn't say that," Sommerlyn said. "You don't want to know what I know, because it will also ruin your life." She stood up and looked at Jill, her tears drying.

"Before you ask me to leave, let me offer you refuge. You and I can drive away from here and back to my home town. My mother will be glad to put you up for a time until we decide what to do. Won't you consider that?"

"They will find me again if they want to. Do you really want your mother involved? You will think that over, won't you?" Unfortunately, Jill knew that Sommerlyn was correct. If inexperienced and naive Jill could find her, a seasoned investigator with an unlimited budget would also. The picture of her mother being around possible violence or murder was not what she wanted to happen.

"I have a little money with me," Jill said. "I can give you what I can, if that will help."

"Run? No, I'm not running again. It won't work, because no amount of money will ever make me feel safe. Bubba has a gun and knows how to use it. I'm as protected here as I could ever be. What happens, happens, and I can't change the past which caused it."

"Please tell me Sommerlyn. I need to know."

"Suffice it to say, Jill Longley, that I did something very wrong, and no one but Manfred knows what it was. If they find him, he'll never tell either. I'll take it to my grave, you can be sure, and I've regretted it my whole adult life. Being in love makes you lose your sense of right and wrong and when you also lose love, it's too late to fix things. ...You have to go now.

Bubba will be back soon, and you don't want to meet him."

"At least tell me if this had anything to do with the child that became Ronald Reagan, who is a candidate for President of the United States."

"No more. Please leave."

"If you were trying to find Manfred, where would you look?"

"I would look at a place that attracts smart people who make their own rules. An organization or country that pays for results, regardless of the cost to humanity."

Chapter Twenty-One

Le Duff

Burns was in a hurry, walking fast with his head down and ignoring the occasional calls from his burgeoning workforce, until one caught him by the arm which forced him to look at her.

"What?" Burns asked, stopping to confront Lila but still impatient to continue on his way.

"I've tried to tell you, Mr. Burns, but you're ignoring me again," Lila said, not letting his arm go lest he get away from her. Burns was finally stopped, and she had gained his full attention.

"There is a man in your office. He wouldn't take no for an answer. Big and rude, if you want my opinion. Says he knows you, and it would be all right. Sorry, I just couldn't make him stop."

"He have a name?" Burns asked, looking at her over his half-glasses.

"Not that he told me. He called you Julius though. I've never heard you called that before. Think you might know him, or should I call the cops?"

"I know him all right. There is only one joker who ever called me Julius. His name is Duffy and as I remember had protruding teeth and red hair. Does that sound like the same man?"

"That's him. Should I have him tossed out?"

"Naw. Couldn't do it anyway. I'll see him," Burns said and abruptly started moving toward his office, his mind twirling with questions. This was the first face to face meeting they will have had since Nam, and lately he had become convinced that Duffy and his connections were nefarious as well as vast. He tried to put on a good face and not give away his suspicions as he approached the closed door.

"Damn if it isn't old Julius! Gotten fat off the land, I see!" Duffy said from behind Burns's desk, his polished cowboy boots crossed and resting on top of some papers. Duffy casually moved and put his feet back on the floor then slowly stood, smiling, with his hand extended.

"*Le Duff*, isn't that what your old Vietnamese mistress used to call you?" Burns remembered, accepting the shake.

"Yeh, but I never liked it. Don't even recall her name. Good to see you, old buddy. Surprised?"

"Surprised to see you behind my desk, likely having looked through every drawer. Find anything interesting?" Burns answered.

"Nothing that I didn't already know. I keep up with my old friends. You should remember that."

"You here to go out for dinner like you always promised, or is there something else?" He saw that Duffy was indeed just an older version of the man he knew, but what he saw through the lens of maturity was a different person than he had retained in his memory. It was the eyes, the narrow, flickering eyes which were the windows that clearly showed there was no soul in Duffy and had never been one. The red hair had nearly darkened to brown, and there were large chunks of it entirely grey, but the lanky, languid body movements were instantly familiar. Duffy had never shown fear, even when there was the threat of painful death all around, and the hammer of fate was hanging just above him. He would just move like he had all the time in the world, like it was a play, the characters ordained to certain words and tasks, the outcome always certain. Later, Burns would agree that Duff had been in his element in combat. He enjoyed it, relished it.

"Dinner? It nearly slipped my mind, Julius. Next time, perhaps, got to go soon but thought I would pop in and give you a salute."

"Salute? Strange coming from you," Burns said. "I remember the Duff who hated saluting officers."

"For all your good work, Julius. Your little paper is on the edge, and everyone is praising it and, especially, your star reporter."

"Jill? Is she why you are here?" Burns could feel himself tense. The last thing he wanted to happen is to have Jill put at risk because of his old connections.

"Naw, Julius. I know all about your little Jill and what she is up to. I would appreciate you telling me what you and she have dug up recently. We were working as a team, Julius. I gave you information. Don't you think you should do the same?"

"Can you be more specific, Duff? This is a newspaper office, and we print what we find. All you have to do is read our paper to find that out."

"I'm talking about stuff you likely won't have the balls to print, Julius. The off-the-record stuff. You know what I mean."

"No, I don't."

"For instance, what did Reagan confide in your star reporter that never made it into print? Another is, what did the Crosby gal tell her while they were in her kitchen the other day? Look, Julius, we do need to share information, because we are on the same team. Always have been."

"You've been spying on Jill?" Burns reacted, trying to look surprised and shocked.

"It's not very hard to do, Julius. You should get her some lessons."

"I'm getting angry, Duff, because you haven't exactly been liberal with your side. You remember cutting me off about Porter and what you know? Why don't you hold up your end before accusing me?"

"Manfred Porter," Duff recalled and whistled softy. "That's someone whom we can't seem to find. He's flat vanished. What did his girlfriend tell Jill Longley?"

"I can tell you that she didn't know anything about Porter for over thirty years. That's a dead end. We have no information for you, Duff."

"Anything else she might have let slip out?" Duffy asked, narrowing his eyes in a threatening way.

"Jill said that she was just a worn out ex-junkie who was afraid of her own shadow. Crosby knows nothing of value or she would have confided in Jill. Now how do we find Manfred Porter?"

"Told you. Porter is gone. It's useless to speculate where. Now the inside story about Reagan. I'm still waiting..."

"Jill is in love with the man, and if she knows anything, I don't think she would even tell herself. Everything she says and writes about him is glowing. As far as she is concerned he is a savior risen to right the world. There are no secrets regarding him."

"You don't say," Duffy murmured and blew out an exhalation as the old insincere smile returned to his face. He looked as though the conversation was over, then brightened, "You will remember, Julius, that I saved your butt a couple of times, won't you?"

"Certainly, you did, Duff. I've not forgotten. My name is still Jules Burns, and I'm the same man I was when I was wearing army fatigues. But you, Duff. What are you?"

"I'm the same also, Julius. Older, that's all, and I've seen more of the hell holes of life than you have. Just a working man like you. By the way, your reporter is wasting her time today interviewing the Townsend family."

She wasn't hard to find at all, or perhaps Jill was improving at being a sleuth. A bit of time spent on the Internet was a lot better than walking around asking people.

"Hi. I called previously. My name is Jill Longley, and I'm expected," she said to the clerk at the main desk. Being in a nursing home brought back all the days she had spent interviewing Mike and Mary before they passed away. She was no longer frightened by a nursing home, because she had learned that it was filled with the lifetimes of people just like her, who each had fascinating and interesting stories that would never be told, the events and people of their past dying with them as the world changed scenes and characters once again.

"You are expected indeed. We all wondered why you weren't here earlier. Mrs. Townsend is looking forward to seeing you!" she said and rewarded Jill with a big smile. "Please come with me." The clerk led the way, her heels clicking against the marble floor in the exact same way as in the retirement home hallway which lead to Mike's and Mary's rooms. She was shown into a small room and in the corner waiting for her was Mildred Townsend, wrapped warmly and in her wooden rocking chair.

"You must be Jill," Mildred said. "I knew you would come to see me eventually."

"You mean because of my pieces about Trey?"

"Yes, and thank you for calling him by his right name. I was sure that he had forgotten it."

"No, he remembers his family with fondness. He's probably changed a bit since you were his mother."

"I don't think so. He may have a different name, but I see his face on television and to me it is the same face he always had, the same voice and the same ideals."

"He was your only adopted child, wasn't he?"

"We had four other children, all natural born. Trey came along somewhere in the middle."

"How did you happen to adopt a child when you already had a couple?"

"My dear, I'm glad you asked, because when I am gone, the story will be forgotten also. It was no act of fortune that we came to raise little Trey. I knew his mother, worked with her, and made her a promise the very day she died. She asked if I would raise Trey, and I made known that I would do my best."

"Worked with her in what way?" Jill wondered.

"At the hospital. I was a nurse, you know. Barbara worked in the lab."

"So you know Barbara McDaniels's whole story?"

"Enough. I guessed a lot, but correctly, it turned out."

"Can you explain what you mean?"

"Barbara was married to a pitiful excuse for a man. Unfortunately, she wanted a child but her husband was just not able, I was told. A lot of girls in that fix might have taken on a lover, you know, the natural way to get pregnant. Not Barbara. She was not that type. Our hospital, as you might have read, had an active fertility lab, with two remarkable scientists heading it. There was so much talk and excitement about that subject that Barbara was convinced that was the right and honest way to go. Frankly, I had doubts and tried to persuade her that it was risky. Well, to make a long story short, it was successful and she did have a baby. Spence, I think that was her husband's name, decided that the baby wasn't from him and took off and left the mother and child to fend for themselves. Men like that...."

"Spence? You knew him?" Jill asked.

"Met him a few times. He had red hair, green eyes and a little chin beard...dreadful little snake. He was drawn and anemic, but he thought he had a way with women. Even hit on me a couple of times."

"If he was red haired, no wonder he had those thoughts," Jill suggested.

"On that, he was correct. Personally, I know that Barbara didn't fool around. It came from our lab. There was a switch or a mistake of some kind, and I know who was responsible."

"Let me guess, he went by the name of Manfred Porter?"

"How in the world did you know that name?" Mildred asked, surprised.

"I'm a reporter. He was the one, am I correct?"

"Yes. I never liked him, but he and Barbara worked together in the lab. For a time, I wondered if he had substituted his own donation to Barbara's pregnancy, if you know what I mean."

"Did he look like Trey?"

"Not a bit. Manfred had blond hair you know. I guess it wasn't him, but I believe he was the one urging Barbara to conceive. After she became pregnant, he constantly worried about her health and kept a close eye on her. He was obviously feeling responsible in some way, but the other nurses and I figured it was a bit of guilt in that he was the one who talked her into it."

"Would, in your opinion, Manfred have been the type to do something illegal or criminal?"

"Heavens, yes, because he did and got fired for it. We never heard exactly what he was supposed to have done, but I would have believed nearly anything was possible from that man."

"Where did he go after he was fired?"

"Just disappeared one day. He never even said goodbye to poor Barbara."

"Did you ever meet a girlfriend he had, also from Great Britain?"

"Seems I heard a name once...funny name like the Hippies used at the time...but no, I never saw her in person."

"Sommerlyn. Was that the name?" Jill asked.

Mildred started to laugh and put her hand over her mouth. "So that's the name. I always thought I heard Summer Wind. Made more sense that way."

"Indeed," Jill agreed. "Say, what kind of boy was Trey when he was with you?"

"Trey was the sweetest kid. Never caused any problems, never brought home a bad report or got in fights. He was on the football team and could have been sent to college with a scholarship but had to let it go because of illness."

"What exactly," Jill asked.

"We don't exactly understand it. He was born with only one kidney, we found out, and the other one was large for some reason. At times, he was crippled with pain...came right out of the blue. Our family doctor said it was some sort of urinary tract infection and always treated Trey with antibiotics and it would go away. He was accepted by the Army so it couldn't have been too bad."

"Would he just collapse and fold up, holding his belly?" Jill asked, remembering a similar episode.

"Yes. It would eventually pass and he would get back up and go on, but it prevented him from rising in the team like he wanted."

Jill paused, considering how to ask her next question. "Mildred...what about girls in his life. Were there any?"

"My, my, there sure were. He was always handsome, but when he got into his later years in high school, remarkably so. In my youth, I had seen some of the old Ronald Reagan films before he got into politics, and I realized the similarity. Occasionally, people would compare Trey with the president, but in a joking, complimentary way. His female classmates were too young to remember the president in his youth, none of them ever viewing old photographs of him in his younger years. It didn't matter a bit, because what they saw in Trey was enough. They called the house constantly, wanting to talk with him, even dropping by on occasion with some excuse to see him."

"And how did he respond to them?"

"He mostly ignored them. Oh, he was friendly enough, he but didn't take any of them seriously. I can't exactly explain it, but it was like he was too old for their antics in some ways. None of them captured his heart and many tried."

"In light of what you said about Porter and his misdeeds, have you ever wondered about Trey's actual parentage?" Jill asked.

"For sure Spence wasn't his father. But Barbara was his mother. I've been around long enough to realize that we all look like someone, often many others. The fact that Trey looks a lot like Ronald Reagan is a happy accident of birth, a unique concoction of genes and a product of possible normal variation. You know the one thing that saddens me?"

"What's that, Mildred?"

"When I heard that Trey was now calling himself Ronald Reagan, it broke my heart. He was raised to be proud of his mother, me and Barbara both, and now he pretends to be someone that he isn't, just because he happens to have that look."

There wasn't any more to cover with Ron's adoptive mother and Jill stood, collecting her purse and jacket, knowing that she may never see Mildred again in this life.

"It's been delightful and informative talking with you, Mildred. I'll leave my card with you, and if you think of anything else, please give me a call."

"I'll do that, dear. Can I ask you a question now?"

"Anything you want."

"Is it true that you are in love with Trey like the papers say?"

"I do love him, but we are not lovers."

"Well, tell him from me that he has my vote, and if there is ever a wedding, I hope to get an invitation."

"Thanks, Mildred. I'll see that you do."

Chapter 21

Chapter Twenty-Two

Many Questions...Few Answers

Jill knocked first and waited for Burns to yell, "come in," often adding a colorful profanity for those who would dare cause an interruption. Instead, the door opened, and Burns used his hand to push her back, the other over his lips in a sign of hush. He was agitated, and his eyes rolled in an unaccustomed way.

"We can't talk in there, Jill," he whispered. Before she could think of a question, Burns glanced at a clock and pointed. "Had supper yet?" he asked.

"No, Boss. It's only 4:00," she answered, wondering just what was happening.

"Come on then. I'm buying, and we can talk there." He didn't wait for acceptance but gently took her arm and started rapidly walking for the exit door.

"Mr. Burns, just what is going on?" Jill asked.

"I'll tell you when we get outside. Say, this is going to be good for my reputation. I mean, a striking female across from me at supper will start a few tongues wagging, wouldn't you say?" he mused, then allowed himself a sly smile.

Jill waited until they got in her car, then she watched him intently, waiting on an answer before proceeding.

"Bugged. That slimy so-and-so put a bug in my desk," Burns explained.

"Who?"

"Damned Duffy, my old pal. I came in to find him sitting behind my desk. He made no effort to hide that he had rifled through it, but what I didn't suspect at the time was electronic eavesdropping. He's determined to find out what we, mostly you, know about Ronald Reagan. And there is more news you have to hear, and I know you won't like it."

A chill ran up her spine. Something had happened to Ron, something horrible. She didn't want to hear it. "Just tell me and get it over with."

"Sommerlyn Crosby is dead."

"Oh, no!"

"Shot by her boyfriend. Police have him in custody. Happened this morning."

"I don't believe it. It's a frame-up," Jill said, gripping the steering wheel with both hands.

"Going by preliminary police reports, the man had a record of violence and incarceration. A 'domestic quarrel' they are calling it."

"What do you think?" Jill asked, still seeing little frail Sommerlyn in her mind's eye. To be shot down like a dog, just for what she might know...

"I don't know what to think, Jill. We have blundered into something very big and evil. I wish I had never asked you to cover the press conference that got us involved."

Jill tried to make herself calm down and view the entire picture. Just what are the motives involved, and who are the ones behind the scenes? She couldn't see it, there was just not enough information to put it all together. One thing was clear, though. It all focused on the birth of Trey Jones and the events surrounding his creation. Some group was trying to seal it off, to prevent the public and its reporters from ever knowing the truth. There were several principal actors involved, all of whom have either died or vanished. Of those left, Jill knew as much as anyone else except...Manfred Porter. He was the one who could put it together. Could he still be alive and hiding someplace on earth? And if he was, how could he be found?

"Boss, are you and I at risk?" Jill asked.

"I'm not, because I've printed everything I know. You might be, because I believe Duffy is following you around and bugging places you might visit. If he wanted you to disappear, he would have done it by now, but I suspect he is trying to find out what exactly you have been told before acting."

"I'm not quitting, Burns, but I'll start writing for one of the big papers if it will insure your safety."

"Hell, gal, you aren't leaving me. You are my star, and if you quit, I might as well also and move to Florida."

"Good. I don't want to write for anyone but you, Jules Burns. Just remember that."

"Now, what's your next step?" Burns asked.

"We have to locate this Manfred Porter and get his story."

"Impossible. If Duffy and his thugs couldn't find him, we never could."

"Perhaps they were looking under rocks. We might instead just look in the obvious places," Jill suggested, an idea forming like a fog clearing.

"Well, I'm looking around, and he isn't in the parking lot. Now where do *you* suggest finding him?"

"Think about it, Burns. All the evidence points to some sort of genetic tampering at the time Ron's mother became pregnant. Manfred Porter was a highly skilled lab technician from Britain who, from what he bragged, was the principal person who did the IVF in Norfolk. Where does a man like that go? I'll tell you what I think...he would go someplace which allowed him to continue to do what he evidently liked and excelled at. Another genetics lab of some sort. And one in a faraway place that is off the grid. He had something to hide and ran away before it came out."

"We need to talk to someone who knows that field...an expert. Let me work on it, and I'll let you know. Meanwhile, you should go find Ronald Reagan and get under his wing. By now, he has Secret Service protection, and you should be safe at least while you are near him."

"That is exactly what I wanted to hear! Thank you, Boss."

A reporter's laminated press card was dangling over her right chest when she boldly walked into the full room, determined to stay toward the rear and escape notice from the other reporters gathered to attend what was announced to be a major policy statement by the Candidate. Her plan was doomed to fail in a room of sharp eyes and minds and being an attractive woman in her own regard quickly led to careful inspection.

"So you are Jill Longley," a grinning man stated while leaning over and reading her identification. In a blink, his comment caused others to take notice and quickly she was surrounded by men, gaping at her and looking her up and down from every angle.

"Wait, boys, aren't you here to report on what the Candidate says and not me?" she complained loudly.

"Sorry, Miss Longley, you are also news or don't you read other papers?" one shot back.

"Is it true, Miss Longley? Are you involved with Ronald Reagan?" another bluntly asked.

Jill stood her ground and stared back at them. "If I were *involved*, as you imply, wouldn't I be up there instead of standing in the rear?"

"Yeah. What happened? Did you fall out or something. Come on, give us a little bit anyway."

A uniformed policeman with a weathered, hard face pushed in between their ranks and grasped Jill by the arm. "You have to come with me, Ma'am," he commanded. He was broad shouldered and had the look of an experienced cop, one that could not be easily refused. The reporters gave way, trying to communally think of a reason for what appeared to be an arrest of a now rather famous insider. Glances were exchanged. Should they protest, who would know what is happening, should they follow along? It happened too quickly for them to become organized, and they all watched helplessly as Jill Longley was led away, the policeman's hands on both her shoulders.

"It's all right, Miss. I was just instructed to help you out. You are not being charged in case you are wondering," he said into her ear as they walked rapidly away. They approached a door, also guarded by a uniformed policeman who held it open. Once inside and the door closed, he let her go. "Wait right here, Miss, and someone will be along," he said, then returned outside into the crowded room.

Jill inspected her surroundings, finding herself in a control room full of large switches and grey metal boxes giving off a low threatening hum. There was one other door at the other end, and overhead, a dim lamp in a shielded housing. The room filled with light as the end door opened and a young well-dressed woman approached her.

"I'm Judy. Please follow me," she requested and beckoned Jill to come with her. They walked without conversation past small groups of well-dressed men, a few of whom had earpieces, muscles and hard eyes. They all appraised her as she passed but made no comment and gave her no smiles or even acknowledgment. She was escorted to a polished wood door and stood by while the other woman softly knocked.

"Come in," Ronald Reagan said.

He was waiting for her, ready with his biggest smile and, after the door was closed behind her, held his open arms to her. She rushed into them and pressed herself against him, taking in his reality, his warmth and his return hug.

"Seeing you again is like breathing the fresh air of the bay. It makes me come back alive," he murmured.

"I've missed you, Ron. Thought about nearly nothing else the entire time, but I've also followed your speeches and your televised appearances. You've been too busy to remember Jill."

"I have not! Where would you get such nonsense! I can tell you that I dream about you so constantly that I spend more time around you than you would think possible. Having you in my arms again is my dream coming true."

"One night, I got up the nerve to kiss the television screen. You tasted like plastic."

"See if this compares," he asked, then found her lips for a long forceful kiss.

"You are right. It's delightfully better. How about another?" she asked, puckering and closing her eyes. Ron wrapped his arms tightly around her and picked her off her feet, swinging her around while they kissed, then very gently put her back on her feet.

"I've only got a moment. They are expecting me to come out there and wow this critical audience. You hang around because I'm not done with you, young lady."

"We have to be careful, Ron. I already was questioned about our relationship this morning. They are watching us like hawks."

"That article your paper published this morning was really good because you were writing like a reporter, not a lover. They are a spoiled rotten bunch of snide opportunists just waiting on a moment to criticize me, instead of doing legwork and proper reporting. I've grown to hate the lot of them...except you, my dear Jill. Ted may have chosen you, but it was a stroke of genius as far as I'm concerned."

"We're ready, sir," a voice announced from the hall.

"I've got to go, Jill. One last thing though…I still love you." He smiled, then headed for the door while adjusting his tie.

"And I love you back," Jill said just as he was opening it. He glanced over his shoulder and winked at her.

After he left, she collapsed into a big leather chair. "Now what?" she asked under her breath. She found herself watching the conference live on a set mounted on the wall. The moment Ron strode confidently to the center of the stage amid loud sustained applause was when tears of joy and respect started in earnest down the sides of her face. She was too busy watching, mesmerized by Ron's command performance, to wipe them away.

"I think you need this," Ted said, offering her his handkerchief. He had come in quietly, his approach not noticed above the noise from the television set. "Wonderful, isn't he?" Ted asked, himself fixated on their candidate.

"You said it," Jill sniffed, embarrassed that Ted had caught her in an emotional moment.

"That mean you are in love with him?" Ted asked tenderly. Jill nodded but didn't look away from Ron's image.

"And he you?" Ted persisted. Jill looked at him and hesitated. "I already know that he is. Even I can tell. You don't need to answer," he admitted.

"Did you like the piece we ran this morning?" she asked offhandedly.

"You are the best thing in the campaign, Jill. It's you making things happen, and I am totally indebted to you."

"Thanks, Ted. You're not jealous, are you?"

"I am, Jill. But that changes nothing. I'm also happy for you both." He shifted in his chair and muted the sound on the set, causing Jill to look his way. "I've come up here to tell you what is happening and which concerns you."

"Let me guess, Ted. You want me away from here so I don't cause some controversy and take the spotlight off of Ron.

"I can't reason with him about you. He doesn't care what anyone thinks. You should see his face when he reads your stuff. In some ways, you have become more important to him than his run for the presidency."

"We may have reached a point of no turning back, Ted."

"If you care about the country and about him winning, you should look at it the way I do, that I must. He is going to win, I have no doubts, but his many enemies are looking for a way to drive a spike into him. Trust me, you don't want to be a tool for them to hammer into Ron. Later, there will be plenty of time for you both. At the moment, this little meeting was all I could manage."

"That was your doing, hustling me away like that?"

"Sure. Hope you didn't mind."

"Seeing him alone was marvelous. Thank you, Ted."

"My pleasure...no, that was not the correct word. More like...my duty. After this conference ends, we are heading out to the West Coast for a series of events. You are not coming with us."

"What will you tell Ron?"

"That you had something you had to do and will catch up later. Of course, later will never come, at least for the time being. I'll get you two together when we are farther along."

"I have no choice, do I?"

"Unless you want to throw a brick through our glass house. You don't want to do that."

"No. I'll go then. Thanks again for the moment with him."

"You can leave by the rear exit. I'll send someone to show you the way. And...keep those articles coming, will you?"

Chapter Twenty-Three

Expert Opinion

F ound him!" Burns's voice crackled over her phone. "Not too far from where you are." Burns appeared excited at his find, but Jill puzzled momentarily over what or more precisely about whom he was referring.

"Found who or whom, Boss? I don't have a clue what you are trying to tell me," Jill responded.

"A genetics expert. You remember we discussed this recently or did reunion with your lover cloud your senses?"

"Let's have the name and leave off the sarcasm."

"Right. Georgetown University has a world-renowned geneticist who was involved in the original human genome project and, I'm told, has a reputation for really keeping up with his profession. He just got back from an extended stay in France, but I managed to wrestle an appointment from his secretary. Dropping your name helped, you should know. Even in France, they write about you."

"I don't feel really famous, Burns, just a little used."

"Been cut off, heh? I know the feeling. You want the name or not?"

"Could I ask how you came up with this name? Not from your buddy, Duffy, I hope."

"Duffy is out of the picture. No, this was from research done by Mabel with a little help from Larry Pendergast. His name is Dr. Michael R. Wenthrop. Your appointment is at 11:15 sharp this morning. And don't be late."

"Genetics Department, Georgetown," Jill repeated, writing it down on her little pad. "11:15 sharp. Thanks, Boss."

The cab swerved and stopped abruptly at the corner, without the cabbie verbally signaling arrival at her destination. Jill glanced back at the intersection, which clearly indicated 37th and O, but where was Reiss Hall? She paid the silent cabbie and got out, looking at the red brick building on the corner and trying to understand why it wasn't evident where to go. She started walking and following students, making toward a nondescript door without markings. Once inside she started following the door numbers until she came to the number written on her pad.

Tentatively, she pulled the door open and came into a small reception area filled with rows of tall green filing cabinets. An unoccupied small desk was pushed uncomfortably in the corner. According to the circular clock above the desk, she was right on time. She waited, standing alone, but listening to muffled conversation from behind one of the doors, words that were just beneath her level of comprehension.

The door opened and an elderly man was looking at her in a questioning way. He wore a well-groomed but entirely white full beard and was dressed in ruffled pants under an unbuttoned sweater vest. "You the reporter?" he asked.

"Yes. I'm Jill Longley."

"Come in then, and let's find out what you want." He impatiently waved her inside and pointed to a well-worn plastic chair. "Sorry about the surroundings, but I had to give up the big suite while I was in France." He went behind his desk and moved a pile aside to give him a better view of her. For a moment, she could tell he was studying her face, his eyes roaming over her features and hair.

"Thanks for seeing me, Dr. Wenthrop. I was told you have limited time this morning."

"That's a bunch of crap. They haven't even got a lecture schedule out for me yet. You can have all morning if you want. I would guess that you've got a lot of German blood in you, am I correct?"

"My mother's side were all German," she admitted.

"Straightforward people, the Germans. I always liked them. Now...why are you here?"

"Have you read any of my articles?"

"Not personally, but I've heard about you and your favorite subject." He rocked back in his wooden chair, studying her like a laboratory specimen.

"So, I'll bet you've figured out why I'm sitting here," Jill ventured.

"I prefer that you call me Mike. Would that be to much to ask?"

"No bother, Mike. Are you avoiding my question?"

"As it turns out, I have been thinking about your likely question for some time. France may seem far away, but we still keep up with the American news. Your problem would revolve around the creation of your rather surprising candidate, unless I'm wrong."

"Right on target."

"My supposition is that you, Miss Longley, have more knowledge about the subject than has made it to print."

"Right again, and please call me Jill."

"Why don't you start at the beginning, Jill, and tell me everything pertinent to the question. Please be specific with any significant dates."

"The story starts with two people, one of them I've interviewed and who was murdered only two days ago. The other vanished many years ago. Both were in school in Cambridge in the late seventies, and both came to the U.S. at the same time. The recently deceased woman was named Sommerlyn Crosby, and she was employed near here as a laboratory technician."

"What do you mean by near here?"

"At GWH, I suppose. In the lab."

"Go on then."

"The fellow was Manfred Porter, a grad student at Cambridge before they left, and he didn't finish his degree. We were told that he was experimenting on frogs. Anyway, he got employment in Norfolk and was involved in the early IVF procedures and claimed that he was the chief technician."

"This is fascinating, but..."

"Wait, it does get more interesting," Jill announced, holding up her hand. "There was a married couple in Norfolk at the time, Barbara and

Spence Jones. She was working in the lab in Norfolk at the same time as Porter. A witness claims that Barbara was convinced by Manfred Porter to undergo IVF to become pregnant. She did and the result was a baby born in late December of 1981 named Trey. The couple split apart, partly because the new baby had no resemblance to the father. After the divorce, Barbara had her last name restored to McDaniels. Unfortunately, she caught a virulent hepatitis and died when the child was young. The rest of the story, you may have heard.

"And your question, Jill? I need to hear it in your own words."

"The obvious one, that is repeated in the press nearly constantly, is how did this child get to look exactly like Ronald Reagan. How was that possible?"

"I would venture that he was fathered by sperm provided either willingly or unwillingly by the president."

"Mike, you do know that Mr. Reagan was about seventy at that time...and president."

"Men can very frequently produce viable sperm at that age. Your problem is to ferret out how his semen made it to Norfolk and got used in their lab."

"I forgot to tell you that comparative DNA analysis does prove a relationship between the two Reagans."

"There you are, Jill."

"No, Mike. There's another thing you have to be told. People have been killed and gone missing concerning the facts we are discussing right now. Something big and evil is running this show. I mentioned Manfred Porter. He got fired from the hospital in Norfolk and has since disappeared."

"A vast conspiracy, you might have called it," he chuckled, shaking his head.

"I'm sure of it," Jill said flatly.

"Still..." Dr. Wenthrop mused and tilted back to watch the ceiling. Jill sat still, allowing him to think it through. Whatever time he needed, as long as they could come up with a plausible explanation.

He sat up and looked around at his stack of books and slowly got up, inspecting the back covers one by one, at last selecting the one he was after. "A moment, please. Something is nagging at me," he said and started flipping the pages. His finger ran down page after page and then stopped. "Ah," he said and put the book aside. "Frog research," he repeated, then turned to his small computer on his desk. "Be patient, Jill, I have to have a few facts in order before I tell you what I'm thinking." He resumed his typing and stopped occasionally to watch the screen. "Interesting," he said.

"You found something?" Jill asked hopefully.

"Pure science fiction, I'm afraid. A rather wild and impossible hypothesis. I can lay this out for you, but I won't claim that it is true in any way, rather, I would state that this theory is bunkum, a simple fantasy of an old man."

"I'm listening," Jill stated.

"You cannot quote me in any way, even obliquely, do you understand?"

"Just between us, Mike."

"Pay attention then because I'm going to start with a bit of scientific history. When I was a grad student, I attended Cambridge for a short while on a scholarship. One of the distinguished professors was a man named John Gurdon, later called Sir John Gurdon, who eventually won the Nobel Prize. A great researcher and a kind and patient man, at least to a young student from the U.S. He had taught in Berkley before that and come to like and respect Americans. At the time, he was famous for being the first to produce a creature, a frog, from a cloning procedure. It had been done previously but not successfully. And, I may add at this time, not in mammals until 1996. He used to say that there was only a thirty percent chance, at best, of the procedure working in frogs. I assume that he may have continued like experiments while at Cambridge but I don't know for sure. You mentioned that Manfred Porter was in grad school and experimented with frogs. You see the connection by now, I'm sure. Manfred may have been taught and developed the skill necessary to remove a cell nucleus and replace it with another. It's not a very elaborate procedure, but there continue to be difficulties and failures with its application. It's never been done with humans and is illegal in most places of the world. And for good reason."

"But Manfred was employed to do IVF. Isn't that just combining sperm cells with a living egg in the lab and then implanting the resulting combination in the mother?"

"Exactly, and that's what I assume he did, only using the sperm from the president of the United States instead of that from Spence Jones," Mike stated, looking directly at Jill so he could be sure she heard him. "At least that's what I assumed until this other fact hit me in the face."

Jill was attentive, her mind twirling with previously unknown possibilities.

"The president was shot in March of 1981 and taken to the hospital only a few blocks from here...where, you told me, a certain woman named Crosby was employed...in the lab. Do you see it yet?"

"Sommerlyn Crosby had access to president Reagan's tissue and blood samples!" The truth slammed Jill between the eyes. It all fit together now.

"What if Sommerlyn stole a small sample from the lab and transported it to Manfred Porter who had the skill and training to try cloning of a human. A clone of the President of the United States! A terrible thing to have done, both immoral and illegal and at that point in history...impossible. Remember that Dolly the sheep wasn't born for twenty-five years after that, and she was a unique success after dozens and dozens of failures. Manfred Porter was the first and only person to create a human being."

"Ronald Reagan is a clone?" Jill heard herself say, more to her unbelieving self than to Dr. Wenthrop.

"Remember what I said, Jill. This is pure speculation, not fact, and a more plausible theory would not involve cloning. I will deny having this conversation with you if any question arises about cloning. Also envision the nearly impossible task of a simple lab tech pulling off a successful cloning of a human just because he knew how to use a micropipette. We should take a swallow of brandy and forget we just met, don't you agree?"

"You realize that the date of late March for the sample and the delivery of Trey in late December is a normal term nine month pregnancy? It fits, Mike. I know you don't want to believe your own theory, but it fits too perfectly not to be true."

"It does, but forget you ever heard it."

"If you were Manfred Porter and had accomplished such a feat, where would you go?"

"I wouldn't tell a soul, first of all. You would end up in prison for several life terms for that." He paused, thinking it through. "There is one possibility, Jill. But you'll never get an interview if the man is still alive. Not in this place. North Korea. We hear about such things coming out of there and most of it is just propaganda. They would like South Korea to live in fear of a cloned army of super humans coming across the border in waves. Really, though, the dynasty there would love a clone or two of their dear leader of the moment. It wouldn't surprise me if Manfred managed to make it to North Korea where he would find all the work he could manage."

"While we are just speculating and theorizing, Mike, why would someone want to cover any trail of Ronald Reagan's birth or creation?"

"If they want him to become president, a son is easier to sell to the public than a clone...and some might raise an issue regarding a third term for the same person. That's what I think."

"Would a DNA comparison prove he is a clone?"

"It would exactly correspond, something that only an identical twin could do. Only, your copy is too young for that."

"They have the test but never released it," Jill confided.

"I can see why. A match would prove my theory correct."

"Can you explain in a little more detail how a cloning is done?"

"I believe what *could* have been done is rather simple. Manfred Porter *could* have promoted a normal fertilization of the egg using the husband's sperm. Then he would have removed the eggs nucleus before cell division occurred, substituting in its place the nucleus of a cell obtained from a tissue or blood sample of Ronald Reagan supplied by his girlfriend. Then the egg was incubated and cell division started before implantation into the mother by the gynecologist."

"It's so simple. Why doesn't it work?" Jill asked.

"There are still unknown factors, but the technique is improving yearly. In the past, and to some degree presently, developmental abnormalities occur which prevent normal maturation of the fetus in the womb. There has been a consensus for a long time that a cloned mammal will have a short life span, although that has recently been challenged."

"You mean even if a baby was born, it may have genetic defects which could shorten its life?"

"I don't think it is currently possible to have a one hundred percent success rate with a human clone.

Perhaps never, and that is part of the controversy surrounding human cloning. In 1981, I think it would have been impossible to produce a perfect human clone."

"I know Ronald Reagan, and he seems completely normal."

"Is he?"

Chapter 23

Chapter Twenty-Four

A Matter Of Theory

Grace was tired of it. It had been three days since Jill returned, and most of the time she had been in her room with the door closed. She was obviously bothered by something but refused any discussion on the subject. Worse were the incessant phone calls, all refused, and most from her own newspaper office. Jill had come down for meals, eaten as if by necessity, and returned to the solace of her old bedroom, closing and latching the door behind her.

Grace sighed and returned to preparing the evening food. The television set blared away in the other room, more for the comfort of conversation for her than interest in the content. She was aware of her now famous daughter's articles having read and reread each and every one, but she, like so many others, could not fathom Jill's personal relationship with the most talked about of all the candidates in her memory. Grace knew her daughter better than anyone in the world and could read her eyes as they both watched Ronald Reagan's face appear, as it did frequently while they were eating. There was deep emotion there, pining and longing...and perhaps, love also. Not that Jill would admit any of those feelings to her mother, but regardless of that, Grace was still absolutely convinced that Jill had been romantically involved just as the other newspersons constantly suggested. Something profound had since taken place that had not removed her love for the Candidate but caused her to want to run away and hide in her room of childhood.

Strident conversation coming from the television caught her attention. They were discussing Reagan again, and this time loudly and argumentatively. Grace went to the door and leaned in, listening and watching.

"Well, I for one don't agree. More money spent on the military is wasteful. We are not engaged in war at this time, and a lot of us feel that money could be spent more wisely at home, repairing our damaged cities and highways."

"Lest you forget, each time our nation has let our guard down we do get into a war and are ill-prepared to do so. We have to protect ourselves as a nation, just as we do in our own homes."

"And who is this Ronald Reagan with the several name changes? Are we to believe that the president has somehow been resurrected or reborn and returned to right all our wrongs? Can you put faith in an unknown just because he resembles someone else? This candidacy smacks of chicanery of some sort. We are being duped."

"And we are the dumbest nation of all if we don't elect Reagan president. He has clear and concise

answers to problems that most of us agree with, even though some on this panel won't admit it."

"Baloney. I don't think we should or can return to the past. Answers and solutions of thirty-five years ago no longer are valid. I wouldn't support this man if he actually was Ronald Reagan."

Grace shut the set down, preferring restful quiet to incessant argument. What was different about today's discussion was the lack of mention of Jill Longley. She had stopped writing about the Candidate and as a result was becoming an unknown as fast as she became the subject of gossip and controversy. Grace sighed again. What will be will be.

A rapping at the door caught her attention. She hoped it wasn't more flowers from Jules Burns. Surely he would get the message by now that Jill was unreachable. Grace peeked and saw a uniformed man holding something. He noticed her face at the window and gave a low bow and a smile.

"She won't see anyone. You are wasting your time," Grace announced when she opened the door.

"Yes, Ma'am. I have a call for her. Thought she would want to talk to Mr. Reagan who is on the other end waiting."

"Just who are you?" Grace inquired, suspicions of a trick were foremost in her mind.

"My name is Juan. I'm an acquaintance of your daughter. She will remember Juan. Please, Ma'am, Mr. Reagan is anxious to speak to Miss Longley."

"Give me that phone," Grace said and reached for it. Juan smiled and punched a button and gave it over with a sly smile.

"Hello. Who is this?" Grace demanded.

"Well, you must be Jill's mother. I've heard so much about you from her. You simply can't be as wonderful as she describes but hearing your voice, I'm inclined to believe her."

There was no doubt. It was the smooth resonant voice of Ronald Reagan on the other end. Grace had heard enough of him over the media to be sure. "Jill hasn't taken any calls for three days, Mr. Reagan. I can ask her, but I'm fairly certain she will refuse."

"She won't refuse me, Mrs. Longley. I'll hold on while you ask. And in case we don't speak again today, let me tell you how much I am looking forward to meeting you in person."

With the phone containing the essence of Ronald Reagan in one hand, Grace knocked frantically on Jill's door with the other. "Jill, open the door, please dear, it's him on the phone." Jill opened it as demanded and saw the phone being offered toward her. "It's Mr. Reagan, Jill, for sure it's him."

"Hi," she said into the phone, then listened, moving slowly backward and closing the door behind her. Her mother shrugged and headed downstairs to tell Juan that a connection had been made.

"I've been informed that you are a hard person to reach at the moment."

"It's just a bit of depression. It'll pass in a few days," Jill responded.

"Anything I did to cause it or anything I can do to correct it?"

"No, Ron. I just need some time to think things through."

"Then it is about me or about us, isn't it?"

"Not the way you are thinking. I still love you...passionately love you. That hasn't changed, you should know that. It's just that I am confused right now. Sorry about the lack of articles over the past several days."

"You remember that I never asked you to write a thing about me, but I was always delighted that you did. Without you I wouldn't have come this far. As for me personally, you never have to write another word unless you want to, and my feeling toward you won't change a bit."

"I can't write a word, good or bad, at the moment, but I appreciate what you just said."

"Something I wanted to tell you, Jill. After that piece you wrote about my adoptive mother, and largely because I was so overcome by your lovely prose, on an impulse I called her and we had a nice long chat. You are the one who inspired me or perhaps shamed me into doing something that I just haven't gotten around to. You made a big impression on her, I can tell you, and she has the highest regard for you and wants to be at our wedding." He chuckled in that old familiar way that always pulled at Jill's heart in some manner.

"Wedding?" Jill asked. "We've only kissed twice. Are you sure you are Ronald Reagan?" she teased.

"Three times. I've kept close track. But for sure, Jill, I am Ronald Reagan, and he would love to get his arms around you again."

"Ted and his group will try and prevent that," Jill predicted.

"I've only recently been made aware of their intentions, and it was true but no longer is. This time, I'm coming to you. Just stay right there with your mother, and soon you will have to give me just one more kiss."

"But, Ron, you kept me at arm's length for so long without explanation, I don't begin to understand what has changed. You said you were protecting me. What has happened?"

"I'll try to explain the best that I can when we are together, something I can't do over the telephone."

"Thanks for the call, Ron. Talking with you has improved my mood tremendously. I can't wait until you arrive. How long will it be?"

"I don't know because they have every second booked someplace or another, but I'll just have to insist on a change of plans."

"Until then, Ron."

"Soon, Jill."

Jill tossed herself on the bed and laid there, arms and legs spread apart, studying the inner space of her mind, crisscrossing details, recalling conversations and, of course, the face of Ronald Reagan. Was he a clone, was it even possible, or was there some other explanation that wasn't so hard to believe? Creating a successful human clone, given the era and the facility involved, didn't even seem laughably possible. It was pure science fiction and speculation. If there was a bit of crooked play, it had to involve a sperm donation from the president. This new thought started to take a life of its own, shutting out all others in a subconscious attempt to restore the man she loved to having been conceived instead of created. There were two questions to be considered. Ted once told her that there had been a genetic test result, supplied by the Candidate himself, which proved a connection to the former president. She wondered, by some magic, if she could get a look at the test results and perhaps confirm them with the reporting laboratory. Assuming that the test was valid and correct, then the question of where the sperm came from was the big problem. She didn't know much about those kinds of medical procedures, but she did know an expert who would.

It took several tries and a long hold, but the voice of Professor Wenthrop at last answered. "This is Dr. Wenthrop," he stated.

"Hi, Mike. This is Jill Longley. Remember me?"

"Of course. It's not often that I get interviewed, especially by someone so famous and attractive. I assume that you have questions regarding our previous discussions?"

"Along a different line, and that's why I need to hear your thoughts on it. I was thinking over your theory..."

"Hold on, Jill. That was no theory of mine, just a possibility. There's a difference to me."

"Sure, I understand, and I appreciate your honesty. Professor, do you know much about frozen sperm used in artificial insemination?"

"I see where this is heading. You want an alternative explanation of events, do you not?"

"It would ease my mind considerably, and you can figure out why."

"The concept of artificial insemination goes back to the late nineteenth century and was a concept designed for the breeders of assorted livestock. As I recall, the first use of frozen sperm didn't occur until 1948 or so. Even though it is, at this time, an accepted and well-used technique, there are still many problems. You have to understand that any technique for using frozen sperm has to involve the rapidity of the freezing process as well as the thawing of sperm. In addition, the presence of various chemicals to preserve the cellular membrane is a field of active study. The fact that freezing and thawing technology is both species specific and even cellular specific, and more importantly, seems to vary from individual to individual makes for a complex laboratory protocol." He paused for a moment, and she could hear rattling of papers before he resumed. "You see that cryobiological properties associated with osmotic changes, such as the membrane permeability to water and factors such as which cryoprotectants are used, means that the particular sperm's osmotic tolerance limits are all critical."

"Hold it, Professor. You are speaking well above my head. What I wonder is a lot more simplistic. Was it possible that preserved sperm was used in the lab to create this person?"

"It is possible, but there are conditions and facts to consider. First, where was the source of the specimen?"

"You know that Ronald Reagan was the governor of California and a rather well-known and successful actor. He had the contacts and the money to have his sperm frozen for what has been called fertility insurance. Surely that was done in the big state of California during those years when Ronald Reagan was younger."

"At least for animals, particularly cattle. That's true, but there is one other troubling fact, Jill. A study surfaced back in about 2003 or 2004 that reported a successful human pregnancy after using sperm frozen for twenty-one years. That, if my memory serves, is the longest for humans thus far, though there were reports as far back as 1970 about successful use of frozen sperm held for shorter than ten years."

"Then it was possible."

"Yes, technically, but proving it would mean finding the storage facility, if it exists, and establishing a trail to the hospital lab in Norfolk in 1981 and all within that twenty year window. Seems to me a task for the FBI, not a single reporter."

"And you recall that I mentioned there was a DNA comparison test which had been run."

"And you recall that I said that this test would be decisive in determining if my original flight of fancy was correct or alternatively confirms your current speculation."

"You have been a big help, Mike."

"Of course I am expecting you to keep me informed as to what you discover."

"I will, you can rest assured."

She wasn't yet satisfied. There were many possibilities, but only one item remained essential to clarify. The DNA comparison test. She had to see it. If it was a near perfect match, then Ron was a clone as she feared, if not...

She dialed again, this time using the number Ted had given her. He answered promptly.

"Hi, Jill. Glad you called because we have a lot to talk about."

"Hello, Ted. I just talked to Ron. He thinks you will let him take a break to come out and see me. Is this going to happen?"

"Is that why you called?"

"No. Something actually more important. Any chance I could see the DNA comparison report Ron gave to the committee?

"The test confirms a match, Jill, or don't you trust me?"

"When you say 'match,' what exactly does that mean?"

"It means that our Ronald Reagan is most definitely related to President Ronald Reagan. What else could match indicate?"

"Well, how exactly? Can you give me a percentage?"

"Gee, Jill, I'm no scientist. Where are you going with this?"

"Can I see it or not? If I write an article about the results, it will calm down a lot of angry folks out there. I can't write about what I don't know for sure."

"But, Jill, any fool can plainly see the similarity. Photo matches and visual recording comparisons are constantly on the air. There is no doubt at all of a relationship."

"Meaning that you're not going to give me a look, are you?"

"I'd have to get clearance. It's not for me alone to decide. Can you tell me why you have entirely stopped reporting? Is there some issue I can help resolve?"

"Get me the test, and I'll give you a great article. Is it a deal?" she asked.

"You will understand that I can't respond to blackmail. It's beneath what I expect from you."

"One more thing, are you going to allow Ron to come here or not?"

"Don't count on it anytime soon."

Chapter 24

Chapter Twenty-Five

The Moment The Phone Rang

Burns looked up from his work, pulled his half-glasses a bit lower and watched her sit down on the other side of his desk. Jill was different somehow, older, that familiar spirit of hers had been dampened. She put her purse on the floor without a word and looked blankly toward him.

"Are you back?" Burns had to ask.

"You see me, don't you?"

"Yeah, and I've missed you. Want to talk?"

"Not here."

"Got room in there for breakfast? I'm buying," Burns offered.

"If you mean my favorite coffee shop, then yes."

"You must mean that place that charges an arm and a leg for coffee," Burns huffed.

"Still buying?" Jill asked.

They sat across a circular marble table top just big enough for two cups of coffee and two top-heavy muffins. The place was busy, as usual, but over so much ambient noise, personal conversations could not be overheard. There was the privacy to be found only in a bustling public place.

"So, what's the news?" Burns asked gently, knowing that Jill had some profound thing she might share if he asked in the right way.

"I talked with Ron. He wants to come here to see me. Ted doesn't want him to."

"Ted wants you to report but not to be news yourself. That's understandable," Burns agreed. "But, I've known you for a long time, and there is something else, a much bigger issue is troubling you."

"Boss, there are things that I've uncovered that even you can't be told. You'll want to drag it out of me, but don't try. Trust me that you don't want that burden on your shoulders."

"By now, I hoped that you would think of me as a friend. If you told me some secret, it would stay that way."

"No. What I've learned would make the biggest news story of all time, but it can't be proven and it's too personal for me to tell anyone."

"My intuition tells me that it's about Ronald Reagan. Something from his past not only very bad but also damaging to his candidacy."

"Burns, you can't guess this one, but let me assure you that Ron is a pure person. He says what he believes and only has the country's best interest at heart."

"Are you two having a lovers' quarrel?

"Let me set you straight on that one. We are not lovers and never have been."

"It's none of my business, but I would have guessed otherwise. So have most others."

"And it's not true. We have strong feelings toward each other but..." She trailed off and sipped her coffee.

"But you would go farther, and I gather he won't?"

"Sounds like fabrication, doesn't it, but that's the fact. I can't explain it even to myself."

"You ever consider that Ron and Ted just used you to write complimentary columns and then discarded you when..."

"Stop!" she snapped, cutting him off in mid-sentence. "Ron cares for me, genuinely cares. That's not it." Her pupils dilated slightly then calmed back to normal.

Burns could tell that the romance subject was off limits. He decided to explore another topic with her. "You met that genetics expert I found for you, I hope?"

"Yes. Good choice, by the way. Dr. Wenthrop really knows his subject."

"Since you are working for me, I need to ask, when you talked with this geneticist, what did you learn?"

"You know the questions I had, Burns, where Ron came from and if he is related to the former president."

"And?"

"The critical bit of information is a DNA comparative test that I was told is being held by the RNC. Ted won't let anyone, including me, get a look at it."

"Did Dr. Wenthrop shed any light on the various possibilities of Ronald Reagan's birth?"

"He concluded that it would take the FBI to track down the details, and it isn't going to happen."

"You shut yourself off from me and the rest of the world, because you couldn't get a look at a test result?"

"It's a dead end, Burns. We have to let it go."

"I guess I could beg Duffy," Burns mumbled, barely loud enough for Jill to hear.

"And that test might just be what someone doesn't want us to see. Don't put yourself at risk, Burns."

"Can Duffy's people guess what you know?"

"Not unless Dr. Wenthrop tells them, and he won't."

Jules Burns's mind burned with questions, but he quickly realized that he already knew the answers. He reached out and patted Jill's hand in an affectionate way. "What do I know, but here is what I can guess, and I'm no genius. The test has been promoted to prove a DNA match. So if that's all it does, there should be no secret about it. If, on the other hand, it shows no relationship between the two Reagans, so much the better. That way we don't have to accuse the former and honored president of something unsavory. There is only one possibility, only one thing truly earthshaking that it could be. They locked eyes, and Burns instantly understood he had hit the nail on the head.

"Don't go there, Burns. Don't you dare," Jill hissed. He sat back and looked at her while thinking it out. Of course, that would explain not only what the world saw, but the way Jill had reacted when she had heard what the learned Dr. Wenthrop had to say.

"So the test would be proof," Burns concluded.

"Yes. But remember there are many other possibilities," Jill warned.

"Of course," Burns answered, using a patronizing tone, not believing there would be any other issue so hidden that it would cause the deaths or disappearance of potential players.

"You may be in danger, Jill. And now, so might I."

"I know, Boss, and I'm sorry..."

"We have only one option," he began, "and that is to publish our suspicions and what we have discovered. It will start a firestorm but then we would be out of any crosshairs."

"We can't do that to Ron. He is a good person and will make a great president. We'll rob the country of something wonderful. "

"You ever wonder why they so badly want this particular fellow to become president?"

"I have constantly thought about that. Perhaps they are good guys, trying to do the right thing for a change."

"Or not."

After dropping Burns off back at the office, Jill found that she couldn't stay there and work. There was nothing at all she could write at the moment, and her emotions would prevent her from either being honest or from hiding the truth. She robotically headed back to her mother's home and the childish security that being in her old room offered.

The phone was ringing, and as she awakened, she realized that it had been making noise for some time. The room was dark and she glanced at the bedside illuminated clock as she reached for her phone. 2:15 AM.

"Hello," she fumbled the word badly, her lips and tongue still not fully awake.

"Miss? This is Juan. Are you awake? Can you hear me?"

"Juan?" she repeated, sitting up, alertness rapidly arising along with her pulse.

"Mr. Reagan was taken to the hospital just now. He asked me to call."

"Hospital! What's happened, Juan?"

"I don't know, Miss. He looks kind of bad. We are in Cedar Rapids, at the main hospital. Mr. Clark is with him. We had just left a rally when it happened."

"What happened? Was he shot?" She was trying to remain coherent but was aware that her voice was rising.

"No. Not shot. He just folded over. I think he passed out for a time. You'd better come."

"I will, Juan. Tell him that I'm coming and will be there by tonight. And tell him to call me if he can, and tell him..."

"Yes, Miss. I know. He knows too."

Chapter Twenty-Six

One Last Time

It was 10:30 PM when the cab pulled up in front of St. Lukes and jerked to a halt. It had been a very long day, and Jill was thinking and moving slowly because of the nervous energy she had expended to get to this very spot in such short order. At each opportunity which had arisen during waits at airports, she had attempted to contact Ted. He never answered nor returned her call, even though she had left pleading messages. The hospital operators clearly and repeatedly stated that they had no authorization to release any information. Whatever had happened since Juan had called her was shortly going to be discovered. She had kept an eye on any developing story on the Internet but, so far, there were none.

After paying the cabbie and giving him a generous tip for making a fast trip from the airport, she picked up her small travel bag and headed through the glass doors. The lobby was devoid of people because of typical hospital rules regarding visiting hours, and she approached the information desk which was staffed by a small woman busily reading a magazine.

"Hi," Jill called out. When the staff person looked at her, waiting on her request, Jill continued, "Can you tell which room Mr. Reagan is in?"

"We're sorry, but it is well past visiting hours. You may return after nine in the morning if you wish."

"I was told that he was brought in as an emergency. Can you at least tell me his condition?"

"We do not disclose patient information of that kind."

"Can you find out if you even have a patient by that name?"

"I'm sorry. No."

"You need to call your supervisor…right now," Jill spat out. There was no way she was walking away without a fight.

It took about twenty minutes, but at last Jill could hear the clicks of high heels against polished stone moving in her direction. A trim well-dressed woman emerged out of a long hallway and headed directly for Jill, who stood up, ready for a verbal contest and a test of wills.

"You are the party asking about a possible patient?" she asked, her thin lips pursed and her face taught.

"I am. The patient is Ronald Reagan. I'm sure you know that name."

"Come with me, please," she said and abruptly turned and started walking away. Jill gathered her pack and followed. Looking around, she became aware that she had seen no evidence of Secret Service protection. None at all. Something was funny about the whole thing. Perhaps Juan had meant the other Cedar Rapids hospital, about a mile away. Could be that she was making a fuss at the wrong location? She was shown into a small interview room, and the supervisor closed the door and indicated that she should sit down.

"You were asking about a Ronald Reagan. We have no admissions by that name. However, it might interest you to know that we have admitted a patient by the name of Trey McDaniels. Could that be the party you wanted to see?"

"I believe that it is."

"And, is your name Jill Longley?" she questioned, looking over a paper in her hand.

"Yes, that's my name."

"You are listed as 'significant other' by Mr. McDaniels and have been given permission to see him. It is after hours for a visit but given the circumstances...."

"Meaning that his condition is serious?" Jill wondered.

"I would rather that a physician discuss his condition. Would you care to see Mr. McDaniels or talk with his physician first?"

"If possible, and if he is conscious, I want to see Trey right away."

"I'll grant that. If you return to the elevator bank that we passed and wait, I'll have an aide show you the way. Anything else?" she asked.

"Where are his Secret Service personnel? Are they with Trey?"

"As far as I know, there is nothing like that in this hospital."

Jill waited alone in the hall, watching the elevator indicators move up and down but never seeming to stop at her floor. At last, there was a clear "ding" and one of the doors slid open allowing a young cheerful girl wearing a pink pinstriped uniform to emerge.

She held the door open and waved to Jill to join her in the elevator. "You are Mrs. Longley?" the girl inquired. Jill nodded, not wanting to clarify her relationship on the elevator. They rode in silence to the eighth floor, and the bell softly signaled their arrival. Jill could feel her pulse increasing as the sounds of a busy surgical ward greeted her. The hall lights had been dimmed, given the hour, but there was still activity at the busy nursing station, and nurses could still be seen in the hallways.

"Hello...Mrs. Longley?" one inquired, giving her a brief welcoming smile.

"Yes. I'm here to see Trey McDaniels," Jill unnecessarily explained.

"This way. He is in our intermediate care unit and may be going to surgery soon. You came in just before his sedation and prep. An attending will be in shortly." Together they walked toward the end of a long hall, the sounds of cardiac monitors beeping from several directions, growing louder as they walked. Suddenly they stopped before an open door, and Jill could see him lying on a big bed, a rack of monitors mounted to the wall above his head. She expected to see Juan or Ted, but the room was empty. Ron turned his head toward her as she approached, his face familiar, but strained, not as confident as the man he was so shortly ago. He extended his free hand toward her and managed a weak smile.

"The person I most wanted to see and here she is. I knew you would come."

Jill looked around the room again, still expecting someone else to be there, if not for protection, at least for comfort.

"Ron. Dear Ron. What has happened?" Jill asked, her voice cracking a little, the emotion welling up involuntarily inside her. Behind her, she could hear the nurse leaving. They were alone.

"Oh, It's one of those times that life starts going a different direction than you plan. A lot can happen in a blink of an eye, and it's always when you don't expect it."

"Are you about to have surgery?"

"They are talking about it. I don't know."

"Are you alone? What happened to the others?" Jill asked, looking around again, sure that someone, anyone would be there.

"I expect so...Don't worry. It doesn't change anything. You are here, and that's all that counts in my book."

"Can you explain things for me? I was only told by Juan to come. So far, I don't have a clue what is wrong or what is going to happen." Jill could feel her tears starting to form and couldn't prevent Ron from noticing.

"I've always been a little different, I guess. When I was young they would give me some medicine and then pat me on the back. The pain came back at odd times throughout my life, but this time it didn't go away."

"Did they tell you what is wrong?"

"A lot, I'm afraid. I always understood that my time might be limited, and this may be the end of it a bit sooner than I'd hoped. You never understood me, because I never explained myself to you. I fell in love with you the moment you came into that room, just like the old song tunes say happens. All I could expect was to make you my friend and be around you. There was always the feeling inside me that I wasn't meant to have a lover, to pass to her or my children whatever was wrong with me. It was a feeling that I was older than everyone else, more expendable, more temporary. For you...I wanted to spare you...but I couldn't really bring myself to push you away because I was in love. Some day, I hope you forgive me for being selfish and letting you get too close."

"You don't have to feel sorry a bit, Ron. I love you and have loved you all of my life. It couldn't be any other way. Please don't leave me now that I have found you."

"If it was for me to decide, things would be different. It is not up to me, and we both know that."

"I expected to see Ted or Juan. Are they coming back?" Jill asked.

"They've gone back to Washington. My campaign for president has ended, and they have to move on. There's no hard feelings about it."

"They just left you here by yourself?" she asked, incredulous.

"Don't be upset about it, because I'm not. Ted has to have another candidate, and there isn't much time left. I let them down, not the other way around."

"I almost didn't find you because you were admitted under your old name. Juan didn't tell me anything."

"Yes, I wanted to spare the hospital all the news people and whatever comes with them. I came into life as Trey, and I might as well go out as him. For a long time, I've known that I am Ronald Reagan. That's who I really am inside and outside. Using my old name is just a way to hide."

"Can you tell me when it happened, the moment you knew who you are?"

"It was in the hospital in Germany. I woke up knowing. For a time, I thought my abductors were responsible for convincing me, but at some point I understood that they only made me see myself as who I really am. There was a lot I had to do before assuming the name, you see. First I had to become educated, gain some experience so that I could ask people to let me lead them. When the moment was right, I changed my name as well as my appearance and walked out into the open. Know what happened right away?"

"No."

"I saw you standing in the middle of the room, all alone, and I seemed to know you, seemed to always know you. It was funny. We had never met but had always been together in some way. I can't explain it."

"You'll pull through, Ron. Don't give up yet. I haven't had enough of you to lose you so soon."

"The country needs me, I know that, and I believe that many of my countrymen think so as well. My only ambition in life was to serve my country. Before

I understood who I was, I still wanted to make a contribution, that's why I joined the Army. There I felt useful, as well as proud that I was with my fellow soldiers. It almost happened, didn't it, Jill? I almost made it."

"Of course you did, and there was never any doubt you would have made a grand president. You had my vote."

"Yes, I could always count on you. It was your reporting that gave me a chance, and this may be the last time I can tell you how much I appreciate it. I love you, Jill."

"I love you, Ron."

A voice was cleared coming from the doorway, and Jill turned toward it. An older, distinguished physician in a long lab coat was standing in the door holding a chart. "Didn't want to interrupt, folks, until you were done. May I enter?" he asked.

"Come in, Doctor Rawles," Ron said and motioned to him with his free hand. "This is Jill. I told you about her."

"Yes, you certainly did, Trey. Glad to meet you, Jill." He started to offer his hand but instead patted her on her shoulder as he approached the bed. "We have some things to discuss, Trey. Is this a good time?"

"I want Jill to hear everything you say. Please," Ron said.

"Then, let me summarize for you, Jill, so that you can appreciate the medical issues involved. Trey came into the hospital with severe abdominal pain and had been semi-conscious for a couple of hours prior to admission. We discovered the uremia first and afterwards the cause. Trey has a single kidney, a product of a birth defect, I believe. The functioning kidney is, unfortunately, failing."

"Can't you do a renal transplant?" Jill asked.

"Normally, that's what is done. Trey has anatomical variations which required some study and consultation before surgery could be attempted. That's what I came to discuss."

"We're listening, Doctor," Ron said.

"We have to admit that you are a very unusual patient, Trey, and you may not have a typical successful result. There are vascular abnormalities near your left kidney which are problematic for placing a transplanted kidney. In the meantime, I have put out a request for a donor kidney, and until we get a match and can all agree on surgery, I am going to recommend dialysis, starting tonight."

"If I am a match, I want to donate my kidney," Jill offered.

"I can't stand to see you do that, Jill. Cutting you to save me...I couldn't bear it. They will find one from their matching system. I'm confident about it."

"We may get lucky, but often it takes a bit of waiting," Dr. Rawles stated. He discretely signaled Jill that he wanted to see her outside. "I'll be back later to get you started, Trey. Anything I can do in the meantime?"

"Don't let this girl donate a kidney. We both know it's a losing proposition, and I'm counting on you to do the right thing."

"You have my word, Trey. Would you mind if I had a private conversation with Jill?"

"We owe it to her. Sure, take your time."

They walked together toward the nursing station. Jill could tell that Dr. Rawles was trying to decide the right way to break some unpleasant news. He stopped in the hall and leaned into the wall, watching her face closely. "Whatever we discuss, you should make an effort to control your emotions. You won't do any good by transferring your fear to him. Keep a positive attitude around Trey."

"I understand. Is it that bad?"

"I've been practicing for a long time, and I've discussed Trey's condition with others equally experienced, but frankly, none of us have seen a case exactly like his previously. He has what I could only describe as multiple system failure. I'm surprised that he has had a productive life, but I'm afraid that his time has run out. I did put in a request for a kidney, and if it is possible to implant it, I will. Though it may not extend his life for very long, even if he survives the surgery."

"You can use mine, and we won't tell him."

"I just made him a promise, Jill, and I think he was right anyway."

"How much time does he have, Doctor?"

"Every moment of our lives is precious, and we should always use them wisely. Go be at his side, Jill. I think that you are all he cares about now that the politics is over."

"You knew who he is?"

"Of course. Everyone would know that face and voice. I am honored to have met him, and I would be more honored to be able to save his life and restore his chance to become president. Lord knows, we need him right now."

"I don't want you to think I don't value your skill or dedication, but do you think he would be better off in a bigger institution?"

"That doesn't offend me in the least and I was ready to send him out as soon as I saw the first image study. I even called Rochester myself this morning. They said the same thing, Jill. There is no reason to put him through that. Be there beside him, that's all any of us can do for now."

Ron was asleep when Jill returned. She pulled the chair closer and slid her hand into his. His face was placid and the fine smile wrinkles had disappeared, making him look younger than he was. He had a noble fine face, one that is unique and imbedded in many memories. Jill had seen all of his movies, most several times. She could still hear his voice speaking his lines and the always present smile. It was the face she had dreamed about as a young girl just coming into awareness of the two sexes, and though still unsure of the meaning of attraction, felt its urges, none ever so strong as when she watched his movies. She saw his face on television after he was president, heard the fine speeches he had given without notes or pauses. The leader of the Soviet Union was drawn to him as well, and in the presence of the American president, Gorbachov seemed to be reasonable, even allied in purpose. Ronald Reagan was a man of the ages, folks said, and his reputation would only grow larger over time. Could this Reagan have matched him, she wondered, then, came once again to the question of the moment. In her heart, she knew that he was a clone of the president, no matter how impossible it was, how unlikely, there he was beside her. He is Ronald Reagan, she knew. He is the same man he always was, inside and out, and she had been lucky enough to call him her love. The tears started in earnest, and the sobbing, her shoulders shaking with the effort to control herself. A warm hand rested on her back and caressed her softly.

"There, there, Jill. No cause for crying here. We are together again, aren't we, or am I hallucinating? Whatever will happen is destiny, and we can't change it with tears or remorse. It was my fate to be born a copy of a famous person and to try to live up to what he was and what he meant for the country. It's been a noble cause, and it was all I wanted in life...until I met you. Holding you at arm's length was the hardest thing I have ever done, but in my heart, I knew that it was for the right reasons and what you see now proves me correct. I told you once that you were too good for me and you are. We can't part until you give me an oath that you will leave me behind, both in body and sprit and go on to have a full, long and rewarding life when this chapter is over." He stopped and looked at her, waiting on her response.

"Ron..."

"You can make that promise, Jill. You can do this one thing for me, because I've never asked anything of you except this promise. I can't leave you until I know you will be happy again without me."

"I'll try. But..."

"Trying is good but meaning it is another. You'll still have my movies if you get lonely." He laughed, showing his even teeth and his smile lines. "Pity that this copy didn't actually make any, but you can pretend. Now I need that kiss you and I promised each other." He gently tugged on her arm and enveloped her with it, pulling her down to him until they were nose to nose. "How lovely it would have been. I've let you down, like I've let them all down. I've tried, God knows, I've tried..."

Jill found his lips and didn't want to let go. This was the first kiss that she was able to pour some of her soul into him, forgetting for a moment where they were and the circumstances. It could have been anywhere and the room, the world and the universe would have waited until they parted. She realized that her tears were flowing onto his face, and she began to taste the salt of them. His eyes closed again, and his face took on that peaceful look, that noble expression that had made him so famous.

Chapter 26

Chapter Twenty-Seven

A Grudging Explanation

You can tell his story now, Jill, leaving nothing out. He can't be hurt any longer...can't you see that?" Burns pleaded.

"One more time Jules, we don't have anything but speculation and conjecture. The facts, if there ever *were* facts, are hidden away and buried forever."

"Then write an emotional impact story and just put down your experiences. You are passing up something awful big, Jill, bigger than either one of us. Right now, the public is clamoring for your views, but soon they will forget and move on."

"Let them. It got too personal for me to tell. I just can't write that down."

"What about when they just abandoned him...dumped him is more accurate...in the hospital and left without another word? What about that? Aren't you angry about it?"

"I'm seething, but Ron forgave them before he died. He said that they had the country to consider and left to promote another candidate while there was still time. He said he understood."

"We would love to see you back at work, Jill. Do you intend on ever coming back, or is this it?"

"I've decided to find Ted Clark and have a face to face with him. After that, I'll come in."

"Give him hell, kid. See you." The phone clicked off, and Jill rolled off the bed, her brain coming alive again after several days of self-pitying remorse after Ronald Reagan was buried. She, Juan and Jules Burns were the only ones present when he was lowered into the ground, forgotten by all the others, even the avaricious, omnipresent press corps. Gone. The columns stopped, the media pivoted to other issues, and the world slowly turned another face, and the dead was quickly forgotten.

Ted never answered her calls, and there was little use in pretending that he ever thought about her or Ron any longer. She and the Candidate were in the past, forgotten and useless. But Jill was going to wake them all up, because she had formed a plan, and when it was executed, it would shake the foundation of the political world.

"Juan. Hi, this is Jill Longley," she said when he answered.

"Hello, Miss. Hope you are back to normal now, because I swear I never saw so many tears come out of one person. Is there something I can do for you?"

"I want to meet with Ted, and I know you can get me in. He hasn't answered any of my calls."

"He's a busy fellow, Miss. When were you thinking?"

"Any time, any place. Ted doesn't have to know I'm coming."

"We are going to the Maryland estate on the weekend. Could you come there, say by Saturday afternoon?"

"I can. Thanks. Are you going to tell the guards to let me in?"

"Sure. They all know you anyway. No problem. I'll call you if things change."

Saturday, about 2:00, Jill's rental car nosed in between the massive iron gates and stopped. She rolled down her window and waited until the guard came around to the driver's side and peered in. "So, you've come back to us?" he said, giving her a welcoming smile.

"Just for the day, Bob. I just need to discuss some things with Mr. Clark," Jill said.

"Anytime for you. A pleasure to see you again, and we're all sorry about losing Mr. Reagan. It's unfortunate for all of us. He was a great man."

"Don't get me crying again, Bob. I have to be dry-eyed when I meet Ted." Bob tipped his hat and pressed the button. With a creak and groan, the gates slowly opened revealing the long row of cultured plants adjoining the winding red stone drive. It was all familiar but had now taken on a threatening look. All the money and influence displayed by this ostentatious estate made her feel small and helpless. Not only that, her visit was a surprise, and Ted was most likely to not be happy to see her. Jill was back to the outsider status she had when attending the original political event when Ronald Reagan was introduced to the public and to her.

She parked right in front of the door, and when an attendant came out to greet her, she waved him away. "Just leave it there. I won't be long." He shrugged and watched as she walked up to the big door and knocked.

When the door opened and Clarissa saw who was standing there, she threw her arms out and whooped, then embarrassed, covered her mouth. "Jill!" she exclaimed. "Are you back to stay?"

"No. Just a visit, Clarissa. How have you been?"

"When the paper announced that Mr. Reagan had died, we all cried. Were you with him?"

"I was right there until the end. He passed away quietly, with no pain."

"You must be here to visit Mr. Clark. He's in the library. You know the way, don't you?"

"Yes, thanks, Clarissa. You don't need to announce me. I'll just surprise him." Jill walked down the long corridor, her high heels clicking softly against the polished wood, toward the library door which was closed. She opened it without knocking.

Ted was in a big leather lounge chair, the one that Ron had also favored. He looked up and put down his paper. "Well, isn't this a pleasant surprise. You look marvelous. Come in and make yourself comfortable. May I pour you a drink?"

"I don't drink, Ted, but thanks." She sat down in her favorite spot, the one that she always chose because of the view and the little stream of sunlight which always managed to find that particular chair. She settled back and looked around. "Nothing changes here, does it?" she observed.

"It was decorated by my father's second wife. I always thought she had good taste so I've become comfortable with it. We never talked afterwards, but you should know I was stricken with grief also. Juan told me how you took it. I'm sorry, Jill. It was just not meant to be, I guess."

"True. I talked with the surgeon. Ron wasn't destined to live a normal lifetime."

"We all should count ourselves lucky with each new day."

"And each new candidate. I understand you've got another one you are promoting. Guess you don't need my help this time."

"It would be awkward, because he already has all the women he will ever need. But you were wonderful with Ron. Without your columns we would have only met with resistance and ridicule. We owe you more than we could ever pay."

"So, I was picked to be Ron's woman?"

"You know that's not true. I wanted to be around you myself, and I'm the one who chose you. But our candidate spotted you the second you came in. He told me in no uncertain terms that I was to find a way for him to get to know you. Compared to Ron, I didn't have a chance. He was the charming one, had the famous voice and face and was going to be President of the United States. I'm just a politically connected rich boy. I don't blame you a bit for choosing him."

"You know that we never became actual lovers, don't you? It was all just a deep friendship," Jill confessed.

"It was more than that. Ron only thought about you after you both parted. I didn't think he was going to last much longer without you being by his side."

"What was so wrong about us being together? Would it have made any difference, really?"

"You have to understand modern American politics. Every petty little thing will be discussed, exaggerated and magnified. I wanted him to focus on policy, and not try to defend his choice of girlfriend every time he was interviewed. You might not think so, but be glad you didn't make it under that spotlight."

"You have been avoiding me, Ted. All my calls have gone unanswered. Can you give me an honest reason?"

"Sure. I know you weren't calling about getting back together with me for personal reasons, even though I would have liked that. You were calling to finish your story, to get all the little pieces to fit together. I don't want the public to dwell on Ronald Reagan any longer. We have to win this election, and it's time to let the past be the past."

"You just said that you owe me. Fine, I'm ready to take payment...today and right now, and you should be warned that I'm not letting this story go just yet. I have to have answers to my questions, or I'll just start writing what I *think* is true."

"Jill, don't make this a confrontation. I'll tell you everything I know, which may not be as much as you already have. Just ask away, but don't get angry with me. Someday when Ron fades a little from your memory, I would like to have a different kind of conversation with you. Right now, he is foremost in your thoughts, but that won't always be the case. It would mean a lot to me to have your friendship and companionship some day when you are ready."

"How did you pick me out of that room with all the choices you could have made. Did you research me and know what you were getting?"

"You just appealed to me as a man. The other was just plain dumb luck. I didn't know anything about you, even your name."

"I believe that Ronald Reagan was conceived in a test-tube by Manfred Porter, using genetic material obtained illegally, probably by Sommerlyn Crosby. What do you know about it?"

"You might be correct. I've seen photos of Trey Jones's father, Spence. It for sure wasn't his sperm."

"Do you know what happened to Spence. Was he murdered to cover that fact up?"

"Spence Jones is, at this moment, in Rio, drunk and surrounded by professional women. When the money we gave him runs out, he'll return to the skunk hole he came from. We just couldn't see the press photos of Spence alongside Ron in the newspapers. So, we got rid of him."

"Is that the truth? You know I can check that out."

"Check it then. It's true, my word on it."

"And Sommerlyn was murdered. She was silenced, and I'm very sure she was involved in some illegal way."

"She was murdered all right, but by her ex-con boyfriend who was in a drunken rage. Don't you read the papers?"

"It's awfully convenient."

"Just what do you think she did that was so important that she would be murdered for it?" Ted asked.

"She stole samples of the president's blood or tissue and gave it to Manfred Porter."

"And just what was Manfred supposed to have done with that?" Ted said, appearing genuinely astonished.

"He created a clone with it, and the egg was implanted into Trey's mother." She had spoken the words at last to someone and for the first time. After all her investigation, speculation and introspection, she had let her certainty spill out of her.

"That wasn't possible. How did you come up with that idea?"

"I worked it out by logic and science, and it is the only conclusion that works. Don't you understand that it fits perfectly? Ron was a clone of the president which is why he was so visually perfect but, at the same time, flawed inside from being a defective clone. Most cloned animals are flawed in some way."

"I'm speechless, Jill. You believe that a procedure, which has only been used on animals so far, was done to create a human being, years before it was even attempted by the best scientists in the world? I should laugh, but I feel like crying for you. One thing for sure. If you publish that, you will be the subject of ridicule throughout the entire world. You won't find even a rock to hide behind."

"If I ever find Manfred Porter, we will know the truth."

"You can give up that idea. I was told that Manfred was butchered by the North Koreans years ago. Why, no one knows. But whatever Manfred did or knew has been lost forever."

"Did Ron ever tell you about his capture and indoctrination?"

"I never heard anything about it. What did he tell you?"

"He was abducted from a train in Poland and held for two years. He killed some people and escaped, but they ran over him."

"That's a new one. The story I heard was that he was hit by a truck in Poland while traveling with a friend. He was treated in Germany at the American military hospital and released. Are you sure he didn't dream that up while in a coma?"

"He was convinced that it had happened, and I believed him. Some group wanted him to become president."

"And so did I, and he would have made an excellent president. I don't understand why he would have believed that fantasy. After his discharge, he immediately started working toward becoming a copy of the president, mimicking his style and way of talking. I was impressed how closely he got it right."

"Will you show me the DNA test now? That will be the final answer, and if I'm right, it will demonstrate a perfect match to the president."

"You have me on that one, Jill. I and everybody else lied about that. Ron did give us a paper with his DNA analysis, but there was never any comparison study. How would he obtain a specimen from the former president? It would take a court order to acquire and process any tissue, if you could even find any. We lied to stop the press from accusing us of dressing up a look alike and calling him Ronald Reagan. It was a way to get them to accept the man and to listen to him. That's all."

"Are you saying that Ron wasn't even related to the president?"

"I don't know the answer to that. Perhaps there was a link that we don't know about. He was uncannily just alike, that *is* for sure. When I was around him, I even believed it myself. But there was no conspiracy to cover up anything, and I had no part in any of it."

"Tell me why you abandoned him in Iowa and just left. I think it is the most hard-hearted act I have ever heard about. I thought you would owe him more than that."

"Remember, that you were on the way to his side. He didn't want to die with all of us around. Just you. Nothing else was left for him but to stay alive long enough to see you once again, nothing else mattered. I didn't want to interrupt that, and given how I feel about you, I didn't want to witness it either. He and I discussed things before I left, and he understood, he even encouraged me to get back to Washington and keep up the fight."

Jill had run out of steam, out of words and out of anger. Everything she held as certain turned out to be explainable, and she began to see it from Ted's perspective. True, Ronald Reagan's genetic identity was still a mystery, but since the public had already lost interest, there was no reason to pursue it any further. Ted was right. In the future, Ronald Reagan would recede in her thoughts. She would never forget him but would, some day, no longer be preoccupied by his memory. It was going to take some time though.

Jill stood up and gathered her purse. "Thank you, Ted, for taking the time and for talking to me. I need to get back to life and pick up my own pieces."

"Can't you stay and have dinner with me tonight? You know there is a room upstairs with your name still on it, and I would feel very delighted and honored to entertain you as my special guest for as long as you like."

"Thanks, Ted, but not yet. I would see his face in my dreams, and each time I came down the stairs, I would expect him to be there waiting, that old smile of his making me feel like we had known each other since birth."

"I know what you mean. We all miss him, and there will never, never be another one who could take his place. Ron was the best speech maker I've ever come across. He was simply magic in front of the cameras."

They walked together to the front door, and Ted stood outside and watched her drive slowly away until the car disappeared from sight.

Chapter 27

Chapter Twenty-Eight

Stalked

Jill's car took the familiar route nearly by habit. She had resumed living in her apartment, and after two weeks of handling the mundane tasks of a small town news reporter, she was starting to feel like the old Jill Longley again. She glanced in her rearview mirror as she slowed the car for a red light. Her father had once taught her the need for keeping aware of traffic coming from behind, and there was one time being alert had saved her from a bad accident. A grey car three back seemed familiar in some way, but she couldn't place the memory of where...then her mind returned to the story she was working on, and she forgot all about the grey nondescript car.

Beckman watched as she calmly pulled away from the light, in no particular hurry. Some feeling, an inner voice whispering, told him that for a moment, she had noticed him. He wouldn't have been surprised, because he had let the traffic patterns get away from him and ended up far too close to her for his comfort. This was the fourth day, and he was beginning to realize that she was very much a creature of habit, nearly down to the second. There weren't many places that she frequented. Her apartment, her mother's home, the grocery store and gas station and, of course, the newspaper office. No boyfriends had appeared and for that he was thankful. Once in a while he had encountered suitors who happened to have been a cop or a serviceman. Those types frequently carried guns and knew how to use them.

Beckman subconsciously felt for the handle of his pistol, a long-standing and very practical habit, even though the gun was always where he put it. Good gun habits are hard to break, such as always checking a pistol to see if it is loaded even though you just put it down yourself. When you live and die by a gun, it becomes one of the most important objects in your life.

What he wanted was to discover when she was most vulnerable, the moment she was unprotected by security cameras or other watchful eyes. So far, she had kept to public areas and rarely ventured out at night alone. Jill Longley was one of those who would be hard to kill and get away cleanly. Nevertheless, he knew from long experience that sooner or later, everybody has a moment of indiscretion or inattention. You just had to keep your eyes open and be patient.

Beckman was using three cars, each one common or ordinary, but not plain like an unmarked patrol car. That kind, ones with blacked out wheels and no chrome, were a dead giveaway. One of his favorite vehicles was a battered minivan. He changed his look as often as the car. At times, he wore black shades and a brimmed hat, at the next outing a farmer's soiled red cap over clear reading glasses. Beckman had never been detected, because the many years he had spent trailing alert and capable Russian spies had honed his skills to perfection. Beckman only needed a moment alone with her, away from any observation, and then his task would be over.

He had kept up with her writing and had to admit that he admired her as a reporter. It was a wonder that she was content to stay in this little town, because, given her celebrity, he was sure that she could do better, even become a nationally respected journalist. Her articles about the Reagan candidacy had stopped for now and that was the reason he was following her. Jill could not be allowed to collect her thoughts and write what she had come to believe even if she could provide no hard evidence. Someone was concerned that it was bound to happen sooner or later. The truth would be dangerous to certain highly placed people who would rather not take the risk that this previously unknown reporter would pick up again where she had left off. Now that she was out of the spotlight, it was time to silence her forever.

Beckman watched his target but also made memory maps of everything around him, every car, every pedestrian, even the store fronts and the bushes. He was trained to focus but have 360 degree awareness. It was the only way to live long enough to make it to the next assignment. There was something that caught his eye, and he almost had missed it a couple of days ago. A bright red motorcycle was present nearly forty percent of the time he had been trailing Jill Longley. The very obvious is occasionally missed, because humans don't see the expected, only notice the unusual. Now that he was clearly seeing a pattern, he deduced that when the motorcycle wasn't present, some other vehicle had taken its place. An old work truck, the kind that is always around wherever you are, fit the requirement. This particular one was always the same work truck. Jill was being followed by two professional groups. One dedicated to her protection, the other for her elimination. Beckman was not the only one looking for an opening, and the task of getting her alone had now become much harder. The question was did the other group have enough training and experience to spot him and had they already done so? It was going to come down to bullets and a sure aim. The one prepared would win, the other die.

The grey car pulled into a gas station and slowed alongside the pumps, inching along, its motor still running. A rusting work truck ambled by, and Beckman got a glimpse of the driver. Young, but adult, yet careless. He had been spotted by Beckman on the second day and now was going to get a taste of what espionage really meant. Beckman assumed, but didn't know for sure, that there were only two men using two vehicles. If the other team were Russian, it would be more like five or six of them, more than two active at any one time. For that scenario, you needed a group of pros, but to handle only one at a time, you simply needed a gun. He fingered his weapon again. It was still resting in its holster clipped inside his waistband, ready for instant use. From experience, he knew that action was better than waiting. If he shot one, the other would have a choice, show or run, either way things would change. He had to make it look like a random, road rage kind of event. The other group might suspect but wouldn't know for sure what they were up against. It would throw them off, so he could get his job done and get away before they reorganized.

A shooting in broad daylight, with multiple witnesses, was an acceptable risk in this case, because the victim would himself be using a false identity, complicating any following investigation. Beckman would vanish from the scene, leaving no connection to the dead man but raising a red flag of warning to the remainder of the other group. He decided to wait for two more blocks, when Longley was scheduled to turn right. That way, she would never notice what was happening behind her. As the moment approached, Beckman started to accelerate, choosing the left passing lane. His car slid by the rusting truck triggering no alarms from the driver who was obviously unaware Beckman was in pursuit of the same subject.

Beckman braced with his foot and gritted his teeth, turning abruptly into the path of the oncoming truck. Predictably, there was a bone-shaking impact as the truck rammed against the passenger side of the grey car. Both vehicles came to a grinding halt, radiator vapor pouring from under the hood of the truck. In his peripheral vision, he could see traffic in the other lanes slow to watch. Time and surprise was of the essence, and he jumped out of his car, waving his left fist in the air and shouting profanities at the truck. His other hand found the handle of his pistol, using the distraction of his anger to cover his intentions. Before the truck driver could understand what was happening, Beckman jerked the truck door open and fired two well-placed rounds at him. Before turning around, he returned the gun to his waist and closed the driver's door. It happened so quickly that the observers weren't sure what had actually occurred. Beckman's car jerked away from the truck and sped away.

Jill was still finishing her sandwich and checking her sentence structure when Burns's face appeared in her doorway. She looked up and found him staring at her, an uncomfortable look on his face.

"Did I do some bad reporting, or are you just coming by to pick on me?" she asked.

"Don't you usually come down Main Street on your way to work?"

"Of course. My apartment is nearly a straight line from here. Is there some reason I should avoid Main Street?"

"Did you see an accident this morning?"

"No. Was there one?"

"A hit, the cops are calling it. Someone got shot after an accident. They don't think it was accident related, but planned."

"Wow, a hit...in this town. Can I have that one?" she asked.

"I've got a bad feeling about this story, Jill. Given the time you arrived here and the time of the shooting, I would venture that the cars were right behind you when it happened."

"So you think I'm connected in some way?"

"Remember what you were doing just last month and the fact that an intelligence agency was bugging the entire place. I worry."

"You know the entire thing is over, Boss. The world, including me, has moved on, and there would be no possible reason that I'm still of interest to anyone."

"You are ordered to keep alert, girl. Please don't get hurt, because I would feel guilty about it."

"How do you think I would feel after getting shot? Seriously, Boss, I want to cover this one."

"I never could refuse a pretty girl anything. If you absolutely insist, then go ahead, but be careful. Remember that."

Beckman was leaning against a wall, attired in blue denim coveralls and wearing his tattered red cap emblazoned with a faded gold image of a tractor. He had observed Longley enter the police station but was more interested in who else may also be watching. His battered mom-mobile was at the curb, innocuous and invisible even though in plain view. In the distance, a flash of color accompanied by a throbbing sound caught his attention. It was a red motorcycle, and that was the second time he had spotted it in the past fifteen minutes. The second member of the other team hadn't taken his message and was still stalking Longley. The sound stopped a block away, somewhere behind where he was standing. There was a narrow alley entrance just fifty feet away and leading in that direction. Beckman had been tempted to use it himself, but he knew from experience that a shadow in an alley attracts cops like garbage does flies. He knew by instinct that the other agent would shortly emerge from the alley and linger there in plain view of the police station entrance.

Beckman started to move in the direction of the alley entrance, slowly strolling away as if he were just killing time instead of an opposing, armed interloper. Pulling the weapon with his right hand, he let it hang straight down along his leg but on the opposite side of the street and police station, out of their view. He crossed in front of the alley without looking right, but his peripheral vision confirmed what he expected. The other man was heading his way. Beckman abruptly stopped and raised his gun, firing three times in quick succession. The shadow dropped to the littered pavement like a sack falling. Beckman unscrewed the silencer and put the gun back in its holster and returned to his van. He pulled away slowly and unnoticed, just another common vehicle on the city streets. By the time the police found the body and studied the surveillance video recording, the van would have joined the grey car as just another burned out skeleton on the city fringes.

It was the end of a long day for Jill. She fell into the sofa and curled up trying to understand what had transpired. After interviewing the detective assigned to the hit, she had followed a squad car out to inspect a burning auto, one that fit the description of the shooter's car. She could see the cloud of black smoke rising from the gasoline and oil fire in the distance, and when she pulled up beside the black and white, it was obvious that she couldn't get any closer without risk of being covered in black soot.

"Is that the one?" she had asked the patrolman.

"Same damage on the left side and same color. We may assume that it is the one and that it has been set ablaze to cover any fingerprints left behind. When it cools off, I'll get the serial number and track it down, but I believe it will turn out to be a stolen vehicle."

Jill flipped on the television and watched the channels go by one at a time, finally becoming tired enough to try to sleep. She turned the set and the lights off and headed for the bedroom.

"Don't turn the switch on, Miss Longley," a deep voice commanded. She remained with her hand hovering just above the switch and facing the voice which came from the corner of the unlit bedroom.

"What do you want?" she asked, sounding more meek than she intended. "Are you going to kill me?" she managed.

"Others were going to try. Soon, I expect. Not anymore, not those two for sure." There was something in the voice that she recognized, a tone or familiar word, then a vision of the parking garage and a man's shadow came to her mind.

"I've heard your voice previously. You are the one who gave me a tip and a warning in the garage."

"Yes," he answered. "I'm here to warn you and give you a way to save yourself. I took out two today who were here to silence you. There will be others. You have two choices if you want to stay alive. Either run away tonight or..." he paused, working out the right words to use. "Or you can publish everything you know or suspect about Ronald Reagan. Everything. If you do that, they will leave you alone."

"My editor said the same thing, but I have no evidence for my suspicions, and anything I print will be refuted. Where should I go if I choose to run?" Images of far away places flickered across her mind. She had no idea of where to start looking.

"There's no place secure enough. They would eventually track you down."

"Why are you helping me, and why did you help me previously?"

"In my job, I am paid to do what I'm told, but at times like this, I use my conscience. If they find out, I am finished. You can never tell anyone about this meeting."

"I know someone, a wealthy, well-connected man who has a private estate. He has guards at the house. Do you think I would be safe there?"

The shadow laughed. "That may be the worst place you could find."

"Then what am I to do? Do you have any meaningful suggestions, or should you just shoot me now and get it over with?"

"I think this is something you can use." An envelope of papers hit the bed. "I'll be around for a couple more days just in case you need the time.

Better start being alert to danger and changing your routine, or they may yet succeed." The voice fell silent, and Jill resisted the temptation to pick up the envelope.

"One more question," Jill said to the corner of the bedroom. "Can't you at least tell me your name?" There was no response. She couldn't even detect breathing.

"I almost forgot to thank you, whoever you are. Thanks!" There was still no response, and her hand eased toward the light switch. In a sudden burst of energy, she raised the toggle, and the light came on. There was no sign of anyone, and the single window was closed. She realized that he must have come by her through the doorway, close enough to touch. In the middle of the bed was a thick white envelope. She picked it up and pulled out the first page. "A Comparative DNA Analysis" the title read.

The End

A Note of Appreciation

The worst and the best writers seek one thing above all others. A reader who not only reads their book, a work of astounding personal effort, but who shares his/her experiences with the world. We want to know what you think about our work. Truly we do. Of course, we want you to like it, and us, and will be so grateful if you take the time to give us even the smallest amount of praise. I really entreat you to do so.

If you have constructive criticism you want us to hear, please, out with it! Writing is such an isolating experience. I begin to live in my books and come to nearly feel that my characters are real. When someone criticizes one of them, I feel their pain. And some of my own.

But if you enjoyed this novel, I beg you on scuffed knee to give a positive review for me. I assure you that is the best way to see more of my work in the future.

Thanks again for reading this far.

Alexander Francis

Novels by Alexander Francis

Are We A Band Yet?
Mick Grundy...Spy Hunt
Mick Grundy...The Russian Connection
Mick Grundy...Elapid
Beware the Exit
The Green Scarf
Revenge of Jesus
Geminknot
An Anthology of Childhood
Schemers and Dreamers
Memory Gap

Please visit afnovels.com